Tandem

TO Hannah,

This is the third book I've signed - I hope it's a lucky one!

Alex

Tandem
By Alex Morgan

Hookline Books

Published by Hookline Books
Bookline & Thinker Ltd
#231, 405 King's Road
London SW10 0BB
Tel: 0845 116 1476
www.hooklinebooks.com

A CIP catalogue for this book is available from the British Library.

ISBN: 9780957695740

Cover design by Donald McColl
Printed and bound by Lightning Source UK

For Trevor

On the road

Paula took off her trainers and rested her feet on the dashboard. She was tired and warm. Closing her eyes, she imagined leaping out into the darkness and running along the hard shoulder, picking up speed until she was travelling faster than all the traffic. She felt the coolness of the road spray on her calves, tasted the bitter, fume-filled rain on her tongue. Outpacing cars, lorries and coaches with long, easy strides, she left every single one of them behind, until she had the motorway to herself. Until there was nothing but the sound of her own feet. Until she was free.

She wrenched her eyes open. "Do you mind if I smoke?"

Stretching down for her bag, she rummaged for the lighter and packet of Benson & Hedges she had bought that afternoon. She couldn't be sure if the nicotine would make her feel better or just string her out even more, but she reckoned it was worth a go. She peeled off the cellophane, dropped it into her bag and prepared to light up.

"I'd rather you didn't," Andy said without taking his eyes off the road.

"But I thought..." She pointed into the footwell at the scrunched up Embassy packet and fragments of ash she had brushed off the seat when she climbed in.

"Ah, no. I gave up a while ago. I just don't clean the van very often. There's not much point when it's usually only me."

"In that case, maybe I'll give up too, if you can call it that when you haven't even started." She returned the cigarette to the packet, lowered the window, and launched the box out into the night.

He gave her a reproving glance. "That wasn't very environmentally friendly."

"It's better than smoking them, and the rain'll dissolve the evidence pretty quickly."

"There's certainly enough acid in it. Let's stop for a coffee to celebrate you giving up."

"Or not starting."

"Whichever. I could do with a break. The wipers are hypnotising me."

Andy pulled off the motorway and into the car park of a service station. He checked his watch. "Meet you back here in forty-five minutes."

Paula pushed her feet into her trainers, relieved he didn't expect them to spend the time together in polite conversation.

There was a queue in the coffee shop. As she waited, she wondered why everyone else was travelling in the small hours. A young man with a drowsy toddler in his arms was placing an order at the counter. His partner sat bleary-eyed at a nearby table, the toddler's baby brother or sister snuffling gently as it slept in a car seat at her feet. An elderly couple were having a disagreement about whether sharing an apricot Danish would be too serious a breach of their diet, and a pair of vast rugby fans in matching kilts and Scotland jerseys were debating whether to have carrot cake or a fruit slice.

Paula knew that, if the last hundred and eighty miles were anything to go by, Andy didn't particularly want to spend the journey chatting either, but it would be rude to doze off, so she ordered a grande Americano with an extra shot and a double chocolate muffin. Their combined caffeine content should do the trick.

She sat down at an empty table and watched Andy help himself to the last sandwich from the cold cabinet. He ordered his coffee to go. She couldn't place his accent but it was definitely British. There was something almost Mediterranean about his looks though: the aquiline nose, chocolate eyes and slightly swarthy skin. His jeans were old and faded, just like the checked shirt he wore with the sleeves rolled up above his biceps. His face was young – relaxed, unlined – and she would have put him at no more than thirty if it wasn't for his hair. The thick black waves he had pulled back in an elastic band were streaked with grey. She had a powerful urge to go over and free them, wrap her arms around his back, bury her face in their softness and cling on for dear life.

She shook her head and took a sip of coffee. He was just a guy who drove a van for hire; she didn't know anything about him. The old Paula would never have acted so irrationally, but things were different now and she no longer knew how she was going to behave. The old

Paula had felt safe and secure. She was sensible and predictable. She didn't smoke. The new Paula was taking things an hour at a time.

She tried to make her coffee and muffin last, but when she looked at her watch it was only two thirty-five, less than fifteen minutes since they had stopped, and she still had half an hour to kill.

The women's toilets were empty. Paula dumped her bag on the long vanity unit, and felt around until she found nail scissors buried among some tissues at the bottom. She regarded herself squarely in the mirror. Fifteen centimetres should be about right. She took hold of a handful of hair and sawed into it just below her right ear, watching as the brown strands fluttered onto the mottled grey and pink melamine.

"Jesus Christ, that girl's giving herself a haircut," squealed a woman in a spangly turquoise cowboy hat, who tumbled through the swing doors with a gaggle of companions. Three of them wore sagging fuchsia boob tubes printed with the slogan *Brenda's hens*. The fourth's said simply *Brenda*. They clutched each other for support as they attempted to process the sight of Paula in mid-snip.

Brenda was the first to collect herself. Swaying on her stilettos like a tree that might fall at any moment, she made a gun out of the thumb and first two fingers of her right hand and pointed it at Paula.

In what she seemed to think was an American accent, she said, "Put those scissors down, lady, and step away from the mirror before someone gets hurt."

Her friends snorted and hiccupped at her wit.

Paula took hold of another handful of hair. "Thanks for your concern," she said grimly, "but I know what I'm doing."

Brenda staggered over and caught her scissor hand by the wrist. "I beg to differ."

Paula tried to pull free. "What do you think you're playing at?"

Brenda eased the scissors from Paula's fingers. "Those things are potentially deadly in the hands of an amateur."

"You tell her, Brenda," encouraged one of the hens.

"Just think yourself lucky the cavalry arrived in time to avert a disaster," another said.

Paula had never been stripped of her nail scissors in a service station toilet by a quartet of sozzled women before. The old Paula would probably have grabbed them back, gathered up her things and made for the door, but the new version was curious to see what would happen next.

"Look what I've found," announced the third hen as she emerged unsteadily from the cleaner's cubicle carrying a wooden stool with a ripped red plastic seat.

"Thank you, Jasmine. If you could just put it there…" Brenda pointed to a spot at the mirror directly in front of a strip light. "That will be perfect for madam."

Jasmine breathed on the seat and gave it a polish with a fake-tanned forearm. "Please, sit yourself down," she said.

Paula hesitated. "Are you actually hairdressers or are you just having a laugh?"

"I'll have you know I got to the third round of South Yorks Young Hairdresser of the Year in 1998," Brenda said huffily. "Now hurry up and park yourself – the rest of the girls are waiting in the minibus."

"I've got someone waiting too," Paula said.

"A bloke?" Brenda asked.

Paula nodded.

"And you don't think I'll get this lot cut quicker than you will? Besides, there's no harm making him wait. You've got to treat 'em mean to keep 'em keen. Isn't that right, girls?"

The hens roared their assent.

"So get your arse on that stool." Brenda pulled a pair of styling scissors from her handbag. "This is my last haircut as a free woman and I can feel in my bones it's going to be a good 'un."

Paula did as she was told and watched Brenda eyeing her in the mirror.

"I'm assuming you don't much care what kind of style I give you, since you were about to wreck it yourself," she said.

The other three crowded round as she made a couple of practice snips in the air.

"What about a fringe?" one suggested.

"Are you out of your tiny mind, Louise?" Jasmine snapped. "Her eyes are her only half-decent feature. Give her a fringe and nobody'll ever notice them."

Jasmine turned her attention to Paula. "Have you thought of trying concealer on those bags?"

Before Paula could answer, Louise said, "Who are you calling out of her tiny mind? I've only had eight vodkas."

"Yeah, but they were all doubles," Jasmine reminded her.

"Ladies, please," Brenda said. "A bit of hush while I'm working, if you don't mind. Now, what do we think about layers?"

"I don't see that you've got any choice with hair like that," said the one who had mentioned the cavalry.

Staring at Paula, she added, "*Have* you tried concealer? You look like you haven't slept in a month."

Paula didn't reply.

"Jodie," Louise scolded, heaving her ample rear onto the vanity unit, "leave the poor girl alone and give Brenda peace to weave some of that South Yorks magic."

"Yes, fuckin' shut up the lot of you," Brenda ordered and began snipping.

Louise handed Jodie and Jasmine each a miniature of Bacardi from her handbag. She held one out to Paula. "Go on," she urged, "you look like you could use it."

Paula hesitated then took the bottle. "Cheers."

"Cheers," her new friends chorused, raising their miniatures.

Paula unscrewed the cap and knocked the contents back in one. "Bloody hell," she gasped.

"Way t'go, girl," Jasmine said and threw hers back. Jodie followed suit.

"What about me?" Brenda demanded.

"You can wait till you're finished," Louise said. "We want her looking better not worse."

"Eck-zacly," Jodie slurred, pulling herself up to sit beside Louise and nearly knocking Paula's bag onto the floor.

"Here, what's this?" she asked, holding up a packet of blonde dye that had fallen out.

"You're a hairdresser," Jasmine said. "You work it out."

"Ha, ha, very funny," Jodie said. Pointing to the cleaner's cubicle, she added, "I wonder if there's anything through there to mix it in."

"You stay here. I'll go." Louise placed a restraining hand on the other woman's shoulder. "You're so pissed you'd probably end up cutting it with toilet cleaner."

"Hang on a minute," Paula said. "Who says I want to dye my hair?"

"What else would you have a box of Natural Born Blonde in your bag for?" Brenda reasoned, snipping away as if she was on speed.

"I wasn't planning to do it right now."

"No time like the present," Jodie said gleefully. "I never go anywhere without my moulding wax." She pulled a huge tub from her bag. "And we can style you with the hand drier."

"But you're all drunk!" Paula exclaimed.

"So?" Jasmine put in. "You're letting her cut your hair."

"It'll take ages," she tried again, "and your friends are waiting."

"They'll be fine," Jasmine said. "There's a full bottle of vodka in the bus." She began massaging Paula shoulders. "Just sit back, chill and in no time we'll have you looking like…" she paused. "Who will she look like, Jodie?"

"Keira Thingy?" Jodie suggested.

"She's far too old to look like Keira Thingy," Louise said.

"Sienna Miller then," Jodie tried.

"I haven't got the cash to look like Sienna Miller or Keira Knightley," Paula protested. "The machine in the foyer was broken."

Brenda stopped snipping. "You don't think we charge for toilet makeovers, do you? You provided your own dye and the hot water's laid on. It would be completely against our code of practice to take money in a public toilet under such circumstances."

Paula held up her hands in submission. "Okay, I give in. Do your worst."

"Blimey, what happened to you? I was beginning to think you'd been kidnapped," Andy said as she climbed back into the van. "And I wouldn't have recognised you if you weren't wearing the same clothes. Since when did they have all-night hairdressers in service stations?"

"They don't. I'm really sorry I was so long. I got ambushed in the toilets."

"If that's an ambush, I hope you got the guilty party's phone number so they can do it again. You look fabulous. Just like…"

"Sienna Miller?"

"That's it."

Paula put on her seatbelt. "Thank you." A trendy haircut and some blonde dye couldn't hide the fact that she was a complete wreck, but it was kind of him to say it.

"Onward and upward?"

"Absolutely. Let's go." She sounded more certain than she felt.

He pointed to the glovebox. "Choose a cassette then."

She opened it and sifted through his collection. It was mostly pensioner music, traditional Scottish and Irish stuff by The Chieftains and Boys of the Lough that was guaranteed to set her nerves even more on edge, but there were a few tapes by bands she didn't know.

She picked one. "What are Seven Hurtz like?"

"Which album is it?"

"Electroleum."

"Brilliant. Perfect if you need to unwind. Stick it on and see."

Paula slid the cassette into the slot and pressed play. Mellow electronic sound filled the warm, still air of the van.

Despite the temperature, goose bumps rose on her arms as they pulled back onto the glistening ribbon of motorway. As a child, she loved being in the car at night, especially if the weather was bad. Tightly belted into her side of the back seat, the reassuring outline of her mum's chestnut bob and her dad's square shoulders visible through the headrests, she snuggled into the upholstery and surrendered to the thrill of being sucked along the tunnel of darkness. No matter how loudly the rain drummed on the bodywork, she knew it could never penetrate this cosy cocoon. Before long, soothed by the lullaby of windscreen wipers and whooshing spray, she slid into sleep. Waking as the car pulled up, there was the sinking realisation that she had squandered most of the magical journey, the knowledge that no matter where they had just arrived, it couldn't offer anything as wonderful as the tantalising expectation and utter security she had just experienced.

If she had known then how much she would long to return to that simplicity and freedom, she would never have allowed herself to miss a second. Now, night-time roads frightened her, menaced her with their destructive power, and yet here she was, making this journey in the dark.

Turning her head, she caught sight of her new short, blonde hair reflected in the window and suddenly she could see Pete as a child. She closed her eyes. They were sitting together at the breakfast table, that day all those years ago when they had become twins. Pete was crying because the kids at school had been mean to him about having a birthday on Christmas day – they said it was no birthday at all. Her dad, who had been doing *The Scotsman* crossword, looked down at his son's tear-streaked cheeks and took hold of his hand.

"We can fix that," he said. "How would you like an extra-special extra summer birthday instead? On, let's see..." He thought for a moment. "How about the twenty-fifth of July? From now on, your extra birthday will be the day your mum and I got married. How does that sound?"

Pete wiped his face on his sleeve. "Will I get presents?"

"You certainly will. You'll get Christmas presents at Christmas and your birthday presents will be in July."

Pete beamed.

"That's not fair," Paula shouted. "My birthday's only nine days after Pete's and I don't have an extra-special extra summer birthday. I want my presents on the twenty-fifth of July too."

Her brother considered this. "If our birthday's the same, you won't be nearly a year older than me anymore." His face broke into a wide grin. "I won't be the littlest in the class and you won't be the biggest. We'll be the same."

"Are you sure that's what you want, Paula?" their dad asked.

She didn't hesitate. "Yes, I want an extra-special extra summer birthday."

"Well, then, from now on you will both celebrate your birthday on July the twenty-fifth, and do you know what that makes you?"

Pete shook his head.

"I do," Paula said triumphantly. "We'll be twins just like the Little Miss Twins. They live in Twoland and say everything twice. Except Pete can't be a Little Miss Twin because he's not a girl. He's a stinky boy."

Pete ignored this insult. "Please, let's be twins, Paula. I can say everything twice. Please, let's. I can, I can. See?"

"Yes," Paula said. "We'll be twins. I'll be the big twin and you'll be the little twin, and I'll always kick anyone that's bad to you."

It was daylight by the time Paula spotted the turning for the village.

She pointed to the rusty black and white signpost poking out of a hedge. "There it is! Down to the right."

Andy grinned. "I know."

"Really?"

"I know the area quite well. I love Scotland."

They were the first words they had exchanged since stopping for another coffee just after the Border.

The van bounced down the twisting, potholed road. "I hope there's nothing fragile in those boxes," he observed. "My suspension isn't up to this kind of thing anymore."

"Yours or the van's?" Paula enquired, hoping humour might dilute the sensation of panic seeping up from her stomach.

But Andy didn't rise to it. Stopping to let a tractor out of a field, he looked round at her. "I don't know what you're running away from, but whatever it is, you couldn't have picked a nicer place to hide."

Paula smiled weakly.

Packing up

The night before, Paula had answered the door to Andy dressed in an old T-shirt and denim shorts. She had felt him looking at her legs as she led him up the hall. They were the only part of her body she really liked, muscular yet lean and shapely. Her mum was always telling her how pretty she was, and Ollie was forever saying she had beautiful skin and gorgeous eyes – they were a pale greeny-grey, with long fine lashes – but Paula invariably gave the same reply: *"Gorgeous won't get you up a hill when you're knackered."*

"Sorry, I'm not quite ready but I won't be long," she said.

"I get the impression this was a last-minute decision," Andy replied.

Paula chewed her lip. "It wasn't exactly planned."

She showed him into the sitting room. There were piles of books, CDs and DVDs everywhere, and four large cardboard boxes sat in the centre of the room. The furniture was modern and simple. An angular sofa, a couple of chairs with cream linen covers and a wall of blond wood bookcases were softened and brightened by arty prints and colourful cushions. The windows had blinds rather than curtains and the floor was pale laminate. The lack of fussy details, ornaments or other knick-knacks pointed to an existence that was normally far more ordered.

"Please, sit down," Paula said, lifting a stack of magazines from one end of the sofa. She gazed around for somewhere to put them.

"There's a bit of space under the coffee table," Andy suggested.

She slid them under the table.

"It's not actually as bad as it looks." She wasn't sure if she was trying to convince him or herself.

"It's good to see you've got decent boxes," he offered. "I once moved a woman who had thousands of books and she'd put them all in carrier bags. It was one of the worst days of my life."

"I can't take credit for the boxes. The flat upstairs just changed hands and I begged them from the girl who moved in."

Paula had called him the day before, after seeing his advert in the local paper. *Van with driver. Reasonable rates. All work considered as long as it's legal. Happy to travel anywhere, particularly north of the Border.* She asked if he meant what he said about going to Scotland. He said he did.

"Could you take me and some stuff to Fife then?" she asked. "The other drivers I phoned didn't want to venture beyond the M25."

"No problem. I enjoy getting out of the South-East. Spend too long here and you start to forget the rest of Britain exists."

"I know what you mean."

"When were you thinking of?"

"As soon as possible."

"Well, if you want to go during the day, next Tuesday's the soonest I can do, but if you're happy to travel overnight we could leave late tomorrow."

"Overnight?" She sounded uncertain.

"If that doesn't suit you, why not wait till Tuesday? Or you could try some more numbers."

"No, overnight's fine." She said it quickly so neither of them had time to change their mind.

She was peering into one of the boxes now, left hand tugging on her right earlobe. She looked over at him. "Sorry, did you say something?"

"I said is he coming?"

"Who?"

Andy leant over and picked up a threadbare stuffed animal with a long tail that was sitting on a pile of books. "Your friend here. Is he a rat?"

She managed a brief smile. "That's Arthur. He's a very elderly dormouse."

"So is Arthur coming to Scotland?"

She held out her hand and Andy passed him to her. She put him in the box nearest to her. "That's the easiest decision I've made all day. I was sure I'd be done by the time you got here, but deciding what to pack's taken far longer than I expected."

"Is it a permanent move?"

She shrugged. "I won't know till I get there."

"That's exciting."

Paula picked up a handful of CDs, checked through them and put them into one of the boxes. Lifting them out again, she discarded a couple and returned the rest to the box.

"If you're not certain what to take, it's probably better to pack too much rather than too little."

"I suppose." She didn't sound convinced.

"Do you want to bring some music for the van? It'll need to be cassettes – the facilities are pretty basic."

"I only have CDs."

"You'll have to make do with my choice then. Most people drive themselves when I move their stuff, so I only have my own taste to consider. I take it you're not a car owner."

"I don't drive. I prefer the view from the passenger seat."

"I love driving, especially long journeys. They give you so much thinking time."

"Was that a hint?" she asked quickly. "I won't intrude on your peace, if that's what's worrying you. I've no plans to tell you my life story."

"That's not what I meant. I was just trying to say I'm happy alone or with company."

"Sorry." Paula gnawed on the corner of a fingernail and glanced around the room.

"Actually, I think I'm the one who's intruding. Why don't I leave you to it for a while? It'll be much easier to get organised without me breathing down your neck."

She ran a hand through her hair. "No, no, it's fine. I'm fine. I really am organised."

It was his turn to smile.

"My dad says I remind him of a swan sometimes," she offered, "desperate to give the impression that I've got everything under control even though it's obvious I'm paddling frantically under the surface."

"We all do that."

She nodded. "I've just got to finish these and put a few last things into a case. Then I'll get changed and help you into the van with the bike." She looked at him pleadingly. "I could make you some tea or coffee."

"No, you concentrate on what you need to do. I'm going to stretch my legs and buy some water for the journey."

"The corner shop at the far end of the road should still be open."

She made to follow him to the front door, but he held up his hand. "You carry on. I'll see myself out."

When he returned twenty minutes later, she had stacked the boxes from the sitting room into the hall, and by the time he had taken them out to the van, two more, one containing a giant spider plant, the other a trio of bushy ferns, had taken their place.

Paula was putting a pair of suitcases by the door when he came back in. "Nearly there," she said.

She reappeared after a few seconds with a sports bag. "That's the last of it apart from the bike. I'll just pull on my jeans."

As she turned to go back into the bedroom, he said, "That's unusual."

She looked at him over her shoulder. "What is?"

He pointed to the outside of her left ankle, where the tattooed characters P&P formed a little curve just above the bone.

"What does it stand for? Not 'Post and Packing' I presume?"

"Not post and packing," she confirmed curtly and closed the bedroom door with a sharp click.

19 Shore Road

"Isn't that wonderful?" Andy inhaled deeply. "There's no smell on earth to beat it."

Paula shivered in the breeze from his open window. "I can't smell anything."

"Give it a couple of seconds. There's no medicine like the sea. It'll lift your heart and blow all the cobwebs away."

She turned away from him to take in the row of Edwardian villas they were passing. They had freshly painted doors and window frames, and their cottagey front gardens were a riot of colourful neglect. The shiny SUVs and people carriers lining the pavement marked them out as weekend boltholes for well-heeled families from the Central Belt. The panorama of fields and trees on the other side of the road offered no clue to what lay less than a mile ahead, beyond where the road dipped out of sight, but before long, their occupants would be gathering up buckets and spades, pushchairs and fishing nets, sand-heavy rugs and carrier bags of swimsuits, and setting out on the day's expedition to the shore. Children would dig holes and hunt for crabs, while parents sheltered with books and newspapers behind striped windbreaks. At lunchtime, they would share egg sandwiches and crisps, and drink through miniature straws from little cardboard cartons of apple or orange juice. Paula smiled inwardly at the thought.

As they left the villas behind, she tried to visualise what they would pass next, but nothing came. The bottom of the dip seemed to signal the beginning of Craskferry proper. There were houses on both sides of the road now, short terraces and a few individual cottages, all with a simple, symmetrical Georgian elegance and all utterly unfamiliar. She had hoped… What had she hoped exactly? That she would recognise everything instantly, after more than twenty years? Perhaps not, but it would have been reassuring if something, some small detail, reignited even a flicker of memory, a glimmer of recognition, just enough to confirm she had made the right decision.

Give it time, like Andy said, she reproached herself silently. There's no rush now.

He pulled up at a T-junction. "Which way?"

Paula consulted the printout of the letting agent's email. "It says turn right at the junction with Main Street."

"Okay, that's here." He flicked on the indicator even though the roads were deserted. "Then what?"

"First left and sharp right takes us onto Shore Road. It's number nineteen."

He followed her instructions.

"Look, the odd numbers are on the beach side. It must have a sea view." He sounded excited.

"The description says it does. You can park there." Paula pointed to a space in front of a four-storey tenement with a crumbling cement façade whose door opened directly onto the pavement.

Andy manoeuvred the van into the space. "So which one is it?"

"This is seventeen so nineteen should be next door, but all I can see is a gap, and the house on the other side's far too grand."

Andy leant over the steering wheel and craned his neck. "What's it supposed to be?"

She rechecked the email. "The ground floor of a charming seaside cottage built in the 1830s."

"Oh dear."

"What do you mean 'oh dear'?"

"You should ask for a refund."

"Why? What's wrong with it?" Paula demanded.

"It looks more 1840s to me."

"Jesus, you frightened me." She bent down to retrieve her bag from the footwell so he wouldn't see how close to tears the harmless joke had left her.

"Do you have the key?" he asked.

"It's supposed to be under a flowerpot to the left of the door."

"Come on then."

The house was set back three or four metres from its much larger neighbours. It had a little front garden, just a couple of beds of blowsy pink roses on either side of a short path of crushed shells. Andy felt under a terracotta pot of orange and yellow nasturtiums.

"Here." He held up a ziplock bag containing a ring with several keys.

Paula selected the largest one. The heavy storm door opened with an easy clunk to reveal a tiled vestibule with a wooden umbrella stand and a single door panelled with intricately etched glass.

"This is strange."

"What is?" Andy asked.

"The agent said it was a flat, with the owner living upstairs, but there's only one door."

"Go in and see then. I'll unload."

Paula took a deep breath and opened the inner door. Directly opposite her, across the dark green linoleum, was another front door where the bottom of the stairs should have been. It had a little nameplate that said *McIntyre.* She could feel her face beginning to crumple.

"That's not on." Andy put the box of ferns down in the vestibule and joined her in the hall. "You can't have complete strangers walking through your flat any time they like to get to their front door. If I were you, I'd phone the agent and ask for something else."

"There isn't anything," Paula said glumly. "This was all she had left. She said it had just come on her books." She waved at the pristine magnolia walls. "Smells like the paint's barely dry. She said the layout was a bit unusual and that was why it was quite cheap. I thought she meant the bedroom was off the sitting room or something."

"Are you sure there's nowhere else?"

"Not a thing. She said I was lucky to find anything at all at this time of year. The village is packed with holidaymakers."

"We'd better get on then." He picked up the box. "Where do you want this?"

"Let's try in here." Paula opened the door immediately to her right.

The square sitting room contained a worn chintz sofa, a couple of matching armchairs and a TV on a small table beside a cast-iron fireplace. The carpet was a swirly mess of red and green. Two net-curtained windows looked out onto the street.

A pair of oak doors in the centre of the back wall led them into a study with an old kitchen table for a desk, and a quartet of empty bookcases. A picture window running the width of the room revealed a long, narrow back garden and, beyond a wall with a gate in the middle, the sea, sparkling gold and silver in the early morning sunshine as it rolled away to meet the perfect turquoise sky.

The beach itself was hidden behind the wall, but Paula could see it in her mind's eye. It was the one thing she could picture with certainty: the wide strip of sand, the peeling paint of the small flights of wooden steps that provided each back garden with its own private access, the disused granary building beside the harbour wall, the cliffs in the distance – they were as sharp as if she had seen them yesterday.

Andy gave an impressed whistle and set the box of plants on the table. "That's some view. Maybe this place isn't so bad after all."

"Maybe not. I'm going to explore."

She found the bedroom opposite the sitting room. It had the same hideous carpet, a small double bed made up with pale blue sheets still creased from the packet, and a wall of wardrobes with white louvered doors. There was a dark wood dressing table in front of the net-curtained window, with a dining chair upholstered in red velvet in place of a stool.

Next door was a shower room that looked as if it had never been used. A tub of grout sat in the white sink and there were two large tins of magnolia paint on the floor by the toilet. She glanced in the mirror. The person looking back had flatteringly cut and tousled blonde hair, but her eyes were dead.

The kitchen was at the far end of the hall and shared the same spectacular sea view as the study. It was clean enough but the avocado units and cream tiles with stylised maroon flowers were pure seventies.

"Where shall I put this?" Andy lent the electric blue tandem against the kitchen door.

Paula looked at it as if she had never seen it before. "I … I don't know. It'll be too long for the cupboard under the stairs but there doesn't seem to be any other storage."

Andy walked over to the window. "What about out there?" He pointed to a large shed halfway down the garden. "Shall I take a look?"

She unlocked the back door and watched as he walked the length of the grass. There was something tremendously attractive, sexy even, about the easy way he moved, a relaxed confidence that said he was completely comfortable in the world.

Andy checked all around the shed, tried the door, peered in the window. "It's perfectly secure and there's plenty of space," he shouted. "All I can see is a lawnmower and a wheelbarrow. Have you got a key?"

Paula examined the ring. "I don't think so," she called back. "The only one left is labelled 'beach gate'."

"Then you'll have to ask your neighbour." He nodded up at the first floor.

Together they lifted the tandem down the outside steps and propped it against the kitchen wall.

"It should be safe enough here for the time being," Andy said.

"The agent said she'd arrange some basic supplies. Why don't I put the kettle on?"

"Good idea. I'll finish unloading."

Paula found a litre of semi-skimmed milk in the fridge along with a small bottle of freshly squeezed orange juice, a block of mature cheddar and a packet of organic butter. There was a paper bag of tomatoes and a punnet of mushrooms in the vegetable drawer at the bottom. A box of free-range eggs, a pack of teabags and a large wholemeal loaf had been crammed into the bread bin. She wondered if the agent was feeling guilty about not mentioning the lack of privacy. She had probably thought Paula wouldn't take the flat if she told her, but a few groceries couldn't excuse such an omission.

She could hear Andy moving about in the hall.

"Do you fancy a mushroom omelette to go with your tea?" she called.

"That would be great."

Paula gathered utensils from the unfamiliar cupboards and drawers. Stooping to light the gas for the frying pan, she felt a draft on the small of her back. She spun round but there was no one there.

"Andy?"

He stuck his head around the kitchen door. "You okay? You look like you've seen a ghost."

"No, no, I'm fine," she said hurriedly. "I thought you came in."

"Nope."

She bit her lip. "Just my imagination."

Her hands shook as she cracked eggs into a bowl. "It's nothing some sleep won't fix." But even as she said it, she knew it wasn't true.

Paula was serving the omelette when he reappeared.

"That's the lot in."

She put their plates on the table. "Sit down. I'll get the toast. I hope you don't take sugar, because there isn't any."

"I gave it up before I quit smoking."

Andy poured the tea and chinked his mug against hers. "Here's to your new home. I hope you'll be very happy."

"That very much depends on whoever's up there." Paula raised her eyes to the ceiling. "Here's hoping they're agoraphobic."

"What brings you to Craskferry anyway?"

She hesitated. "I came across it in a Sunday supplement feature on Scottish seaside villages and thought it looked…" She had been going to say familiar but realised that would only invite more questions. Instead she concluded limply, "like a nice place to spend some time."

It was obvious from his expression that he knew he was being fobbed off.

"Sorry, I…" she tried again.

He silenced her with a wave of his fork. "It's okay. None of my business. And what I said earlier about running away, I'm sorry. I was tired and being flippant, and I shouldn't have. I should stick to driving and humping boxes." He took a mouthful of omelette. "This is excellent by the way."

"Thank you. Things are a bit complicated right now. I mean I've got a lot going on and I… I've got to get settled here, find a solicitor..." Paula lifted her mug with both hands and swallowed some tea. "The past few weeks…"

She shook her head and looked down at the red gingham tablecloth, unable to continue.

"It really is okay. Remember what I said about the healing power of the sea? It can fix things if you let it."

A tear slithered down her cheek. She went to wipe it away, but he took her hand in both of his. Her instinct was to pull away, but the warmth of his touch dissolved the tension in her hand and arm and she felt herself relax.

"You're going to be fine," he said with absolute conviction.

"Am I?" Paula whispered. "How could you know that?"

Tiredness was making her head swim. Feeling weightless, she leant across the table towards him. The urge to wrap her arms around him, to let go of everything and take refuge in his quiet strength was as powerful as it had been the night before. Their lips were almost touching. He was going to kiss her.

A soft voice observed from the doorway, "You must be Miss Tyndall."

Andy let go of her hand and jumped to his feet. Paula started to get up as well.

"No, no, stay where you are." The stout, grey-haired woman had a wicker shopping basket over one arm. "I was on my way out and wanted to make sure everything was all right."

"Are you Mrs er…?" Paula struggled to recall the name on her upstairs neighbour's door. Her memory was constantly letting her down these days.

"McIntyre. Well, if you have everything you need, I'll leave you and your…" She looked at Andy. "Your friend to finish breakfast."

To Paula's horror, Andy said, "I was just leaving actually. I have a dentist's appointment to get to." He patted the right side of his bottom jaw. "Oil of cloves can only do so much for toothache."

"Aye, there's nothing worse than a toothache. I'll bid you good day then." Mrs McIntyre headed back down the hall.

Paula willed Andy to sit down again but he didn't.

"It was great to meet you," he said. "I think you'll find what you need here."

"You can't leave yet." The feeling of panic was overwhelming. He was going and she would be left alone. She reached out for his hand but he slid it into his pocket and followed Mrs McIntyre.

It took Paula a moment to react and by the time she caught up with him he had reached the front doorstep. She grabbed his arm. "Please, don't you want to stay and… I thought maybe… that you wanted to…"

He gently removed her hand from his arm. "I can't stay, not when you're like this. It would be wrong and we'd both regret it."

She made one final attempt. "But you can't drive all that way without any sleep."

He stepped out onto the path. "I'm only going as far as Edinburgh. I've got an old friend there who's a dentist. I'll get some sleep at his place."

Before she could humiliate herself any further by getting down on her knees to beg, or ripping off her clothes, some deeper part of her took charge. “Have a safe journey then, and thank you,” she heard herself say. “I’ll recommend you to anyone who needs their stuff moved.”

Running on sand

When she opened her eyes, an unfamiliar white paper lampshade dangled above her from an intricate ceiling rose. She gazed at it, enjoying a sensation of utter weightless absence, of not knowing – or caring – where she was or why she was there. It lasted barely a few seconds. As her mind emerged from the numbness of sleep, the pieces of the puzzle clicked back into place. The sudden realisation pressed so heavily on her chest that it forced the oxygen from her lungs and left her gasping for breath: he was gone and she was alone in her new home.

She threw off the duvet and sat up. Was it morning or night? The light edging around the curtains implied morning, but she couldn't be sure. She turned to the alarm clock on the bedside table, seeking confirmation. The display read 20:45. She had been out for more than ten hours. She hadn't slept so long, or so soundly, since before it happened. Since then, even a few hours felt like a miracle. Most nights she simply dozed and woke, dozed and woke. And each time she woke, she faced the same terrible reality. Everything had changed – forever. It was like running at full tilt into a brick wall whose existence had temporarily escaped her. The result was always the same: winded and dazed, she was left wondering how she could have possibly forgotten.

As she struggled to get her breathing under control, it hit her that there was something else. Even in the midst of this, when nothing else should matter, something did. Then it came back too. Andy: she had thrown herself at Andy, a man she had met only the night before. He could have been married or a psychopath. Pathetic and needy, she had virtually begged him to come to bed with her. And he had said no.

Paula extracted her spongebag from the chaos of half-unpacked clothes and possessions and went through to the shower room. The paint tins and grout tub were gone. She faced herself in the mirror above the sink. Tendrils of her new blonde hair clung to her forehead and cheeks. She swept them back with both hands.

"Fuck." She shook her head. "How am I going to get through this? Can you please tell me that? How do I hold it together?"

No one answered.

She brushed her teeth, turned on the cold tap and splashed her face until it was numb. Back in the bedroom, she pulled on cycling shorts, a sports bra and a fresh vest top from a suitcase, socks and running shoes from her sports bag. Clipping her iPod to the waistband of her shorts, she set it to shuffle. It didn't matter what was playing as long as it was loud enough to drown out the insistent, subliminal message woven into the white noise in her head: he's gone, he's gone, he's gone. She used to run for the love of the movement, the soaring feeling of lightness and being in tune with her body. Now she did it to try to leave that hateful reminder behind, but no matter how far or fast she went, she couldn't outrun it. It was always there: he's gone, he's gone, he's gone.

Paula let herself out of the back gate. Five weathered wooden steps led down to the sand. Pausing at the top, she enjoyed a brief moment of triumph. It was just as she remembered: the beach, the steps up to all the other gates, the cliffs far along to the right beyond the houses and the high dunes, the paddling pool a little way to the left and next to it, the red sandstone of the harbour and the granary.

She saw herself running barefoot towards the pool, shrimp net and bucket in hand. The sun was shining and she had on pale green shorts and a faded pink and white striped T-shirt. Heat oozed through the stretched fabric onto her tummy as, on sandy soles, she hopped over the smooth warmth of the rocks and scooted nimbly between clumps of crispy black seaweed to reach her goal.

Paula shook her head. It might have been fifty-one years ago not twenty-one. She walked slowly down to the wet sand, did some stretches and turned to face the cliffs. The display on her iPod said 21:02, but it was as light as mid-afternoon. She knew daylight lasted longer in the north but it just didn't feel right. She didn't feel right. Her mind said run, but her body was weighed down with the dull, bruised ache of jet lag. After weeks without proper rest, the overnight journey and a day in bed, her internal clock could no longer tell day from night. Her head was thick and heavy, legs weak. For a moment, she considered returning to the flat and crawling back into her strange new bed. If she did, sleep might provide release for another hour or so, but after that there was only the prospect of another endless, wakeful night.

She shook out her arms and legs and began a slow jog. It was like trying to run in the dead weight of an old-fashioned diving suit. Using willpower in place of energy, she forced herself to move faster, dragging each leaden leg in turn from the sand's sticky grasp and throwing it forward to take the next unsteady step until, finally, the muscles began to co-operate and her movements took on a momentum of their own. Sprinting now, she passed dog walkers and couples out for an evening stroll, her feet, more than a match for the damp suck and pull beneath them, easing into a familiar rhythm. Before long, she had the beach to herself, and suddenly there it was – the lightness, the wash of elation she had so longed for, that she had so badly needed.

Head back, she drew in a long breath of relief. It smelt, tasted, salty and fresh. Andy was right about the healing power of the sea. Everything was going to be all right. She pulled her shoulders up to her ears and let them fall, feeling the remaining tension slip away. She was gliding across the sand, barely skimming its perfect surface. There was no fear, no pain, no nothing. It was glorious.

And then it was over. For a tiny joyous moment, she was empty and free. Then, as inevitable as the tide, the knowledge came pouring back in, reclaiming the void with a roar that filled her ears and threw her off balance: he's gone, he's gone, he's gone. She stopped and bent over, gasping for air. Moisture oozed down her cheeks.

Straightening up, she demanded out loud, "Why can't I get through this?"

She could make her body do anything she wanted – run ten kilometres, cycle a hundred and fifty, swim, hike, anything – but she couldn't control her emotions.

"Why? Why can't I?" she asked furiously as she began to run again.

By the time Paula reached the cliffs, she had to squint through the tears to make out the figures on her iPod. It had taken just twenty-five minutes to complete what in that long-ago summer would have seemed a hugely ambitious journey, capable of filling half a day as every rock pool was checked for life and every pretty shell and colourful pebble examined to see if it was worthy of joining her collection.

The tide was too high for her to go any further, even if she could see clearly to place her feet safely on the slippery rocks. She leant back against the cliffs' unyielding sandstone, her whole body vibrating as tears poured down her face and dribbled onto her vest. Desperate to feel something, anything other than this, she turned the volume right up. Amy Winehouse's *Rehab* filled her head. Beating her fists on the stone behind her in time to the music, she mouthed the chorus over and over.

The light was starting to fade. Oblivious to her scratched and bruised hands, she pulled off the soggy top and used it to blot her eyes and cheeks. Stuffing it into the waistband of her shorts, she jogged past the high dunes and towards the village once more. "This is the last time I'm going to cry," she told herself.

Passing houses and people again, Paula noticed a girl of about eleven or twelve in lilac pedal pushers and a matching hoodie walking a tall, thin dog on a short lead. They were dawdling along the edge of the water roughly opposite her new home. The girl wore her white blonde hair in two spiky bunches pulled high on the sides of her head and appeared to be watching something. She would walk a few paces, turn and retrace her steps, bending occasionally to stroke the dog, but her gaze never wavered from whatever was holding her attention.

The closer Paula got the more certain she became that it was her house the girl was scrutinising. She could see now that the dog was a greyhound, its velvety coat a blurry mix of fawn and pale grey, and each time the girl went to pat it, her lips moved beside its ear, as if she was relaying her observations.

Paula veered up the beach and stopped at the bottom of her steps. They were just a few metres apart now and for an instant their eyes met. The girl's were ringed with black eyeliner, her lashes thick with mascara. She turned away and Paula bent over to catch her breath. When she straightened up seconds later, the girl was gone.

Fish supper, no sauce

Paula woke with a start, immediately conscious she had forgotten something, and for once it wasn't her loss. That was with her, like a physical presence in the bed, filling the space so she barely had room to move. She tried to think what other fact might have been misplaced. Making a complete fool of herself with Andy? No, unfortunately that memory was as fresh as when it happened.

The bedside alarm said 10:00. What day was it? She struggled to focus on this more basic question. Sunday, it was Sunday, and that meant a big pile of newspapers with glossy supplements.

Arthur, the dormouse, regarded her from the neighbouring pillow.

"You don't know how lucky you are being a stuffed toy," she said, poking him in the stomach. "No stress, no worries – no emotions at all. You've no idea how much I envy you."

She was heading out the front door, keys and purse in hand, when she remembered what she had forgotten. The tandem was still out in the garden. She had left nearly five grand's worth of racing bike propped up overnight under the kitchen window.

"No need to panic," she thought as she rushed down the hall. "The back gate's locked and no one knows it's there. It'll be fine."

Gripping the edge of the sink beneath the window, she stretched up on tiptoe to try to catch sight of the bike, but the wide stone sill got in the way.

"It's definitely down there," she told herself. "I just can't see it."

But as soon as she stepped out of the back door she saw it was gone. A hand flew to her mouth but it was too late to stifle the cry of anguish.

An upstairs window opened and Mrs McIntyre stuck her head out. "Another fine day, the day. You'll mibby find what you're looking for under the big window."

Paula glanced to her right and there was the bike, leaning unharmed beneath the study sill.

Relief flooded through her. "Did you move it?" she demanded.

"I'm seventy-four, I've got arthritis and I live alone. I couldnae be hauling that huge thing about the garden even if I wanted to," Mrs McIntyre responded evenly.

"But who else could have? I locked the gate when I came in last night."

"If I were you, I'd check what's been left down there."

Before Paula could ask what she meant, the old lady had bowed back inside and closed the window.

Paula turned and looked down the garden. The greyhound from the beach was standing patiently at the bottom of the path, its lead tied to the handle of the gate. As she approached, the dog regarded her with its head cocked slightly to one side. Paula held out the back of her left hand so it could smell her before she went any closer. It gave a brief sniff and tried to lie down but the lead wasn't long enough.

"Hello there," she said. "How did you get here?"

She checked the gate: it was still locked. Crouching down, she felt round the dog's collar for a tag but there wasn't one.

"So you're incognito. Did that girl leave you here? How did she manage to get you through the gate, or did she haul you over the top?"

Paula glanced down onto the beach. Half-a-dozen plastic fish crates lay in a heap at the bottom of the steps.

"Those weren't there last night, were they, dog? Did your friend borrow them from the harbour to make some extra steps? She must be stronger than she looks."

Paula bent down and stroked the dog's narrow head. It leant against her. "Was she the one that moved my bike? Why did she leave you behind?"

"If that's Bovis you're talking to, don't expect any sensible answers," a voice said from the other side of the gate.

Paula peered through a knot hole in the blistered green slats. A woman of about her own age with close cropped red hair looked back at her.

"I don't know what he's called," Paula said. "He's not wearing a tag."

"That'll be Bovis." The woman climbed the steps and put her head over the gate. "Hello you," she said to the dog. "Has that scamp left you as bait?"

"The girl I saw with him on the beach last night?"

"He's a she actually."

"Oh, sorry." Paula leant down and addressed the dog. "Sorry for getting your sex wrong, Bovis."

"Nora Roberts," the woman said, offering her hand. "I live a few doors along. And this is Terry Two." She pointed towards the sand. Paula leaned over the gate. A fluffy West Highland terrier puppy on a long lead was sniffing a piece of seaweed.

"Is there a Terry One?"

"He's at home waiting to be fed. We've been out so long he's probably got his own breakfast by now."

"He must be a clever dog."

"I'll tell him you said that. He'll be flattered."

Paula let the strange comment pass. "Isn't it confusing them both having the same name?"

"We manage. This one was already called Terry when I got him from the rescue centre." Nora addressed the puppy. "Weren't you, sausage? He had a difficult start in life and I didn't want to make things worse by confusing him with a change of name." She turned back to Paula. "Are you the new tenant?"

"I arrived yesterday."

"Staying long?"

"For the summer at least, maybe longer." Paula managed a brief smile. "I'm not making any plans just now."

Nora climbed back down the steps and onto the beach. "Once you've stayed for the summer you won't ever want to leave."

Paula shrugged. "I spent the summer here once before and managed it."

"But you're back now," Nora said over her shoulder. She gave a little wave and walked off along the sand.

Paula turned her attention to Bovis. "What are we going to do with you?" She scratched behind the dog's ears. "I should have asked Nora where that strange girl lives, so I could take you home and find out what she was up to."

She glanced over the wall. Nora had vanished, probably into one of the other gates.

"Let's untie you for now so you'll be a bit more comfortable and I'll go and see if Mrs McIntyre can help. I wonder what Nora meant when she said you were left as bait?"

There was no answer when she knocked on her landlady's door.

Paula got a padlock and chain from a box of cycling stuff Andy had left in the corner of the bedroom, and secured the tandem to a drainpipe. Then she walked up onto Main Street. The first shop she came to was a newsagent. She chose a *Scotland on Sunday* and *Sunday Herald* from the display outside and went in.

"That'll be £3.40," the man said.

She handed over the money. "I don't suppose you know where a blonde girl with a greyhound lives? I found her dog and I want to return it."

"A blonde girl?" the man repeated.

"About eleven years old, with a pale fawnish greyhound."

He snapped his fingers. "I ken the dog you mean. That moth-eaten thing's perfectly capable o' findin' its own way home."

"I'd like to return it anyway," Paula said firmly.

"In that case, you want to go up to they new houses at the top o' the hill behind the harbour – Kirkcaldy Close. Let me just check ma book for the number – mum gets *Ok!* and *Hello* delivered."

He pulled a ledger from under the counter and thumbed through to the right page. "Aye, Carole McCormack: *Ok!* and *Hello*. Seven Kirkcaldy Close. Do you ken how to find it?"

"It can't be that difficult."

"No, this isnae exactly the metropolis."

Paula thanked him and headed back to the house. Out in the garden, the tandem was chained up under the study window where she had left it, but there was no sign of the dog. She checked the gate: still locked. She looked over it. The fish boxes were neatly piled on the top step.

By the time Paula had eaten a couple of poached eggs on toast, watched Katharine Hepburn and Humphrey Bogart in *The African Queen* on BBC2 and read all the papers, it was half-past nine. She stretched and got up from the sofa. Mrs McIntyre had passed the closed sitting room door a couple of hours before and she could hear her moving about upstairs.

She pulled a fleece over her T-shirt and set off along the beach to the harbour. The granary must have been redeveloped into flats because there were lights on every floor. She followed the harbour wall to the furthest point then retraced her steps, turning down a ramp to stroll along the sand of the next bay. The sky was tinged with grey by the time she headed back towards the village. When she reached the harbour once more, she walked up a cobbled lane that led onto Main Street. It wasn't until she saw the blue neon sign for Felice's Fish Bar that she realised she was hungry.

A man of about forty in a white nylon overall, his thick black curls held in check by a net cap, was shovelling chips into cardboard cartons for a couple of teenage girls.

"Salt 'n' sauce?" His accent was a mixture of Scottish and Italian.

They nodded and he sprinkled the chips with salt and topped them with gloopy brown liquid from an old lemonade bottle. Closing the boxes, he wrapped them in shiny white paper and passed them over the counter.

"Anythin' else?"

"Big ginger an' two heart attacks," the thinner of the girls said.

Paula watched with a mixture of fascination and horror as he took a pair of Mars Bars from the shelf behind him, tore off the wrappers, dipped the chocolate in a washing-up bowl filled with batter and dropped them into one of the fryers. While they sizzled, he retrieved a two-litre bottle of Irn-Bru from the bottom of a glass-fronted fridge and rang up the girls' purchases.

"What can I do you for?" he asked Paula.

"What do those taste like?" She nodded towards the parcel of fried Mars Bars the girls carried.

He shrugged. "No idea, hen. They make a right mess of the fryer though. You wanna try one?"

"Y'should. They're pure brilliant," the thin girl offered as she followed her friend out of the shop.

"No thanks. I'll stick to fish and chips. What kind do you have?"

"Maris Piper." The man lifted one of the hinged baskets of chips, gave it a shake and returned it to the bubbling fat. "They're always Maris Piper, except when they're King Edwards."

"I meant the fish."

He studied her for a moment. "You're no' Scottish are you?"

"I'm English."

"London?"

"Yes."

"You need to learn the lingo then. Up here battered fish is always haddock. Fish 'n' chips is a supper, Irn-Bru is ginger and a fried Mars Bar is a heart attack." He grinned. "Got that?"

"A fish supper," Paula repeated. "I'd forgotten that."

"So you did know."

She smiled. "I lived in Edinburgh for four years when I was small."

"That's virtually England, but we'll no' hold it against you." The man grinned. "So what'll it be?"

"One supper, salt, no sauce and I'll skip the ginger and the heart attack. Oh, and a small bottle of sparkling water."

He winced. "This is a chippy, no' the Ritz. How about a fat Coke? You look like you could do wi' the calories."

"Fat Coke's fine."

"One supper, salt, no sauce, wi' a fat Coke coming right up." He dipped a huge white fillet into the washing-up bowl and tossed it in the fryer.

As he wrapped her supper, she asked tentatively, "I don't suppose you've got a plastic fork?"

He snorted.

"Okay, no fork."

"You're gettin' the hang o' it now."

Paula walked back along the beach to the steps of her new home. She sat down and opened the sweaty parcel. By the time she had finished eating, it was completely dark. She put the empty box and can on the sand, and felt in the pockets of her fleece for a tissue. Her fingers closed around her mobile phone. Without thinking, she switched it on and checked for new messages. There were two.

"Hi, darling." It was Ollie. "Your bike's ready. I think you'll be really pleased with the gears. I've put on the Dura Ace ten-speed cassette, a new chain and replaced the broken lever. If I don't hear from you by tomorrow morning, I'll pop round with it in the afternoon. Hey, and if you change your mind about Dan's party, give me a shout and I'll pick you up on the way. I know how you're feeling – I feel exactly the same – but I think it would be really good for us both to put in an appearance. No one'll expect us to stay long."

The electronic voice said he had called the day before at half-past five. Paula pressed delete. The second message was Ollie too.

"Paula, where are you?" He sounded frantic. "What's going on? I'm outside your flat with the bike. I just looked in the sitting room window. Half your stuff's gone. Please tell me you've been burgled, because if you haven't, the only thing I can think is that you've done a runner. For God's sake, call me as soon as you get this. I need to know you're all right."

The message was left at four o'clock that afternoon. She pressed delete again and waited, knowing what came next.

"First saved message," the electronic voice said.

"Hiya, babe." It wasn't Ollie this time. "You all set for tomorrow morning? We're gonna be great. They won't see us for dust. Don't forget you said you'd get more High5 for the bottles. I'm just going for a quick blast on the solo. Call me when you get this."

Paula's finger moved to select delete but something stopped her. "You bastard," she murmured into the phone, tears she had sworn not to shed muffling the words. "How could you abandon me? I would never have done that to you."

She hurled the handset into the blackness. There was a small splash.

"There, the tide can have you and you can sail away to Norway for all I care."

She scrambled to her feet, grazing already battered knuckles on the wall as she fumbled for the right key. Kicking the gate closed, she strode up the path.

Shopping with Sanders

Bovis was stretched out in the sun at the bottom of the steps, snout resting on her paws, when Paula got back from her run the next morning. A boy with shaggy collar-length blond hair, wearing a faded orange T-shirt and denim cut-offs was sitting cross-legged on the sand beside the dog, poking at the toenails of one of his bare feet with a small stick.

She stopped beside him, leaning forward slightly with hands on hips while she got her breath. The boy squinted up at her, revealing exactly the same snub nose and wide mouth as the girl Paula had seen on Saturday night.

"You okay?" he asked.

She paused her iPod. "Will be in a minute. Hot today, isn't it? You looking after Bovis?"

"That's right. How'd you know her name?"

"A woman called Nora from along the road told me."

"Why are you staring at me?"

"Am I? Sorry." Paula scanned the beach. There weren't many people out yet. Just a couple of dog walkers and one young family setting up camp a little way along the sand. The father was using a stone to bang in the poles of their windbreak, while the mother unpacked rugs, towels and swimsuits. A pair of little boys hopped about impatiently.

Without looking at him she said, "I saw her with a girl before. Are you brother and sister?"

He sniffed. "What makes you think that?"

"You're so alike." She smiled fleetingly. "You could be twins."

"Sandra said someone'd moved in."

"Your sister?"

"Aye."

Paula took out her earphones and sat down on the steps. "I think she climbed over the gate into my garden and moved my bike."

"Why would she do that?" he asked without much interest.

"I was hoping you could tell me."

He shook his head. "Nope."

"She also left Bovis tied to the gate."

Shielding his eyes with a stubby hand, he gazed out to sea. "Did she?"

Paula stretched down and knocked some wet sand off her trainers. "Any idea why she would do that?"

"Possibly."

"Nora said Bovis was bait."

The boy considered this. "Mibby."

"So your sister was testing me in some way?"

He turned and looked at her. His blue eyes were so pale they were almost transparent. "If she wanted to know what kind of person you were, she could of left Bovis to find out. You know, see how you'd react."

"She'd have had to be spying from somewhere then. I wonder where she could have been."

He shrugged. "There's plenty of rocks to hide behind and she's got ears like a bat."

"Does she often do that kind of thing?"

"You'd have to ask her." He grinned, revealing a mouthful of small, perfectly even teeth. "But Bovis definitely likes you."

"How can you tell?"

"She told me."

"Right."

"I don't mean she can speak," he said quickly. "I mean she tells me things by the way she behaves. See how she just shifted, so the tips of her paws are covering the end of her nose? She only does that when she's dead relaxed. If she likes a new person she leans on them, or rests her head on them, but if she doesn't, she'll turn away and, if I let her, she'll just walk off. When we're at home if someone she doesn't like comes into a room, she gets up and goes somewhere else." He rubbed the top of Bovis's head. "But you must be a nice person because she's comfortable with you."

"I like her too." Paula stood up. "But I've got to get on."

He looked disappointed. "Don't go yet. I could tell you some jokes. I know hundreds. How do penguins drink their Coke?" Without waiting for a response he carried on. "On the rocks. What's black and white and goes round and round? A penguin in a revolving door."

"That's very funny, but I really have to go."

"Wait, wait." He held up his hand. "Have you heard the one about the frog that went to McDonald's? He ordered French flies and a diet croke. What does a spaceman keep his sandwiches in? A launch box. What d'you call a vampire who likes cooking? Count Spatula!"

Paula couldn't help smiling again. "They're really good, but I'm off now. Will you tell your sister I'd like to speak to her?"

The boy stood too. "Where are you going?"

"To have a shower. I need to buy some food if I'm going to have any breakfast."

"So we'll wait here for you."

"Why?"

"You're new. We can show you the shops."

"Are there that many?"

"Of course not." He rolled his eyes. "This is Cra'frae."

"Cra'frae?"

"Only visitors call it Craskferry, and it's not that big."

"I know, that's what everyone keeps saying: this is not the Ritz, this is not London or Edinburgh, not the metropolis," Paula recited. "Anyway, I'm going."

She turned to leave but he touched her arm. Paula spun round as if she had been struck.

He pulled his hand away. "No need t'be so jumpy."

"Sorry. What do you want now?"

"Someone left a fish 'n' chip box and an empty can beside your steps. I put them in the bin." He pointed to a large black dustbin along the sand.

"That was kind of you. They were mine. I forgot to get rid of them last night."

"Did you have a heart attack?"

"Hilarious."

He held out his right hand. "Sanders McCormack."

Paula shook it. "I know. The McCormack bit at least. Sanders is unusual."

He wrinkled his nose. "My sister's Sandra."

"You said."

"We are twins," he said, excavating a lump of seaweed with his toe. "We were conceived in the toilet of a fried chicken restaurant."

"Of course you were."

"We were!" he said indignantly. "Anyway, what's your name?"

Paula opened her mouth to tell him but something strange happened. "PT," she heard herself say.

"Pete-y? That's more like a bloke's name."

"PT. It's a nickname. It's from my initials – P for Paula, T for Tyndall."

"Fair enough." Sanders sat down again. "We'll see you here in a bit then, PT."

"I'll be a while. Don't feel you have to wait."

"We're in no hurry. Bovis and me have had our breakfast."

"Shouldn't you be at school? It is Monday, isn't it?"

"Doh, it's the holidays."

"But it's only what, the fourth of July?"

"You're in Scotland now. We get our holidays earlier than English kids."

"So you do – I keep forgetting things these days."

"It's probably your age."

"Thanks, Sanders. See you later."

Back in the kitchen, Paula found a key lying on the table. A note scribbled on the back of a used brown envelope said simply, "Shed key for bicycle." It was signed "B McIntyre".

Sanders and Bovis were waiting when she went back out half-an-hour later.

"Where's your shopping bag?" he asked.

"I don't have one. Don't tell me shops here won't give you plastic bags?"

"Everybody knows plastic's bad for the environment. Mrs McIntyre sometimes uses a tartan trolley. You could borrow that."

"I wouldn't be seen dead with a tartan shopping trolley."

"But it's very nice tartan. It's Henderson. Betty was a Henderson before she married into the McIntyres, so that trolley means a lot to her. It's part of her heritage."

"You're talking nonsense."

Sanders gave a snort of laughter. "Aye, but it sounded good, didn't it?"

"Come on, I want to get to the newsagent's before all the papers are gone."

When she reached the front of the queue, the newsagent suggested, "If you're going to be here for the summer, you could put in an order. Lots o' visitors do. That way, the paper's on the mat for breakfast just like at home."

"That's a good idea," Paula agreed. "I'll have *The Scotsman* and *The Guardian* plus *Scotland on Sunday* and the *Sunday Herald*."

"I see you found them," he observed as he wrote her address in his book.

She glanced over her shoulder at Sanders, who was hovering in the doorway with Bovis. "Yes, but it was his sister I was after."

The newsagent handed Paula her papers. Looking at Sanders, he said, "You can tell yon sister o' yours I watched her palm that packet o' Maltesers the other day. If she tries anything like that again, I'll call the cops."

As Paula turned away from the counter, she saw Sanders stick his tongue out at the newsagent. She frowned at him.

"Old Renton fancies you," he said as they walked down Main Street.

"Who?"

"Him in there, the newsagent."

"Don't be daft. Anyway, he's not old. He couldn't be much more than thirty."

"That's ancient."

"Careful, it's my thirtieth birthday soon." Tears pricked behind Paula's eyes.

"He was talking to your chest the whole time you were in there."

She swallowed hard and blew her nose. "No, he wasn't."

Sanders squinted at her. "You don't know him. He told Sandra he'd give her fifty quid if she had sex with him and a hundred if she brought a friend."

"That's a very serious accusation. Did she really tell you Mr Renton said that? If it's true, she needs to go to the police."

"No." He picked at a loose thread on Bovis's lead. "But I bet he'd like to."

"You can't go around making up things like that about people."

"He deserves it."

"Is this to do with him spotting Sandra shoplifting?"

"Mibby. What's next on your list?"

"I need vegetables."

"My mum goes to the Co-op because it's cheap, but you're a bit posh so you'd probably like it over there." He pointed across the street to a shop with a huge chestnut tree outside. A sign running across the sunshine yellow frontage read, *Linton's Fruit, Vegetables, Groceries and Whole Foods.*

The pavement was stacked with crates of fruit and vegetables. A handwritten card propped up beside a sheaf of brown bags at the back of a box of aubergines read, *ALL ORGANIC. SERVE YOURSELF.*

Paula began filling bags with apples, cherries, oranges, onions, an avocado and handfuls of dark green spinach.

"What's that goin' to make?" Sanders asked.

"I hadn't thought." She passed him a couple of bulging bags. "Make yourself useful and hold these."

"You might be overdoing it a bit on the vitamins."

"What do you think I should be eating then?"

"Something with lots of sugar and calories and stuff. You're pretty skinny even if you have got quite a big chest."

"How come everyone round here thinks it's okay to make personal remarks?" she demanded. "The man in the chip shop said I needed fattening up."

"That's Felice," he said eagerly. "He's married to my mum's friend Kyoko."

"Right." She picked up a cauliflower.

"Chocolate cake would be good – to fatten you up. It was my twelfth birthday last week and I had an excellent chocolate cake."

"I doubt this place sells chocolate cake."

"It does but it's not the real thing. It's that carob crap." He made a face and stuck his tongue out again.

"I think I'm about done here."

Sanders tied Bovis's lead to the railings and they went inside. Paula laid her bags on the counter while she chose a loaf of wholemeal bread and some other items from the shelves. A man in a navy and cream striped Breton top nodded to Sanders, and began weighing her purchases and noting figures on a scrap of paper. When he finished he said, "That'll be £14.80."

Paula retrieved her purse from the pocket of her jeans, and took out a ten pound note and some coins.

Before she could pay, Sanders said firmly, "She's local. She's staying downstairs at Betty McIntyre's."

"In that case, welcome to Cra'frae," the man said. "I'm Adrian Linton."

"Paula Tyndall." She held out the money but Sanders pushed her hand out of the way.

"Sanders!" she exclaimed. "What are you doing?"

"I said she's local," he repeated.

"And it's still £14.80."

"Aye right and I'm a penguin." He turned and walked out.

Adrian gave a sigh of exasperation but didn't say anything. Paula handed over the money.

"What was that all about?" she asked when she got outside.

"He always adds 50p to visitors' bills."

"Don't be silly."

"It's true. My nan used to work there sometimes and he made her do it too."

Paula rubbed her temples. She could feel a headache coming on and her hands were starting to tremble. "I need coffee."

"We could go to Nora's Ark."

She looked at him quizzically. "Is that another of your inventions?"

"No, it's a café. Honest. It's where Mum got my cake. It belongs to Nora, the lady you met on the beach. She's my mum's friend too."

"Okay, just point me in the right direction. You don't need to come."

He beamed at her. "I don't mind keepin' you company."

She sighed. "All right, fine. I'll treat you to a slice of cake if you promise to bugger off and leave me in peace as soon as you've eaten it."

"Deal."

The façade of Nora's Ark was painted bright pink, and a wooden sign above the door showed a stick figure with a cat tucked under one arm and a rabbit under the other standing on the deck of a little boat.

"That's Nora," Sanders said. "She likes animals."

"I gathered."

He tied Bovis to a metal ring under the window, which had an enamel dish of water beside it.

Nora appeared from the kitchen as they were sitting down. "Morning, Sanders," she said. "You've brought me a new customer."

He nodded at Paula. "This is my friend PT."

"Paula," she corrected. "PT's just a nickname. I'm sorry, I should have introduced myself the other day."

"It's nice to see you again." Nora took a pad and pen from her apron pocket. "What can I get you?"

"Chocolate cake and a Tizer float, please," Sanders said.

Nora shook her head. "I don't know why I bother asking." She turned to Paula. "Sanders is a regular. He always has the same thing. What about you?"

"A big pot of coffee and I suppose I'd better keep him company with the cake."

"It doesn't have to be chocolate. I've got coffee and walnut, apple and cinnamon, banana loaf, millionaire's shortbread and lemon meringue pie today." She pointed to a row of clear plastic domes on the counter. "Go and see what you fancy."

Paula glanced at Sanders. He mouthed, "Chocolate."

"My nutritional adviser seems to think I should stick with chocolate."

"It's my favourite too," Nora said. "It's the white chocolate icing with Smarties on top."

She brought over their order then went to serve a pair of elderly ladies who had come in.

Paula tried a forkful of cake. "This really is good. Does Nora make it herself?"

"Aye. She makes all thc cakes and tray bakes," Sanders replied through a mouthful of crumbs. "The millionaire's shortbread's my second favourite. That's what I have if she's run out of chocolate cake."

Paula took a sip of coffee. "What's millionaire's shortbread?"

"Doh, it's like shortbread with chocolate and toffee stuff."

"It would have to have chocolate. Is there anything else you like to eat?"

Sanders thought about this. "Ice-cream, and my mum makes nice soup. Cock-a-leekie's the best."

"That's leek and something, isn't it?"

He raised his thick eyebrows. "It's chicken 'n' leek. Don't you know anything?"

"Apparently not."

He picked up Paula's *Scotsman* and began leafing through it.

Nora came over. "What rubbish is he telling you?"

Looking out from behind the paper, he crossed his eyes, opened his mouth as far as it would go and let his chocolaty tongue loll out in a passable impression of a village idiot.

Nora ignored him. "Are you settling in all right?"

Paula swallowed a mouthful of cake. "I am. I need to sort something out with a solicitor though. Is there one in the village?"

"No, but there are a couple of firms along the coast in Westwick."

Sanders stuck his hand in the air. "Please, Miss, permission to speak?"

"What now?" Nora demanded.

"You could try Rhind and Gibson in Edinburgh." He put on a posh voice. "I hear they're terribly well thought of."

"What on earth do you know about Edinburgh lawyers?" Nora asked.

Sanders put the paper down and tapped the side of his nose with a finger. "I am not at liberty to divulge my sources."

Little Paula

Paula sat opposite Caroline Gibson of Rhind and Gibson in her vast wood-panelled office. She had found the firm's advert in *The Scotsman* moments after Sanders left Nora's Ark.

When the secretary had shown Paula in, a short, wide woman of about forty-five dressed in a navy trouser suit rose from a desk at the far end of the room and stepped forward to shake hands.

Caroline indicated a pair of leather sofas in front of a marble fireplace. "Let's sit here. It's more comfy than the hard chairs at the desk."

An immense gold-framed mirror above the mantelpiece reflected a row of portraits of austere, whiskered gentlemen hanging on the opposite wall. "This is the most splendid office I've ever been in," Paula remarked.

"Every single building in the New Town was like this originally," Caroline said. "The Georgians built this whole section of Edinburgh to represent the very height of classical order and elegance."

"Does Rhind and Gibson fill all of this one?"

"It does. It was the original Mr Rhind's home and this was the drawing room." Caroline smiled. "One of the benefits of being senior partner is you get the swankiest office. I found it quite daunting at first with my predecessors watching over me, but after I gave them nicknames they didn't seem quite so scary."

She pointed to the portrait nearest the door. "That's Auld Wullie, William Rhind. He founded the firm in 1829. The old buzzard next to him is Crusty Chris – his son, Christopher Rhind – and next to him is Malky, Malcolm Gibson, who joined the partnership in 1878, and over there, on the other side of the door, are the Two Ronnies, Ronald Gibson senior and junior, Malky's son and grandson."

"They still look terrifying to me," Paula said. "I can't imagine they'd approve of being given nicknames."

Caroline laughed. "They were probably birling in their graves anyway with a woman taking over as head of the firm, except maybe Ronnie junior. He was my grandfather and a really sweet old bloke." She clasped her hands under her chin. "So, let's get down to business. When you spoke on the phone to my assistant you said you'd just moved up to Craskferry from London?"

"That's right and I'd like some advice."

"Marion explained your situation to me, and I believe she told you, Miss Tyndall, that it may not be possible for us, or any law firm, to help you at this stage."

"She did, but I'd still like you to try," Paula said firmly.

Caroline nodded. "I think Marion also told you that you could have saved yourself a journey across the Forth and consulted a firm in Fife. It's not that we want to turn away business, Miss Tyndall, but I have no doubt any lawyer would give you the same advice. A Fife firm would be cheaper too." She waved her hand at the room. "They don't have our overheads."

"Your assistant explained all that, but I wanted to make the trip to Edinburgh. I lived here when I was small and I've not been back for years. My dad's an accountant with one of the City firms and he was sent up here to set up a new office. I spent my first three years of school at St Andrew's in Morningside."

"My niece goes to St Andrew's. It's a good school." Caroline picked up a pen and tapped it against her front teeth. "Well, if you're certain, tell me the whole story and, while I must stress again that I don't think it's likely anything can be done, I will look into it."

"Well, as I explained, I have a legal obligation, but I don't want to… I simply can't…" Paula ran a hand through her hair. "I want to find a way out of it."

The clouds were all wrong.

Glowing huge and heavy with sulphurous intent, they belonged in a different sky, one that matched their mood.

Yet they were gliding towards her across the intense blue, purposeful, unstoppable, like a squadron of bombers on their way to annihilate an enemy village.

She stood quite still, just watching, breath held high in her chest, as their giant frown unfurled across the sand.

She was unsure how she had got there, uncertain what she had intended to do next. She knew one thing instinctively though: the threat they posed went far beyond ordinary rain. The slightest movement, the tiniest twitch of nerve or crackle of thought would attract their poisonous, burning, devastating attention.

Paula assumed she was alone on the beach until she saw the girl.

She was running along the edge of the sea in the direction of the cliffs, the sparkling foam nipping like a terrier at her pink plastic sandals, then retreating just as fast. She was eight or nine years old, and as she ran she threw her head back, laughing, drawing the warm air deep into her lungs, blind to the threat from the sky casting its shadow across her tanned skin.

In her right hand, the girl held the string of a kite. It was the old-fashioned fabric kind, made up of alternating triangles of red and green, with a fluttering tail of yellow and blue bows. It dipped and wove in a breeze far more benevolent than the one carrying its evil burden so high above them.

Paula felt a recognition she could not place.

Suddenly, the girl stopped, turned round and began walking towards her. The design on the front of the pale blue cotton pinafore was as familiar as if Paula had seen it the day before. The skirt had a wide pocket embroidered to look like a row of flowerpots filled with pink and white blooms. It was bulging slightly. She smiled internally at the memory of what it contained: hundreds of tiny cowrie shells gleaned from the sand that morning. She could feel their weight and the way they ground damply against each other as she ran.

The girl paused. Paula and her childhood self were standing not more than three metres apart.

"Hello," little Paula said.

Paula willed herself to speak. She wanted to warn the girl of the horror lurking so close by, to step forward, put an arm around her fragile shoulders and lead her to safety, but she couldn't.

Fear had pushed speech and movement so far beyond her grasp she could not recover them.

Little Paula waited a few seconds, then shrugged.

She turned and ran back towards the water's edge, skipping around the glossy piles of seaweed that dotted her path. A pair of seagulls circled above, calling raucously to each other, as she raised the arm holding the bobbing kite once more and resumed her journey to the cliffs.

Adult Paula could only watch as she faded into the distance.

Her cheek was pressed against the cool pane of a window and she could feel rough upholstery on the bare skin of her legs. She must have dozed off. She rubbed her eyes and focussed on the moving vista beyond the glass. Sea and shore. A row of houses, some trees, more sea. She was travelling along the coast on a train, but where was she going?

A recording of a woman's voice came to her rescue. "We will shortly be arriving in Westwick. Westwick next station stop."

She had been to Edinburgh to see the lawyer and this was where she caught the bus back to Craskferry. It wasn't until she was on the platform that she began to think about the dream. Almost every night for more than a fortnight, it had come during her fitful hours of sleep. Then, after she arrived at Craskferry, nothing – until now. But this time it was different. It was the first time the girl, her childhood self, had turned and acknowledged her.

Paula checked the timetable in the bus shelter outside the station. She had a few minutes to wait and a phone box sat on the other side of the road. She hurried across and dialled her parents' number.

Her mum's voice was flat. "Barbara Tyndall."

"It's me."

"Paula, thank God." Relief lifted her tone. "Are you all right?"

"Getting by. How are you two? You sound wiped out."

Her mum ignored the question. "Where on earth are you? Every time I've called your mobile it's been switched off. Ollie rang yesterday crazy with worry. He said you weren't at the flat and you hadn't answered his messages. He seemed to think you'd disappeared."

Paula let out a long breath. "I'm fine. I haven't disappeared. My mobile's knackered."

"But where are you?"

"I'm in Craskferry."

"Craskferry! What in heaven's name are you doing there?"

"I needed to get away, to be somewhere that didn't have any memories of, well, you know."

There was a short pause. "Are you really okay?"

"Yes, I'm really okay. Look, if Ollie calls again, don't tell him where I am. I can't cope with him just now. Do you understand?"

"I do, Paula, but you know he's upset too. Promise me you'll ring him."

"I will. I've got to go, my bus is coming. Give my love to Dad. Take care of yourselves. I'll call again soon."

Paula made it back to the shelter just as the bus was pulling away. She waved frantically at the driver and he stopped and opened the door.

"Hurry up then," he grumbled. "I huvnie got all day."

She showed him her return ticket and threw herself into the nearest empty seat.

"I thought all you young people had mobile phones," said a voice close by.

"Pardon?" Paula turned to the woman next to her. It was Mrs McIntyre. Just her luck – a twenty-minute journey stuck making small talk.

"I said I thought you all had mobile phones."

"I don't."

Mrs McIntyre adjusted the weight of the wicker shopping basket in her lap. "Well, you cannae rely on call boxes to keep in touch with the world. There cannae be more than a handful still working in all o' Fife."

"I don't really need to keep in touch at the moment."

"You needed to phone somebody just now."

"I was just catching up with my mum while I waited for the bus."

"And what if she needed to contact you?"

Paula shrugged.

"I've got a spare phone upstairs. You can plug it into the socket in the back room."

"That's very good of you, but I really don't need to speak to anyone."

Mrs McIntyre took a small spiral-bound notebook out of her handbag, tore a page from the back and wrote down a number. She handed it to Paula.

"Give this to your mother and let her be the judge."

"All right, thank you." Paula folded the paper and put it in the pocket of her fleece.

"Someone said I should get yon broadband for tenants with computers."

"It would save them having to use an insecure, open network."

"Aye, well, that's all Greek to me, but I might look into it."

"Not on my account," Paula said quickly. "I don't plan to be online that much, so I'll risk the open network."

Mrs McIntyre looked out of the window and Paula followed her gaze. There were thick hedges on both sides of the road, and beyond them rolling fields filled with pale golden crops or flocks of peacefully chomping sheep. Occasional patches of dense woodland, cottages or groups of farm buildings broke up the uniformity.

"Thank you for the shed key," she said when she couldn't bear the silence any longer.

"Did you find out who moved your bicycle?" Mrs McIntyre enquired, eyes still on the view.

"It was just a kid."

Mrs McIntyre turned to regard her. "It's very precious to you, isn't it?"

"Tandems are expensive and this is a good one. It was stupid of me to leave it unlocked overnight."

"I didnae mean its cash value," she said gently, resuming her scrutiny of the passing countryside.

Sir Nils Olav

Paula leant her bare shoulders against the rough sandstone cliff face and gazed out to sea. The breeze that was carrying a flotilla of little yachts across the bay was chilly on her sweat-damp skin. Shivering, she wrapped her arms around her body. Tendrils of newly short hair whipped across her face. She tucked them behind her ears, but the wind threw them back into her eyes and tugged on the flex of her earphones. Black Eyed Peas' *Pump It* came on and she turned the volume as high as she could bear.

As the track ended, a familiar voice broke into the momentary silence. "PT, are you deaf? I said cheer up."

Something contracted in the centre of her chest. She closed her eyes and pressed down on her breastbone. Just breathe, she told herself. Breathe slowly. It'll pass. There was a soft thud. She opened her eyes to find Sanders crouched by her feet. Bovis landed beside him and shook herself down, peppering Paula's legs with sand.

She paused the music. "I didn't hear you. Please don't call me that."

"You said it was your name."

"Well, it isn't. It's Paula."

"Aye right." He made a face. "Suit yourself."

She adjusted her expression into a smile. "So where did you spring from?"

"Up there." Sanders indicated a ledge about ten feet up and a little further along the cliff. "Didn't you see us climbing down?"

"I was watching the boats. How did you get Bovis up there?"

"There's a path from the top."

"Your sister not with you?"

"Nah."

"I still want a word with her. What mischief is she up to today?"

"Dunno." He scratched his nose. "Would you like me to tell you some more jokes?"

"I don't think so."

"You sure? You look miserable."

"Do I?"

A gust of wind turned his over-grown blond hair into a halo. "You look sad even when you're smiling."

"Go on then." Paula sighed inwardly. She took the phones out of her ears. "Make me laugh."

He thought for a moment. "What's black and white and red all over?"

She groaned. "That was ancient even when I was your age."

"So what's the answer?"

"Now, let me see." She put a finger to her lips and cocked her head. "I wonder, could it be a newspaper?"

"Wrong!" Bovis looked on patiently as Sanders did a little victory dance, punching his arms in the air. "You're absolutely wrong. I said r-e-d not r-e-a-d."

"In that case, I don't know. You'll have to tell me."

"A penguin with sunburn!" he declared gleefully.

"I'd better get on with my run before I seize up."

"Where are you going?"

"Since the tide's out, I was planning to go round into the next bay and follow the coast for a bit."

"Can we come?"

"And run?"

"I'm really good at running and Bovis is pretty fast when she wants to be."

Paula looked down at his feet. He was wearing purple ankle-length wellingtons. "You wouldn't get far in those. I don't know how you got down the cliff without killing yourself."

"Ninja."

"Even ninjas can't run over rocks in wellies."

He looked crestfallen. "Please, please, pretty please."

"All right, all right, but we'll walk, and no more jokes."

"Don't you like penguins?" he asked as they set off round the headland.

Breathe, she told herself again, just breathe. When they were little, Pete had loved visiting the penguins at Edinburgh Zoo. He used to imitate the way they walked. Once he was laughing so much he tripped and gave himself a nose bleed. "I haven't got an opinion about them one way or the other," she said.

"They're very interesting creatures, y'know."

"And I suppose you're going to tell me why."

"If you like. There's one at Edinburgh Zoo who used to be a wing commander."

"Is that another joke?"

"No." Sanders sounded wounded. "He's been promoted and he's a sir and the colonel-in-chief of a regiment in the Norwegian army now."

"You're talking drivel again."

"Honest I'm not. He's a king penguin and his name's Sir Nils Olav and he's the mascot of the Royal Norwegian Guards. It was in the paper. There was a picture and everything – I cut it out. He's 80 centimetres high, and a load of soldiers came over from Norway to give him a medal. They pinned it on a band round his flipper and patted him on the shoulders with a big, shiny sword. They even put a statue of him outside the penguin enclosure. Mum was going to take me to see last summer, but Nan got sick and we couldn't go. I really want to go and see him."

"Does he wear his medal?" Paula enquired trying to sound serious.

"Course not. It's only for special occasions."

"So how do people know which one he is?"

"Duh! They ask a keeper. The statue's nearly as tall as me and it's made out of bronze."

"Sounds like you're quite a penguin fan." She wondered if Nils Olav had been there when she and Pete used to go. "How long do penguins live?"

"Fifteen or twenty years usually, sometimes longer."

Probably not then.

"People think they're dull because they just waddle about and swim and eat fish and crap all day, but they're not dull at all." Sanders unclipped Bovis's lead from her collar and she galloped towards the water's edge, sending a group of seagulls, which had been bobbing in the shallows, flapping and squawking into the air.

He lowered his voice and leaned towards her. "There's a gay penguin at Central Park Zoo in New York. He's called Silo and for six years he had a boyfriend called Roy. The keepers gave them an abandoned egg after they tried to hatch a rock and they looked after it and raised the chick together. It's called Tango."

"How on earth do you know all this?"

"It was in one of Mum's magazines. Anyway, this girl penguin called Scrappy arrived from another zoo and Silo dumped Roy and built a nest with her. Isn't that sad?"

"Very sad. What happened to Roy?"

"It didn't say." Sanders kicked over a mound of seaweed, releasing a cloud of tiny black flies. "What's your favourite animal?"

Paula thought for a moment. "I don't know really. I quite like donkeys. They're so velvety and placid. I think they used to have some on the beach here."

"What were they doing on the beach?"

"Giving rides to children."

"There are donkeys up at Mr Thompson's farm."

"I don't suppose it's the same ones. This was more than twenty years ago. They're probably long dead."

"They might not be. They live even longer than penguins. I went once with Nan, and Mr Thompson let me pat them. He said they could live to be over forty."

"You're a bit of an animal expert."

"Well," he said, shoving his hands into his pockets, "they're nicer than a lot of people."

"I'd have to agree with you there."

"What else do you like?"

"Other animals?"

"Anything."

"That's a big question." She stopped. In the distance, Bovis had caught up with another dog – it looked like a spaniel – and they were chasing each other in and out of the sea. "I like reading historical biographies and novels."

"Books about dead people?" He screwed up his face. "What for?"

"Because they're interesting. Their lives were so different to ours and yet in so many ways they were just the same."

"Do you watch TV or is that too modern?"

She couldn't help smiling. "I like romantic films and comedies."

"I hate all that romance stuff – there's too much kissing and blubbing."

"What's your favourite programme then?"

He grinned. "The Simpsons."

"They're fab. I love Marge's mad hair."

"I like Oor Wullie too."

"Oor who?"

"Wullie. Haven't you heard of him?" he asked aghast.

"He sounds vaguely familiar but I can't think why."

"He's only the best cartoon character ever."

"On TV?"

"No, in the *Sunday Post.*"

"What's that?"

"It's a newspaper and he has his own annual at Christmas – I've got lots of them. You really, really don't know anything, do you?"

Paula grimaced and sat down on a rock. "Sanders, you're very rude sometimes."

He pretended not to hear. "So you haven't seen him?"

"Not that I can remember. I think I've seen the *Sunday Post* in the newsagent. It looks like a paper for pensioners. What are you doing reading it?"

Sanders chuckled. "My nan gets it. It's got the Broons too. They're good, but Oor Wullie's my hero."

"Why? What's he like?"

"He looks a bit like me – messy hair and a wee round nose. He's only eleven though. Did I tell you I'm twelve?"

"You did."

"And he wears dungarees and sits on a bucket. He rides around in a go-kart made out of wood and gets into all sorts of trouble."

"Sounds like your kind of guy."

Sanders grinned. "What other things do you like?"

"I like running and I love cycling."

"On that bike with two seats?"

"On the tandem," Paula confirmed. "You've seen it?"

"I saw it over the gate."

Closing her eyes, she saw herself climbing onto their first tandem. The assistant had wheeled it out of the shop and was holding it steady on the pavement for them. She was thirteen years old and her leg shook with a mixture of fear and excitement as she lifted it over the crossbar and settled her weight onto the back seat.

"That looks a good fit for both of you," the assistant said. "Are you ready to take it for a spin?"

"Right now?" she heard herself asking.

"Come on, PT, don't be a coward," Pete chivvied. "There's no point getting it if you're not going to ride it."

She sucked a huge breath into her lungs and let it out slowly. "All right, I'm ready. Let's go."

"Hold on tight and pedal," he called over his shoulder.

The assistant stepped back and the bike bounced off the pavement into the road, as they began to turn the cranks, legs moving in absolute unison thanks to the chain that linked them.

Paula's stomach tightened to a fist of anxiety as the bike wobbled from side to side. They were going to fall in a heap on the tarmac any second.

Then, suddenly, something unexpected happened: they were under control, picking up speed and heading down the road in a perfectly straight line.

She began to relax.

They reached a set of traffic lights just as they turned to red. "Stop pedalling, foot down," Pete instructed.

She did exactly as she was told.

"Okay, pedal up, push on."

They pulled away as smoothly as if they had been riding together all their lives. Rounding a bend, they found themselves at the top of a sweeping hill.

"Tuck in," he ordered, "we're going for warp speed."

Paula crouched down until the crown of her head was touching the small of his back. Tucking elbows and knees in as far as she could get them, she glanced down. The road was a dizzying streak of grey under her feet.

When they reached the bottom, she lifted her head and let out a whoop. "That was amazing."

"Wasn't it magic? I told you we'd be good at this."

"You two are naturals," the assistant observed as they reluctantly slowed to a halt in front of the shop. "You'll be winning races before you know it."

"Did you hear me, PT?" Sanders tugged on the hem of her T-shirt.

"Sorry, no."

"You were miles away."

"I was." She rubbed her eyes. "What did you say?"

"I said Bovis and me have got to get back now. Nan's expecting us for lunch."

"Okay, on you go. I'm going to run a bit further."

Paula made a ham and tomato sandwich and took it through to the study. Her laptop was on the desk, untouched since she had unpacked it. She switched it on, found an open network and within seconds emails were pouring into her inbox. Most were the usual spam – carelessly spelt sales pitches for replica watches, dodgy mortgages and loans, fake Viagra and university degrees where the only qualification was to be in possession of a credit card.

She kept her finger on the delete button until there were just two messages left. The subject line on the first read, *Please get in touch!!!!!!*

She clicked it open and began to read. *All right, I get it,"* Ollie had written. *"You don't want to speak to me. But please, please, please reply to this. Just a single line to let me know you're okay. I'm missing you dreadfully. Don't cut me out of your life, not now, when we need each other so much. I couldn't bear it. Ollie.*

She was about to hit delete, when she noticed the PS – *If I don't hear from you by Wednesday evening, I'm going to call the police.*

It was already Wednesday afternoon.

Can't talk right now, she typed furiously, *but I'm okay. Need you to leave it at that.* She hit send.

The next message was from Jen. *How are you doing, girl? Ollie reckons you've gone away somewhere. Good idea, I say. He was convinced he could persuade you to come to Dan's party. I don't know what goes through that man's brain sometimes, but I do know he's in a pretty bad state. He got pissed out of his head on neat vodka – I thought Poles could hold their drink – and cried on my shoulder for most of the night.*

Anyway, I'm not going to ramble on. Just wanted to tell you I'm thinking about you. Do you know if you'll be back for your birthday? We don't have to go out or do anything. At least promise you'll be back in town by September for mine – I can't face the big three-oh without my best girl. I'm planning to get hammered on tequila slammers and fizz, take my top off, dance on the bar, fall off and chuck up all over myself, so I'll need you there to pick me up, put me in a taxi and remind me all about it the next day. It'll be brilliant!!

Wherever you are and whatever you're doing, take care of yourself, and if there's anything I can do, you only have to ask. Love you, Jen xxx

Paula closed her laptop and pressed her fingers to her eyelids. Her birthday. Her extra-special extra summer birthday, the one she shared with Pete. She couldn't bear to think about it.

Sandra on the run

Paula was coming out of Adrian Linton's shop when she spotted Sandra and Bovis turning down the cobbled lane that led to the harbour. She made it to the corner in time to see Sandra's pink ra-ra skirt disappearing around the side of the granary. Paula ran along the front of the building, carrier bag of groceries thumping against her thigh as she weaved between the strolling holidaymakers. She was certain she would to catch them as they emerged at the far end, but there was no sign of them on the harbour wall or behind the granary.

She was about to head back to Main Street, when an exceptionally tall woman in her mid-twenties stepped out of the building's front door and into her path.

The woman smiled at her. "Hello. Are you Mrs McIntyre's new tenant?"

"How did you know that?"

She held out her hand. "Rachel Fanshawe."

Paula racked her brain as they shook hands. Then it came to her. "Of course, the estate agent. Sorry, I'm not quite with it today."

"It's the warm weather," the woman said pleasantly. "It slows the thought processes."

"How did you recognise me?"

"I was driving past and saw you and Mrs McIntyre going into her house the other day."

"We'd bumped into each other on the bus from Westwick."

"How do you like the place?"

"It's lovely, but it's a bit strange having her coming and going through the hall."

"It is a slightly unusual arrangement." The woman smiled again. "Betty converted the house to give her extra income, but she was adamant she didn't want the vestibule carved up. She said if she keeled over it would cost too much to undo when her children wanted to sell."

Before Paula could respond, she caught sight of Sandra and Bovis on the crowded beach, trotting along the water's edge. She spoke quickly. "It was nice to meet you, but I've got to go – I can see someone I need talk to."

Paula jogged down the slipway. As she came close to catching up, she called out, "Hang on a minute, Sandra, I want to speak to you."

The girl glanced over her shoulder, but instead of stopping, she broke into a run. Soon, she and Bovis were sprinting flat out across the sand towards the row of steps belonging to the houses on Shore Road. Making a sharp right turn, they disappeared through a gap between two garden walls.

By the time Paula reached the same spot, the narrow alley was empty.

The kite dipped and soared above little Paula as she skipped along the water's edge. Giggling, she dodged the foam's darting encroachments and jinxed around the tangled piles of glossy green, brown and black seaweed. The breeze tugged at the hem of her blue and white pinafore and pulled playfully at the string wrapped around her hand. The seagulls called to each other as they circled effortlessly overhead, buoyed by the warm air currents.

Suddenly, the girl turned and faced her watching adult self. She took a couple of steps forward and opened her mouth as if to speak again. Then, changing her mind, she swung round and resumed her journey along the beach.

Paula felt something grip her arm and shake it.

"PT, wake up."

Sanders.

He shook her again. "Wake up, you were talking to yourself."

She forced her eyes open. She was sitting on the top of the beach steps with her head leaning awkwardly against the gate. Sanders stood on the sand beside her.

"God, no wonder I can't sleep at night. I've got to stop dozing off like this." She rubbed her neck. "I told you not to call me PT."

"You were saying, 'Talk to me, talk to me'."

"Was I?" Paula stretched. "I saw your elusive twin earlier, but she scarpered when I tried to speak to her. I got the distinct feeling she was avoiding me."

Sanders sat down beside her. "Can I ask you something?"

"Go on."

"Who do you ride your tandem with?"

She sat up straight. "Why do you want to know?"

He stuck out his bottom lip. "No reason. Just you're always on your own and you need two people and I thought mibby..." His voice trailed off.

"Have you been spying on me as well?"

"No, but..."

"Sanders, what are you trying to ask me?"

"I thought mibby, if you didn't have anyone else to ride it with, well, mibby I could."

Paula stood up. "I don't think so," she said coldly. "I have to go."

"Wait." He wrapped both hands round her calf.

"Sanders, what are you doing?" She grabbed the top of the gate to stop overbalancing on the rickety step.

"You must want to or you wouldn't have brought it."

"Sanders, get off my leg."

He let go. "Sorry."

"I brought the tandem because it's important to me, but that doesn't mean I was planning to ride it."

"But you could. I could go on the back."

Paula shook her head. "Absolutely not."

"But why? It'd be fun."

"I said no."

"I'm big enough." He jumped up and stood on tiptoe. "See, I'm taller than I look, and Mum says my legs are quite long for my height. It would be great. We could visit the donkeys at Mr Thompson's farm. You'd enjoy it."

"Sanders, no."

"But why won't you give me a chance?" He was almost in tears.

Paula sat down. "I've only ever ridden it with my twin brother," she said quietly.

"You're a twin?" he asked, cheerfulness instantly restored.

She ran her fingertips over the tattoo on her ankle. "I was." Her voice was a whisper.

Sanders climbed the steps and sat beside her. "What do you mean?"

"He died."

"How?"

"In an accident."

"When…"

Paula held up a hand. "Enough questions."

She looked past him. The beach was packed with families enjoying the sunshine. Over by the rubbish bin, Bovis was ripping at a bulging black plastic sack. "You'd better go and deal with your dog before she makes herself sick eating whatever's in that bag."

An only child

Paula was sitting down to eat a piece of toast, still wearing the pyjama top and knickers she had slept in, when the doorbell rang. She decided it was probably the postman for Mrs McIntyre. When her landlady didn't come down after the third ring, Paula went to answer it.

"This had better be good," she muttered as she unlocked the storm door and peered around it.

Sanders stood on the step. He held out a carrier bag. "I brought a picnic."

"Did I miss something? I don't remember agreeing to a picnic."

"That's because it's a surprise."

"Okay, I'm surprised."

"So can I come in while you get ready?"

"Hold your horses, cowboy. Where exactly do you think we're going?"

He grinned. "To see the donkeys. I've made tuna sandwiches and I've got some carrots. Donkeys love carrots."

"At the farm you were talking about?"

"Yes."

"How far is it?"

"Dunno. Mibby ten miles."

The vestibule tiles were cold under Paula's bare feet and she shifted her weight between them. "And we're getting there how?"

He put his hands together as if he was praying. "Pretty please, on the tandem."

"Sanders, I told you, you're not riding the tandem."

"You're just being mean."

"No, I'm not. I'm just being…" Paula paused. What was she being? She had no idea. But she did know one thing: she wasn't going out on the tandem with him. "Why don't you go and play with your friends?"

"I don't have any." His lip was trembling. She couldn't tell if he was genuinely upset or if it was another of his fabrications.

"Your twin sister then. Go and play with her and leave me in peace."

She closed the door and had gone a couple of steps down the hall when the letterbox opened.

"I don't have a twin sister," he yelled.

The flap snapped shut again.

Paula made for the door. As she stepped out, one foot caught in the handle of the carrier bag he had left on the step. Next thing she knew, she was on her hands and knees on the path of crushed seashells that led to the front gate. Wincing, she picked herself up. Fragments of shell were pressed into her palms and all the way down her shins. Blood oozed from a particularly large piece just below the right knee. Brushing them off, she hobbled to the gate. She checked the road in both directions but Sanders was gone.

A man driving past hooted his horn and whistled through his open window. Paula looked down. She was standing in the street in nothing but a pyjama top and a pair of knickers. She went inside, rinsed her bleeding leg, stuck a plaster on it and got back into bed.

Hi Jen, she typed. *Sorry to vanish without saying – I needed to get away from everyone and everything, especially Ollie, poor thing. A friend in need? Not me. Just can't do it right now. Is that really rubbish of me? Don't answer that. I've run away to the seaside – Craskferry, to be precise, look it up on a map – but please don't tell him. It's peaceful, which is exactly what I need, if a bit surreal at times.*

I seem to have been adopted by Dr Jekyll and Mr Hyde reincarnated in the body of a twelve-year-old boy. He's utterly endearing one minute and a total monster the next. I actually feel quite sorry for him. I think he's lonely and he seems desperate to be liked. We fell out earlier this morning though. My fault. Why am I such a cow just now? Don't answer that either.

I haven't decided how long I'm staying, but I'd like to get a few more things from the flat – I did a crap job of packing. I want to get my solo bike too – Ollie said he'd finished it. Any chance you could get him to drop it at your place? If I do you a list, could you pick up the other stuff? You've still got a key, haven't you? If that's okay, I'll arrange for someone to collect everything. Let me know if there's any interesting looking post (there won't be). I've done one of those redirection forms, so there shouldn't be much. Thanks a million, darling. Love you forever! P xxx

She hit send without bothering to read the message over, grabbed her purse and headed for Main Street.

Nora's Ark was packed and she had to wait at the door until a pair of elderly men in tracksuits left so she could take their table. After a couple of minutes, a teenage girl came over.

"The lunchtime specials are up there." The girl pointed to a blackboard. "Do you need time to think or can I take your order?"

Paula ran her eyes down the board. There was watercress soup with a herb scone, baked potatoes with chilli, cheesy baked beans, or hummus and roasted peppers, and a choice of several salads. She ordered a Greek salad with focaccia and a pot of coffee.

As the waitress turned to go, Paula asked, "Is Nora around?"

"She's in the kitchen."

"Would you see if I could have a quick word when things die down? Tell her it's Paula, Mrs McIntyre's tenant."

She had finished her salad and was onto her second cup of coffee when Nora emerged from the kitchen, carrying a mug of her own.

"Okay if I join you?" she asked. "I haven't sat down since eight o'clock. It's been pandemonium today." She surveyed her domain. "This is the first time since eleven that I've seen empty tables. Kylie said you wanted to speak to me."

Paula nodded. "Sanders came round this morning. He said something very odd. I thought maybe you could explain it."

"Fire away, but I can't promise to shed much light on anything that charming little horror says. He's far too bright for his own good and a bit of a Walter Mitty."

"His grip on reality does seem a bit tenuous. He told me the other day that he was conceived in a fast-food restaurant."

"Ah." Nora lifted Paula's milk jug. "May I?"

"Go ahead."

She poured milk into her coffee. "Unlikely as it may sound, that is true. I probably shouldn't be telling you this, but Carole – his mum – had a serious drug problem in those days. She was meeting her dealer and didn't have the money to pay, so… well, you can imagine the rest."

"How dreadful. Does Sanders know that part?"

"Not about the drugs. I don't think any of the people who remember would be cruel enough to tell him. He was nagging her about who his father was."

"He can be pretty persistent."

"He certainly can, so Carole said they met in the queue and that she never saw him again."

"That's nearly as bad. Couldn't she have made up something a bit nicer?"

"That's Carole for you. I've known her since we were kids and I'm very fond of her, but she doesn't always think before she speaks."

"I assumed he was talking nonsense."

"Understandably. So what did he say today?"

Paula sipped her coffee. "Well, he was bugging me and I told him to go and play with his twin Sandra. He'd talked about her before and I've seen her around the village a couple of times, but suddenly he's insisting that he doesn't have a twin sister, and there was something about the way he said it..." Paula shrugged.

Nora spooned a few grains of sugar from the bowl into her coffee and stirred thoughtfully. Eventually, she said, "You're going to have to speak to him about Sandra. All I can tell you is that he's not lying about that either. Sanders doesn't have a sister, twin or otherwise. He's an only child."

Drowning

Other than the usual junk, there was only one message in her inbox, a single line from Jen. *No probs, toots, just tell me what and when.* Paula hit reply and typed in the list she had already put together in her head. She shoved Mrs McIntyre's bedding in the washing machine, remade the bed with her favourite pink sheets, and gave the flat a cursory tidy.

Before long she would have to catch up on some work. She had passed her new jobs on to colleagues but she still had several family trees to finish. When Paula had told Sylvia, her boss at Genus Genealogy, about the accident, she had let Paula's clients know there would be a delay in producing their work. Even so, they would want their reports. Soon, she would deal with them soon.

She picked up her purse and keys and headed down the garden path. There was no sign of Sanders on the beach, in the bay beyond the harbour or on Main Street. Paula got a takeaway cappuccino from Nora's Ark and wandered over to a small play park behind the war memorial. Several parents were supervising young children as they scrambled up the steps of the slide, excavated the sandpit and tested their weight on the seesaw.

She sat down on a bench next to the swings and considered where to try next. Along at the cliffs? His house? Or maybe she should just go back to the flat and tackle one of those reports. After all, why should it matter to her whether Sanders had a sister or not? She had come to Craskferry to get away from other people.

She watched a father pushing a delighted toddler back and forth on a kiddie swing. A boy of about seven ran in circles round the swing set, inexpertly dribbling a football. She wondered if they had any brothers or sisters. When she was small, she always had someone to play with, to share stories, schemes and jokes, to dress up with and pretend to be pirates or explorers or spacemen. They had pitied all the other kids who weren't like them, the lonely ones without a twin.

Paula drained the last of her coffee and dropped the cup into the bin beside the bench. As she stood up, she caught sight of Bovis, weaving across the grass with her nose to the ground in pursuit of some smell.

"Here, girl," Paula called.

Bovis raised her head and, scent trail forgotten, loped over.

Sanders trotted through the park gate. "Come back here, you bad dog," he shouted.

Bovis ignored him. When she reached Paula, she lay down, placed her head on Paula's foot and let out a long sigh.

"Get over here, now," Sanders called, but Bovis didn't move and he was forced to come across.

"Hello, Sanders," Paula said. "I'm sorry if I was mean to you yesterday."

Sanders bent down, attached Bovis's lead to her collar and hauled her to her feet.

Paula put her hand on his arm. "Please, wait. I really want to talk to you. Will you sit with me for a while? I want to know what you meant yesterday."

"I don't want to talk about it." He shook her off and began dragging Bovis towards the gate.

Paula fell into step beside him. "All right, we won't, but I thought we were friends," she pleaded. "If you stayed for a bit, you could tell me some more jokes."

"I don't feel like telling jokes."

"We could talk about something else then."

He let the lead drop and Bovis romped off towards an Alsatian, trailing the lead behind her. "I haven't got long," he said as they walked back to the bench. "We're having tea at Nan's at five."

Paula looked at her watch. "It's not four yet so you can keep me company for a while."

He eyed her suspiciously. "I thought you liked being on your own."

They sat down. "I thought so too but I'm not sure any more." She fixed her gaze on a clump of trees at the far side of the park. "Can I ask you a question?"

"Mibby."

"You don't have to answer if you don't want to."

"Ask and I'll decide."

"Are you an only child?"

He pulled a splinter of wood off the bench seat. "Why d'you want to know?"

"Well, if that wasn't your sister I saw on the beach, who was it? She looked exactly like you."

"You said you wouldn't ask about that."

Paula chewed her lip. "I know but I'm trying to understand. Will you please explain to me?"

"Only if you promise you won't be horrible to me again."

"I promise."

He leant forward, cupping his chin in his small hands. The nails were bitten down so far that the sight of them made her wince.

"There's just me," he said quietly. "I don't have a twin or any other sisters or brothers or anyone."

"Who's Sandra then?"

"Me. I'm both of us."

Paula tried not to let her voice sound shocked. "Sanders and Sandra?"

"Aye."

"That was you watching my flat?" she asked. "With your hair tied up and make-up on?"

He nodded.

"You moved the tandem and left Bovis?"

"Aye."

"But why?"

"I saw a bloke getting the bike out of a van. I liked it because it was for two people and it looked like it'd be fun to ride. When I came past again, you and the man came out. You looked upset, like you'd had a row, and he drove off and left you. When we were on the beach later, I looked over the wall and the bike was there, and I wondered who you were going to ride it with if you'd fallen out with your boyfriend."

"He's not my boyfriend."

Sanders didn't give any sign he had heard her. "Then you came out and started running. We waited till you came back to see if you were friendly, but I couldn't tell, 'cos you just looked sad and your face was all swollen up like you'd been crying. So we came back really early next morning and I climbed in the garden for a look at the bike. It wasn't chained up, so I got on to see if I could ride it, but it was too hard on my own." He spoke without looking at her, words tumbling over each other. "I thought if I left Bovis, I could watch and see what you'd do. I thought if you were nice to her, it might be okay to ask if I could ride it with you, if that man wasn't going to."

"Bloody hell, Sanders. You were spying on me. What's so interesting about me?"

He picked at a scab on the back of his hand. "I told you, I liked the bike – I've never seen one for two people before – and I wondered why you were so sad. I didn't think just having a row could make someone cry so much their face swelled up like a football."

"Thanks, Sanders. But how come I didn't see you except when I came back from running?"

"I'm good at hiding."

"So it would seem. Where were you?"

"That's my secret."

"Okay, but let me make sure I've got this clear. You're Sanders and Sandra."

"Aye."

"I see."

He turned to regard her. "No, you don't. You don't see at all. How could you?"

"Sorry, that was a stupid thing to say. Of course I don't. Tell me then, why do you dress up as Sandra?"

"To help me decide."

"Decide what?"

He put his hands over his eyes, opening and closing his fingers as he spoke. "Who I'm going to be."

Paula frowned. "But you're Sanders."

"I was, and I am for now, but I'll have to make my mind up soon."

"I'm sorry, this is all a bit much to take in. Are you sure you're telling me the truth?"

He jumped to his feet. "I knew you wouldn't believe me," he shouted. "I shoulda never tried to tell you."

He stomped off across the park to recapture Bovis.

"I'm sorry. Please don't go," Paula called after him.

A couple of parents looked over at her, but Sanders ignored her. He got hold of Bovis's lead and they jogged towards the gate.

"Well done, Paula," she said to herself. "Another diplomatic triumph."

Closing her eyes for a second, Paula leant her head back as far as it would go. She drew in a long breath of salt and seaweed and warmth, letting it out in a slow sigh. Things were different now, she was sure of it, and everything was going to be all right after all.

The clouds had passed, taking her paralysis with them, and the beach was exactly as it should be, sea and sand shimmering in the pure light. Her heart and limbs were weightless, thoughts clear.

She stretched out her arms, reaching into the still heat with each finger, and began to turn, feeling the dry grains that had once been stones and shells shift and tickle between her toes. There were no families, no dog walkers. The bay was all hers.

"Paula!"

She swung round. It was the little girl, her childhood self, standing at the foot of the steps leading to Mrs McIntyre's garden. She wore that same familiar dress and held aloft the string of her gently tugging kite.

"Hello," Paula called back.

"Will you play with me?" little Paula asked.

"Of course." She took a step towards the girl. "What would you like to play?"

"No, stay there. We'll play hide and seek. Shut your eyes really tight and count out loud to a hundred."

"One, two, three…" As she counted, she heard the soft crunch of little Paula's plastic sandals drawing nearer. "Sixteen, seventeen…"

"Count louder," she ordered.

"Twenty-eight, twenty-nine…"

She was standing so close now Paula could feel the heat of her body, feel the air being displaced as the girl slowly circled her.

"Forty-two, forty-three…" she counted on.

The crunching grew distant again.

"Don't count so fast." Her voice was far away.

"Fifty-nine, sixty…"

"Count louder." Further away still.

"Seventy-two, seventy-three..."

Paula had to strain to hear the words. "Promise you'll come and find me."

"Ninety-nine, a hundred." She opened her eyes to see the yellow and blue tail of the kite flicking out of sight through the gap between the garden walls that had swallowed up Sanders and Bovis a couple of days earlier.

"Promise…" The plea was so soft, so distant, she might have imagined it.

Paula began to run towards the entrance to the alley, but she had gone only a few metres when she realised something was wrong.

Her feet were sinking, her movements slowing and becoming more laboured with each step.

She looked down. A mass of shiny blue-black seaweed was tangled around her feet and it was spreading, sucking and crackling, as it raced across the sand in every direction. In seconds, the entire beach was covered.

She pulled one foot free to take another step. It was coated with dark slime. Over at the water's edge, a trio of penguins cried plaintively as they struggled to free themselves from the rampant weed. After each desperate flap, they sank deeper, their once white stomachs stained the colour of ink.

Paula bent down and dipped a finger in the gloopy mass. She sniffed it. Oil. The seaweed was covered with oil, and the level was rising.

It was up to her knees. She tried to take a step but it was so thick she could barely lift her foot and the swirling undertow threatened to tip her over.

"Help me! Someone, please, help me!" she shouted, but there was no one to hear.

Even the penguins were gone, pulled under by the horrible blue-black tide.

When she glanced down again, the oil was half way up her thighs.

"Please," she yelled to the empty beach. "I can't move."

It was around her waist and, though the surface was smooth and still, she could feel its strange currents tugging at her legs. Everywhere she looked there was oil. The sea had vanished; the wall, the gates and steps were all disappearing. Before long the buildings would be beneath its greasy surface. Even the sky was turning black, as a thunderous curtain of cloud rolled across the estuary. She needed help – soon.

Opening her throat as wide as she could, Paula shouted again. "Help me, please. I'm going under."

In the distance there was a rowing boat with a man at the oars. It was Pete. He had come to rescue her.

"Pete, I'm here, over here."

Frantically, she tried to pull her arms to the surface to wave, but she couldn't lift them. The oil was round her chest. Lapping at her neck. Seeping up her face. She stood on tiptoe. The boat was getting smaller, shrinking every second as it pulled away across the bay.

Paula closed her mouth and held her breath. The oil trickled into her ears, rose in her nostrils, crept between her eyelashes.

All the panic and fight were gone. She surrendered to the inevitable. Shivering, she let her jaw relax and the cool liquid oozed into her mouth. Moving slowly like treacle, but far more bitter, the poisonous oil rolled down into her lungs.

Paula stripped the sweat-drenched sheets off the bed and put them in the washing machine. She had a shower, drank a glass of orange juice and sat down at her laptop. It was time to do some work. Upstairs, Mrs McIntyre seemed to have visitors – she could hear occasional footsteps and laughter. It felt good to have a bit of life going on around her, above her, but with no one expecting her to join in.

When she checked her watch, it was almost nine. Her stomach contracted, reminding her that she hadn't eaten all day. She closed the laptop and went through to the kitchen. Flicking the kettle on, she shoved a teabag into a mug and dropped a couple of slices of bread into the toaster.

Hit and run

Paula opened the storm door before he had a chance to ring the bell. She stood half-concealed behind the inner door, uncertain how to behave until she saw how he would be. He was just delivering her solo bike and some other stuff, yet when she had got up from her desk to shower away the stiffness of another long day of work, she had put on her favourite top and a skirt. She wished now she had stuck with her usual uniform of jeans and T-shirt.

Andy stepped into the vestibule. "How are you doing?" he asked.

She could feel her cheeks flushing. Bending forward he rested a hand lightly on her sleeve and kissed her cheek. "You look good."

She tensed at his touch and made no move to respond. "Is this how you greet all your customers?" she said stiffly.

He took a step back. "Only if it's repeat business."

She heard herself ask, "Did you get everything?"

"I'll unload," he said.

Paula watched from the sitting room doorway, arms folded across her chest, as he wheeled her bike into the hall. "Careful, that was expensive," she said.

"Don't worry, I'm insured."

"That's a comfort," she said sounding sarcastic.

"Where do you want it?" Andy asked evenly.

"Rest it there for now." She pointed to a stretch of wall. "I'll put it in the shed later."

He brushed past leaving her momentarily dizzy. She willed him to reach out and pull her close, imagined the feel of his arms wrapped around her, his touch on her skin, his thick wavy hair between her fingers.

"Might as well do it now. Have you got the key?" he asked.

She got it from her bag.

He opened the kitchen door and they were enveloped by a rich herby smell. "What are you cooking?"

"Spatchcocked chicken with rosemary, thyme and red onions," Paula said flatly.

She watched as he unlocked the shed and carefully balanced the solo against the tandem. Back inside, he carried the boxes he had collected from Jen into the study.

"That's everything then. Apart from this." Andy pulled a folded magazine from the back pocket of his jeans. "The cover caught my eye in a service station. I thought you might want a copy."

Paula took the magazine without looking at it. As he walked to the door, she willed him to turn round and say something, anything, to give her a sign that she should ask him to stay. That the effort it had taken to plug in Mrs McIntyre's spare phone and dial his number had been worth it. That his kiss was actually something more than a polite greeting. That her rudeness hadn't spoiled everything.

He was halfway down the path when she tore the door open.

"Andy," she called. "Sorry, I can't believe I did that."

She held out a handful of £20 notes. "I don't know how we both forgot."

He pocketed the money. "Thanks."

"Thank you."

Paula went back inside and closed both doors. She watched from behind the sitting room curtains as he drove off. When the van was out of sight, she sank down onto the sofa. Pulling her legs under her, she unfolded the magazine. It was *Cycling Monthly*.

The letters formed a banner across the front page: *Pete Tyndall: tragic death of tandem champion.* The feature inside, headed *Tandem star killed on training run*, covered two full pages. There were pictures of Pete and her competing, and panels down the sides of the spread were filled with tributes from leading figures in the cycling world.

She began to read the main article: *The death of tandem champion Pete Tyndall, following a hit-and-run incident while he was returning home from a training run last month, has shocked the cycling community.*

Paula's eyes filled with tears.

Tyndall, 29, was out alone on a training ride near his South London home, just before 10pm on Friday, June 10, when he was hit by a car as he crossed a junction. The Renault Megane Coupe did not stop.

An off-duty paramedic who was passing on his motorbike summoned an ambulance and gave emergency first aid, but Tyndall, who suffered serious head injuries and multiple fractures to his body, was later declared dead at the scene.

Inspector David Mallone, of the Metropolitan Police, told Cycling Monthly: "CCTV footage showed Mr Tyndall rode through a red light. However, the driver of the car had a legal obligation to stop, which he did not do. He was later apprehended and charged with failing to stop after a collision."

In May, the respected English teacher and his cycling partner, sister Paula, achieved their best-ever result, when he piloted them to a new UK hundred-mile mixed tandem record of three hours, thirty-one minutes and fifty-seven seconds, in the annual McQuarrie Memorial Event held by Southend Road Club in Essex.

The day after he died, they had been due to compete in a twelve-hour event in Norfolk, where they were hotly tipped favourites. The pair also held national records at fifty, twenty-five and ten miles.

In addition, Tyndall held the UK men's fifty-mile tandem record with Ollie Matraszek, the twins' coach for mixed events, as stoker.

Tyndall, who rode for Tooting Flyers RC, had enjoyed considerable success as a junior in solo events, and his club records for fifty, twenty-five and ten miles still stand.

His father, Derek Tyndall, who held the UK twelve-hour record from 1972-5, said: "No son could have made his family more proud. We still can't believe Pete is gone, taken from us by a momentary loss of concentration. He was such a cheerful, upbeat personality, full of energy and humour, and equally gracious in victory and defeat.

"For Pete, everything was a challenge to be seized with both hands. Nothing was ever a problem or an obstacle. Cycling and teaching were the matching pillars of his life. He was a wonderful son, a wonderful competitor and a wonderful human being. The loss is unbearable."

Pete Tyndall started cycling competitively at the age of eleven on a Peugeot Triathlon that was a birthday present from his parents. He began riding a tandem with his sister as stoker a year or so later, and they were soon winning local races and setting new club records. They were victorious in their first national competition, over ten miles, aged just sixteen.

Ollie Matraszek said: "Pete and I were best mates for more than twenty years, right from the week we moved to the same primary school at the age of eight and the teacher sat me next to him. We competed against each other in junior events and later I became part of team Tyndall on the tandem circuit.

"Pete was a formidable rider, even more so with Paula as stoker, and he was a brilliant friend, funny, loyal and supportive. His determination was an inspiration to everyone who knew him. No one could have had a better riding partner."

Tooting Flyers president Vic Hartnet added: "Pete had been with the club since he was eleven years old and he had many good friends here. He devoted much of his spare time to coaching and encouraging the club's younger members. He will be sorely missed by us all.

"To see Pete's life ended in this way is devastating, nothing short of a tragedy."

Tyndall's sister Paula was unavailable for comment.

Paula closed the magazine and stuffed it under a cushion.

"So that's what it all boils down to, eh Pete?" she whispered to the empty room. "A couple of pages in *Cycling Monthly*. You thought you were invincible. You couldn't be arsed to stop at a red light and you were pushing so hard you didn't even check the road. You fucking idiot."

Wiping her face with the back of her hand, she went through to the kitchen and switched off the oven.

She leant against the units and gazed upwards. "I made a pretty spectacular mess of that earlier, didn't I? Andy must think I'm completely crazy, all over him one minute and unable to say a civil word the next. Well, that's about par for the course at the moment. Ollie, Andy, even Sanders – as soon as anyone wants to be nice to me, I push them away. What the hell's the matter with me?"

She dug her nails into her palms. "Come on explain it," she demanded more loudly. "You can't, can you, you selfish bastard? Because you bailed out on me. You're gone and I'm stuck here on my own. And that's all there is to it. That's the beginning, middle and end of it. You're gone and I've got to get on with it. Just like all those poor singletons we used to laugh about."

She sat down at the table and rested her head on her arms. "If they can do it, why can't I? Tell me that, Pete. Why can't I function? How am I supposed to do that without you?"

Tears soaked into her sleeves. "Please, help me," she begged, her voice almost inaudible.

Services rendered

Paula edged the storm door open. Andy stood on the doorstep. "Could we start again, please?" he asked. "That was awful."

She nodded but couldn't meet his eyes. "I know. I was horrible."

"Can I come in then?"

"What? Yes, of course." She stepped back and pulled the door fully open. "See, I'm doing it again. I don't know what's wrong with me. Please, come in."

"Hang on. I need to get something from the van."

"Please don't drive off again."

"I won't."

He was back in seconds holding two bottles wrapped in blue tissue.

"I didn't know if you preferred red or white, so I got both."

At last she met his gaze. "Wasn't that a bit presumptuous?" She winced at her own clumsiness. She had meant it to be a light-hearted remark but it came out sounding almost hostile.

"Optimistic. I think that's a better word, don't you?"

Andy smiled but his eyes were uncertain. She didn't know which of them was more nervous. She must try to relax. The wine would help.

"Optimistic." She repeated. "Yes, that's good. Come through to the kitchen then, Mr Optimistic."

He followed her down the hall, and she retrieved a corkscrew from a drawer.

"I was optimistic too," she offered.

"Really?" He passed her the bottle of white. "This needs a while in the fridge."

She tested it against her cheek and nodded.

Andy opened the red. "How did your optimism manifest itself?"

She felt him watching her as she stretched up to get wine glasses from the top shelf of a cupboard, revealing several centimetres of taut stomach. He kept his gaze on her as she adjusted her top, checked the glasses for dust and placed them on the counter. "I made dinner."

"The chicken was meant for me?"

She grinned sheepishly. "You're not a vegetarian are you?"

"I'm not. *Slainte.*"

"What does that mean?"

"It's Gaelic for cheers. You should reply '*slainte mhor*'."

"*Slainte mhor.*" She clinked her glass against his. "What did I just say?"

"Cheers more."

"Fair enough." She sipped the wine. "This is really nice. It tastes like plums and vanilla."

"Better than our last toast."

"Toasts don't really work with tea."

"They don't." He swallowed some wine. "I read the article. I'm really sorry about your brother. This must be a terrible time for you."

She looked away. "That's no excuse for taking it out on everyone around me."

He touched her hand. "It's okay. There are no rules for this kind of thing."

Paula's eyes welled up again.

"Can I do anything to help with dinner?"

She blew her nose on a square of kitchen towel. "I was just going to boil a few potatoes and make an avocado and tomato salad."

"That sounds fabulous. Shall I do the salad while you organise the potatoes?"

Paula took another mouthful of wine. It really did taste good. She pointed to the fruit bowl. "The avocado nearest you should be ripe."

He helped himself to a chopping board and knife that were lying on the work surface.

She watched him slice the tomatoes with neat, economical strokes. She was so clumsy these days that if she picked up a knife, she either cut herself, or whatever she was slicing flew across the room. Andy didn't look like someone who ever cut himself.

"Do you enjoy cooking?" she asked.

"I love it."

She felt herself smile again. "So do I."

As they ate, they chatted about food and restaurants, films and books, and both said a little about their work, but that was it. Nothing significant was discussed – and that felt fine.

When they were finished, they took the second bottle of wine to the sitting room. Paula sat down. She felt slightly drunk, her senses a little blurred.

Andy wandered through to the study and began examining the piles of CDs she had dumped on the bookshelves. His hands moved slowly as he picked up the discs one by one. Mesmerised by his movements, she knew she was staring but was utterly unable to turn away. Every time he lifted a box or turned it over to read the track list, she felt his long fingers were caressing her skin. Her mouth was dry and she longed for a glass of water but she couldn't move to get one. Her breathing grew shallow. If she didn't pull herself together soon, she would pass out.

"This is your chance to get revenge for my musical taste," he said without looking up. "What shall I put on?"

She took a gulp of wine. "What about The Chimes? They're great chilled, evening music."

"I haven't heard them for years." He selected the disc and glanced around. "Where have you hidden the stereo?"

"I use the laptop. I've got decent speakers so it sounds as good a stereo. At least it does to me. I know the music I like but I'm not into all that stuff about woofers and tweeters." Shut up, Paula, she told herself sharply, you're jabbering like an idiot.

Andy slid the CD into the laptop and came back through. He hesitated in the centre of the room. She guessed he was deciding whether to sit beside her or on one of the armchairs.

She patted the cushion next to her. "I promise not to attack you."

He smiled and sat down.

She held her glass in both hands so he wouldn't see how badly she was shaking. "*Slainte.*"

"*Slainte mhor.*"

She drew in a deep breath. "About before, when you brought me up here… I don't normally throw myself at men like that. You must have thought… well, I don't know what you must have thought."

Andy shook his head. "Nothing bad, if that's what you mean."

Paula gulped some more wine. "But did I misread the signals? Please be honest with me."

He stared at the carpet for a moment. "What happened over breakfast was just so quick and you seemed so fragile." He turned his glass in his hands, studying the wine. "But you didn't misread the signals. I panicked. We'd barely met and I didn't want to take advantage, to do something you might regret later."

He looked up at her. "I couldn't stop thinking about you after I left. I was so pleased when you asked me to bring some more stuff. But when I arrived and you didn't seem exactly delighted to see me, I told myself that you'd changed your mind and I'd misread the signals."

Paula felt herself blushing. "No, you didn't and I didn't, change my mind I mean. I was just being useless. I was excited about seeing you again and I panicked too and, well, everything seems to come out wrong these days."

"So you weren't just being kind inviting me in and feeding me when I came back?"

"I wasn't being kind, but what made you come back?"

Andy chuckled. "I was driving out of Craskferry and this voice in my head was going, "Don't be so stupid. She's gorgeous and interesting, and you blew your last chance. You blew it. You really blew it." It wouldn't shut up, so I decided I'd just have to prove it wrong."

It was her turn to smile.

"So." He put his glass on the floor. "Where does that leave us?"

Paula placed hers beside it. "I don't know." She clasped her hands to conceal the tremors.

Andy leant across and put one hand on the back of her neck. He drew her towards him. "Did I tell you how much your new hair suits you?"

"You did but you could tell me again."

When he kissed her she floated upwards, weightless, free at last. Everything really was going to be all right.

His arm was wrapped around her, his torso nestled spoon-like against her back.

"Ollie?" It was out of her mouth before she could stop it.

Andy stirred slightly but didn't respond. Slowly easing herself round, she watched as he slept, utterly peaceful and very beautiful in the early half-light. His skin was the colour of milky coffee, his chiselled yet delicate bone structure from another time entirely. He could be a young senator in ancient Rome or a famous Renaissance artist. She placed a cautious hand in the centre of his smooth chest. The skin was warm, heartbeat slow and steady. His grey-black hair, released from its elastic band, lay in thick waves on the pillow. She wriggled closer until she could bury her face in it.

Ollie would never forgive her if he found out what she had done. He was part of her old life, a life Andy had no role in, no knowledge of. The person she was then would never have betrayed Ollie. But that Paula was gone, taken, obliterated. The one left in her place to cope couldn't stop herself, hadn't been willing to. She had wanted, and needed, Andy. It was as simple as that.

Paula ran the tip of her left index finger down his profile. He shifted a little, stretched out an arm and pulled her close. She smiled and closed her eyes, allowing herself to drift back into relaxed, dreamless sleep.

She was woken by Andy tweaking the end of her nose.

"What are you doing?" she murmured.

"Retaliating." His arm tightened around her. "I felt you earlier."

"I thought you were asleep."

"I was until you started mucking about with my nose."

"It's a very splendid nose."

"Is that a polite way of saying it's big?"

"No, it's very distinguished."

"Admit it, it's big, or…"

"Or what?"

"Or…" He thought for a second. "I'll tickle you until you beg for mercy."

Paula was squealing so loudly she didn't hear Mrs McIntyre come downstairs and collect her post from the vestibule.

There was a sharp rap on the door.

"Are you all right in there?" her landlady demanded.

Andy's hand flew up to cover Paula's mouth.

"Yes, Mrs McIntyre," he called out.

Paula struggled to gag him with her hand before he could say any more, but he was stronger than her.

"We're both absolutely fine," he continued brightly.

They heard the sound of footsteps, then the old woman's front door banged shut.

"I can't believe you did that," she exclaimed. "I won't be able to look her in the eye ever again."

"Sorry." Andy lowered his gaze in mock contrition. "I couldn't help it. Now, where were we?"

They were sitting on the beach steps drinking mugs of tea, plates of toast and marmalade balanced on their knees, when Andy touched the tattoo on her ankle with the side of his bare foot.

"It's Pete, isn't it?" he said. "Paula and Pete."

"Yes," she said quietly.

"You must miss him a great deal. I can't imagine what it must be like to lose a brother or sister."

"He wasn't just a brother. We were born the same year – me in January, him in December. He was my little twin and I was supposed to look after him, stop bad stuff happening to him." She laid her plate on the step and studied her hands. "When I was small I used to love imagining our family tree. I would make up stories about who had gone before us and all the exciting things they'd done in their lives. I used to draw it out over and over again in coloured felt pen. The names and stories were different every time, but one thing stayed the same. It was always upside down, with me and Pete together, side by side, at the top. Everything led up to us, the two of us."

When she finished speaking, Paula slumped over until her chest touched her thighs and let her hands rest on the weathered wood between her feet. The sand under the steps was a tangle of driftwood and seaweed that had been sucked up by the tide, thrown around in the swirling water, then dumped as it raced carelessly away. She let out a long sigh. If only Andy hadn't spotted the magazine. She hadn't wanted him to know. She had wanted to keep that part of her life separate, hidden, so that being with him wasn't tainted by the shared knowledge –

and for that small, infinitely valuable portion of time, it could be as if Pete had never died.

Andy put his arm around her. "I'm sorry. That was insensitive. I shouldn't have brought it up."

Paula swallowed. "It's been so lovely not thinking about it for a while."

"Please forgive me."

She nodded. "Pete named me in his will as his executor, but I can't. You know, I just can't face it. I've got a lawyer looking into it, to see if she can get me out of it."

"That's good."

Paula rested her head on his shoulder. "Oh, Ollie, what's going to happen to me?"

"Ollie?" Andy pulled away from her. "That's the guy in the article. What's going on between you and him?"

"What?" Paula's face burned. "What do you mean? There's nothing going on. It was a slip of the tongue."

He stared as if he was seeing her for the first time. "Once maybe, but not three times."

"Three times? I didn't…"

"You called me Ollie last night when we were making love."

"I couldn't have."

"You didn't even notice you'd done it. I told myself I'd imagined it, that it was just one of those weird things that happen sometimes. His name was in my head from the magazine and I was tired and a bit drunk. But then you did it again this morning. You didn't realise I'd heard and I wished I hadn't, so I pretended I was asleep. I thought if I told myself I'd misheard or imagined it, if I really tried to believe it, it could be true."

He still hadn't taken his eyes off her. "But I didn't mishear, did I? You and Ollie are a couple."

"No, yes, I mean…" She felt sick. "Oh, God. Please don't hate me."

Andy stood up and looked down at her. "I don't hate you. I feel sorry for you, but I can't be in a relationship that isn't based on trust. I know things are hard for you right now, but before this goes any further, you need to decide what you really want. Here..."

He slid his wallet out of his jeans pocket, counted out the cash she had given him the night before and placed it on the step beside her.

"For services rendered." The contempt in his voice was almost more than she could bear.

Free at last

Paula pressed send and the family tree and report winged their way back to Sylvia. It was good to have started work again, to have made the first step towards getting one part of her life back under control. There were several more reports to finish though, and it would be a while before she was ready for any new projects – no matter how keen Sylvia was to give her them. When Paula had told her boss she would be spending some time in Scotland, she was delighted.

"We've always got more Scottish work than our researchers up there can handle," she said. "The world's full of expats wanting to trace their Highland heritage. Let me know as soon as you feel able to take on some new challenges, and I'll get one of the team in Edinburgh to show you the ropes. Things are a bit different up there. Actually, they're easier because the Scots have always been such great record keepers. It'll be like a holiday for you."

Paula checked her email. There were messages from Jen, Ollie and Caroline Gibson. She opened the lawyer's first.

Dear Miss Tyndall,

Having checked the English legal situation, I regret to inform you that, as I suspected, it is no longer possible to commute your executorship of your brother's estate. Had you acted sooner, it could have been achieved, but the legal process is now too far advanced and you are bound to carry on with your obligations. I'm sorry – I know this is not the news you wanted to hear. If I can be of any further assistance, please do not hesitate to contact me. The firm's bill is attached.

Yours, Caroline Gibson,

Senior partner Rhind and Gibson.

Paula rested her head in her hands. "Pete," she said quietly, "why did I agree to this? I should have known I couldn't bear it. We both thought we were indestructible, could never have imagined it would come to this. But how can I go through your things, pick through your life? It's too much, just too much."

In a bid to focus on something else, she opened Jen's message.

Wow! He's sex on legs. Where did you find him? Does Ollie know??? Jx

She hit reply.

If you're referring to Andy, he's just a white van man I found in the local paper. There's nothing for Ollie to know. Px

It was the first lie she had ever told Jen and it didn't feel good. They had been best friends since the first day of senior school. After Pete, Jen was the person she was closest to in the whole world. They always told each other everything, but she couldn't bear to explain the events of the previous night – or this morning.

Jen responded immediately. *So you won't mind giving me his phone number??? I need to find out if he's single!!*

Paula answered quickly. *Don't even think about it. He's bad news.*

Jen's reply was one word: *Boo!*

Reluctantly Paula opened Ollie's message. She didn't need to read it to know what it would say. It was a miracle he had left her in peace for the best part of a week – her mum must have had a word with him.

I'm glad you're okay. Jen says she's had a couple of emails from you and that you sound like you're getting by. I got the impression she knows where you've gone, but she wouldn't say. Please, Paula, tell me where you are! I need you right now and I think you need me too. No one else can truly understand what we're going through. I love you. Please get in touch. Ollie.

Ollie, she typed, *I'm so sorry to leave you like this. You're right, no one else can know what it's like, but that's exactly why I can't see you just now. I can't deal with you knowing, with your grief – I'm having enough trouble keeping myself on an even keel. And yes, I know you think you can help me, but I don't want to be helped. I just want to forget. To stop thinking.*

Paula sent the message and closed the laptop. She had had enough of other people's frailties – and her own – for one day. It was almost six. She made a cheese sandwich, took it into the sitting room and switched on the TV.

She woke up, with the empty plate still on her lap, as the Channel 4 news was starting. What she needed was some exercise. She was in the bedroom pulling on a pair of cycling shorts, when she heard Mrs McIntyre closing her front door and crossing the hall. Her landlady's footsteps sounded less brisk than usual, tentative almost, as if she was tiptoeing.

Paula opened the door a few centimetres. "Good evening, Mrs McIntyre," she said.

The old woman scowled at her, but Paula pressed on. "I wanted to apologise for earlier. I'm very sorry if we embarrassed you. We were just messing around."

Mrs McIntyre didn't reply but her lips made a sound like air escaping from a balloon. Paula interpreted it to mean, "I know perfectly well what you were doing."

It was hard work riding up the hill out of the village. Paula told herself it was natural after a month out of the saddle and no exercise apart from a few runs on the beach. But it wasn't really lack of exercise making her weak. She and Pete had been due to go for the twelve-hour record and they were both so fit everyone said they would smash it. Ollie reckoned they would beat it by at least ten miles, but Pete was convinced they could add twenty.

It was different riding her solo to the tandem. Not just because on the tandem she gave up responsibility for the gears, brakes and steering to Pete. Sometimes on particularly steep hills, she would close her eyes as she counted out each painful and desperate rotation of the pedals: push with the left, one, two, three, four, five; push with the right, one, two, three, four, five; pull with the left – praying the cleat locking her shoe to the pedal would hold – one, two, three, four, five; pull with the right, one, two, three, four, five. She had shut her eyes on really fast descents, too, the better to feel, hear, smell, taste the whooshing, nerve-tingling speed.

But that ability to hand over responsibility for everything apart from her share of the physical work was not the real difference. It was about being part of a team, something bigger, better, stronger than herself. Alone she was good, she could hold her own, but she wasn't a champion. She had always known that – it was why she never bothered to compete solo. Winning simply didn't matter enough for her to dig so far beyond her comfort zone that she might actually unearth the strength and determination it required.

Together, though, it was another matter. Right from their first race, Pete's desire to win was so strong it fed them both and lifted her to a level far beyond what she would have achieved alone.

Her mind might be letting her down over the day-to-day stuff, but seventeen years on, the memory of that day was still fresh.

Pete's breaths echoed her own, each gasped intake a fraction behind, each ragged exhalation a reminder of her own pain.

Concentrate now, focus, make them match. Find a distraction – anything apart from what her body was feeling and her mind knew was coming.

Her feet had never turned so fast. Her calves and thighs throbbed with lactic acid as they fought to keep up. Over forty miles an hour they were doing, well over, and there was a roundabout at the bottom of the long hill.

Cold sweat slicked Paula's hairline and trickled down the back of her neck. There was no way they could make the turn, no way on earth. She wanted to pull her feet off the pedals and throw out her arms and legs like a sail to slow them down.

They had ridden the course before, but never like this: at this speed, with the road so slippery, with so much at stake. When they crashed, they would break their necks. If they survived, they would be left speechless, brainless, immobile, trapped in wheelchairs forever.

Was it worth it? Every muscle, every bone, every blood vessel screamed no, no, it isn't, but still she turned the cranks. She had to do it for him.

She glanced up from her handlebars. The giveway line was seconds away. Slow down, slow down, Pete, please. She could move nothing but eyes and feet as the fear pressed down on her shoulders.

"Please God, let us make it in one piece."

The tandem swung out as it crossed the greasy white line and Pete leant them into the tight curve of the roundabout, a thin cushion of air between their exposed flesh and the jagged teeth of the tarmac.

"Please God," she prayed, "please, let us win."

Now, she was left alone to struggle against the rising road and her own fragility. Where would she get her inspiration to carry on? She had competed because it was what he wanted. She had done it for him, the other half of herself, the embodiment of the characteristics she lacked and admired. He had a mental toughness, a steely core she could never hope to share. He rode to win. She rode so he could win. Without him, there was no point.

Maybe it was fitting that her body seemed to be giving out. Why should she go on riding without him? A part of her had died with him and what remained couldn't survive alone. The knowledge of what had happened was with her every morning when she woke, the combination of panic and anger constricting her heart and lungs, twisting her intestines and weighing on her arms and legs until they ached. It buzzed in her head all day and filled every millimetre of air around her. It made her hands suddenly start shaking when she tried to do the simplest tasks, like brushing her teeth or tying her trainers, and it made her throat constrict when she went to speak. She had never felt so out of control in her life – hurtling downhill at forty-five miles an hour on the back of a tandem couldn't hold a candle to this. The only time she had felt truly at peace since it happened was when she was in bed with Andy, and look how that had turned out.

Paula lowered her head and dug in. This was nonsense. She had to stop thinking like this. What would Pete tell her? Focus, focus on the road, focus on your legs. Focus on spinning those bloody cranks as fast as humanly possible. That was all that counted for him.

Gradually, her muscles warmed up. Stretching out and releasing the tension of inactivity, she started to feel as if she was in control again. Maybe it was just a question of focus. Maybe she could still do it. Turning down the road towards Westwick, she slid into that familiar groove. Fields, hedges, trees and sky scudded past in a blur. She was flying, light, fluid and unburdened. The earth and all the misery it contained could not hurt her now. The secret power of her own body had snapped that hold. This was true freedom.

Cake and donkeys

Paula had ordered a cafetière of coffee from Kylie in Nora's Ark, and was trying to decide between the lemon drizzle cake and the peach loaf, when she caught sight of Sanders and Bovis mooching along the other side of Main Street. Sanders had his hands in the pockets of his shorts, Bovis her nose to the ground as she followed some trail only she could sense.

Paula rapped on the window but Sanders was too far away to hear.

"I'll be back in a second," she told Kylie.

Sticking her head round the door, she shouted his name. He stopped and glanced over.

"I'll treat you to some cake."

"No thanks," he yelled back.

"Go on, chocolate cake and a float?"

He thought for a moment then crossed the road. Paula returned to the table, where Kylie was waiting.

"I'll have the peach loaf and Sanders will have the usual."

Sanders tied Bovis's lead to the ring outside, came in and sat opposite her.

"I've ordered for you," she said.

He nodded but didn't speak.

"I remembered a joke," she offered. "Do you want to hear it?"

He put his forearms on the table and rested his chin on his clasped hands. "Go on then," he said without enthusiasm.

"Okay. I'm not very good at telling jokes so you'll have to bear with me on the delivery, but it goes something like this. What do you call a donkey with a limp?"

He looked up at her. "Dunno."

"A wonky donkey."

"Is that it?"

"No, there's more." Paula waited until Kylie had unloaded their order from her tray and moved off to serve another table.

"What do you call a donkey with a limp and a twitch in one eye?"

He shook his head.

"A winky-wonky donkey."

Sanders smiled and took a big bite of cake.

"What do you call a donkey with a limp and a twitch in one eye that likes to play the piano?" she persevered.

He swallowed. "Don't know, tell me."

"A plinky-plonky, winky-wonky donkey. And what you call a donkey with a limp and a twitch in one eye that likes to play the piano and dance?"

He was grinning now, chocolate crumbs all round his mouth.

She stretched out her hands to show that this was the finale. "A honky-tonky, plinky-plonky, winky-wonky donkey."

Sanders clapped. "That was pretty good."

"I didn't do badly, did I?" She poured some coffee, added milk and took a sip. "Could we be friends again then?"

He sucked up a strawful of red fizz streaked with melting vanilla ice-cream. "Aye, okay, on one condition."

"What's that?"

"If I tell you something, you'll believe me."

"I'd like to believe you, Sanders, but…" She didn't want to drive him away again but she couldn't lie. She had done enough of that in the past few days.

"But what?" He was watching her intently, a forkful of cake suspended halfway to his mouth.

She pursed her lips. "It's very difficult because before, well, you told me a few things that weren't true." She swallowed some more coffee. "That makes it hard for me to know when you're telling the truth."

"When did I lie to you? I was joking when I told you that stuff about Mrs McIntyre and her shopping trolley."

"I wasn't thinking about that."

He frowned. "What then?"

Paula pushed her plate away. "You said Adrian Linton over-charged holidaymakers."

Sanders shrugged and unloaded the fork into his mouth.

"And that the newsagent..."

"Old Renton." His voice was muffled by the cake.

"That Mr Renton offered Sandra money for sex, and we both know that couldn't be true."

He opened his mouth as if to defend himself but shut it again without saying anything. He began sucking noisily on his straw.

"See what I mean?" Paula ploughed on. "I like you a lot, Sanders, and I know you like telling stories, but sometimes it's better to just run with the truth. Believe me, I know. I wish I'd done more of it myself recently."

He tapped the rim of his glass with a chewed fingernail, and the moment seemed to stretch. Paula let him be, and eventually he spoke.

"I've got something really important to tell you."

"And?" she prompted.

Sanders looked nervous, and she couldn't help feeling sorry for him.

"It's really, really important." He whispered, and Paula leaned in towards him.

"Why don't you just tell me, Sanders?"

He looked around at the tables filled with people. "Not here. I'll tell you tomorrow when we're on our own."

"Okay," Paula said. "Tell me where and when, and I'll be there."

"The farm," he said. "Mr Thompson's farm. We could go on the tandem."

He looked up at her hopefully, but Paula just shook her head. She felt utterly exhausted. "I have to go." She stood up.

Sanders got to his feet. "Okay, okay. We'll go on the bus. I'll bring sandwiches. Meet you at your place at eleven?"

"Okay, Mr Thompson's farm on the bus."

She went straight home and switched on her laptop, hoping that, in spite of everything she had said and done, there might be a message from Ollie: something simple and reassuring and familiar to hold onto, an anchor to keep her from drifting even further out of her depth. But there was only one message. The subject line read: *Viagra, half price. Don't miss it!*

She hit delete.

Winky-wonky donkeys

Paula wasn't sure if she felt better or worse the next morning. Her dream had changed a little. The oil was gone and everything was back to the way it had been before. When her childhood self ran across the beach and darted through the gap between the garden walls, she was able to follow. When she got there, there was no sign of little Paula, but at least she was no longer drowning in suffocating black slime.

In her waking world, everything was the way it had been too. In spite of the dreams, she looked forward to sleep: it was an escape. Awake, she had to face reality: Pete was gone and she was alone. She tried not to think about Andy, but it was difficult when the memory of his touch was so vivid.

It wasn't until she was eating breakfast that she remembered her promise to Sanders. She wondered briefly about finding an excuse to cancel, but he wanted to share a secret and she couldn't let him down.

She was standing in the back garden, crumbing a piece of burnt toast for the birds and wondering if he was going to turn up – it was already ten past eleven – when his head appeared over the gate.

He came in without closing it. "Hi, PT. Sorry I'm late – we'd run out of carrots so I had to go and buy some."

"Morning, Sanders. Could you just try calling me Paula, like everyone else?"

"You said PT was your nickname."

"It was but I shouldn't have told you. It was Pete's name for me because it was so like his own. He was the only one who used it and I want to keep it that way."

He shrugged. "Okay, PT."

"If you're going to be a smart arse, you can turn round right now and head for home."

"Sorry. Is sliced pork all right? It was the only thing in the fridge. I put in some salad cream and slices of cucumber, and I got a couple of bags of crisps, and loads of carrots for the donkeys."

Paula dusted her hands on the legs of her jeans. "That's fine. We'd better get going." She threw him her keys. "Lock the gate – we'll go out the front."

"Hang on a sec." Bovis loped into the garden.

"What's she doing here?"

"Mr Thompson won't let her on the farm in case she chases the animals."

"Obviously, but why's she here?"

Sanders affected a wounded expression. "Can't she stay? The garden's all walled in. I can't leave her at home. She ate Mum's purse this morning and Mum said if I didn't take her away she'd make her into a new one."

"Can't you leave her at your granny's?"

"She's gone to St Andrews to get new false teeth."

"Couldn't you just stick Bovis in her back garden?"

"Nan lives in a flat. She hasn't got a garden."

Paula knew she should ask Mrs McIntyre's permission, but if they didn't go right away, they would miss the bus. "All right, fine," she said. "You can leave her. Now come on."

The bus dropped them at the farm gate. They walked up the track and Paula knocked on the open back door. A rotund man of about fifty wearing jeans and a stained green sweatshirt emerged.

He smiled, revealing a missing front tooth.

"Are you Mr Thompson?"

"I'm a Mr Thompson, hen. This here's my brother Jim's farm. He's ower by the animals, if you're needin' to see him. I'm Bill Thompson."

"We've come to see the donkeys," said Sanders, who had been busy stroking one of the farm cats.

"Well, that'll be fine, I'm sure. Don't go feedin' them any rubbish though." He winked at Paula.

"We brought carrots," Sanders said. "They're not rubbish, are they?"

Mr Thompson smiled again. "Naw, carrots are good for donkeys and wee boys."

A slightly older man dressed in muddy blue overalls climbed over a stile and walked across the yard.

He waved to Sanders. "Howdy, wee man," he said. "Is your nan with you?"

"Not today," Sanders replied. "I brought my friend Paula to see the donkeys."

"D'you ken who this wee fella is, Bill?" Jim Thompson asked his brother.

Bill frowned. "Should I?"

"It's Agnes Clapperton's grandson."

Bill broke into a wide grin. "Naw! Fancy that. Long time ago, before I moved away to work on the rigs, I was good friends with your nan – and your ma. You tell your nan, Billy Thomson's back and he was asking after her."

A swirl of cool air gathered the dust from the farmyard and blew it around in a little cloud. Paula shivered and zipped up her fleece.

"Aye, it's a fine, breezy day," Bill said. "Typical Scottish summer. Away an' say hello to your furry friends."

A couple of donkeys strolled across to the fence when they saw Paula and Sanders approach. Sanders held out a carrot to the closest one. Gripping the end between its teeth, the donkey crunched it up. He handed another to Paula and she fed its companion. Other donkeys trotted over when they realised there was food on offer.

Sanders handed out more carrots. They were nibbling up the last of the orange crumbs that had fallen on the grass when Jim joined them. The donkeys crowded even closer to the fence, stretching their necks so he could stroke their soft grey and brown noses.

"They're completely useless and they eat me out o' house and home, but I cannae help being fond o' them," he said.

"Are they the ones that used to be on the beach at Craskferry?" Paula asked.

"Aye, the very same, but that's a good long time ago. They havnae worked for the best part o' twenty years."

She smiled. "I went for rides on them when I came for the summer as a child. It's lovely to see them again."

"Bill used to run them for me, but we're all getting on now, aren't we?" He rubbed one of them behind the ears. "I retired them after he went offshore. There's no demand for donkey rides anymore.

The PC brigade don't like it. Nothin' left for it but to grow old gracefully. Isn't that right, fellas?"

Jim left them alone with the donkeys, and Paula marvelled at the way Sanders stroked them and gently untangled the burrs from their stubby manes. He was calm now, and she wondered if he needed this time to work up to whatever it was he wanted to tell her.

Sure enough, when they had left the farm and strolled into a small wood, where they sat together on the trunk of a fallen tree by a little waterfall, he finally came out with it.

"I've got to choose," he said, standing up to throw the last of his sandwich into the water.

"Choose between what, Sanders?" Paula asked gently. She didn't want to push him – she could see from the concentration on his face that he was trying to say something important.

He joined her back on the trunk and helped himself to a bag of crisps. "You know how most babies are born boys or girls."

She swallowed. "I thought they all were."

"Not all. Some are kind of stuck in the middle and someone has to choose what they'll be. Sometimes they get to choose for themselves later.."

Paula laid her sandwich down. "Like a…" She searched for the word. "Hermaphrodite? I thought they only existed in Greek myths and things like that."

This had the makings of another one of Sanders' bizarre stories, but the tone of his voice, his facial expressions, his whole demeanour told her that it was different.

"Aye, kind of. I think a hermaphrodite is both. You know, a boy and a girl. I was born with something wrong with me that means I'll start turning into a girl soon. I have to decide what to do about it." He shoved a handful of crisps into his mouth.

Paula felt as if someone had punched all the air out of her. She wanted to tell herself that, regardless of what her eyes and ears told her, he was lying again, but she knew utterly and instinctively that, for once, he wasn't. Even Sanders couldn't make this up.

"Bloody hell, Sanders," she blurted out.

"It's rude to swear."

"Sorry, you're right. Have you always known this?"

He nodded but didn't look at her. "Mum said I was special because I'd been given a choice other people didn't get." He grimaced. "I don't want a choice though."

"But you're a boy just now. I mean, you were born a boy, weren't you?" she floundered.

"They covered me up before Mum could see. She says she knew right away something was wrong. She started shouting because they wouldn't say if I was a boy or a girl."

"Why wouldn't they say?" Paula's voice was almost a whisper.

"That's what Mum wanted to know. She heard them all talking outside the room. They were saying I wasn't right down there." He pointed to his groin. "The doctor came in and looked at me, and after that, when they went out again, she tore my nappy off to see for herself. After that they had to give her an injection to stop her yelling. Next day, they took me away to do some tests and more doctors came. They said they'd decided that even though you couldn't tell for sure by looking at me, genetically, I was a boy."

"Blimey." Paula massaged her forehead with the tips of her fingers. "I still don't really understand."

Sanders held up his right hand, the thumb and forefinger a small distance apart. "When a boy baby's born, his penis is like this, right?" He moved his fingers until they were almost touching. "Mine was like this. It was so small it was like a girl's thingy. The rest was a bit more like a boy though. That's why they weren't sure."

He bit into another sandwich.

Paula waited for him to continue.

Eventually, he said, "The doctors told Mum I had a thing called partial androgen insensitivity syndrome."

"Had?" Paula queried.

"Have. It doesn't go away. It means one of my genes doesn't work, so I don't respond right to the stuff that makes you a boy."

"Testosterone?"

"Aye, that's it. When a baby starts to develop in its mum's womb, at first it isn't anything, but then it turns into a boy or girl. The doctors said I was meant to be a boy but, because I didn't react enough to the testosterone, I didn't develop right. I stayed sort of in the middle." He scratched his ear. "Some people are much worse. Even though they're boys inside, they're exactly like girls on the outside, so they get brought up that way. Fran, my psychologist, says most of them grow up as happy as anyone else."

"Maybe they're the lucky ones then," Paula observed.

"Mibby." Sanders picked at one of his dirty, bitten fingernails.

"I still don't see why you have to make a choice though. Can't they just operate to make you look more like a boy? I mean, people have sex changes all the time, and it's not as if they'd have to do anything that extreme, is it?"

"It's not that simple. They can change a boy into a girl, but it's much harder the other way round." He fixed his gaze on the other side of the river. "I have to sit down when I go to the toilet. I can have an operation to change that, but I'll always look different. They can't make me exactly like a boy."

"So what'll happen to you?"

"You know how boys get muscles and go all hairy and their voices get deeper? I won't grow muscles and hair, and my voice won't change. I'll grow a chest like a girl, and if I want to get rid of it they'll have to cut it off. If I decide to stay as a girl, I'll need other operations to make me right." He indicated his groin again.

Paula shook her head. "Sanders, this is so awful I can hardly take it in. Does everyone at school know?"

"They know I have a medical condition but they don't know what it is. I use the cubicles when I pee and I'm careful when I change for gym."

"What about your close friends?"

He glanced down at his feet. "I told you, I don't have any. It's easier."

"But haven't people seen you dressed as Sandra?"

"I've only been out a couple of times and the first time it was getting dark. I don't think anybody noticed apart from you. Mum says people don't really look at other people because they're too busy thinking about themselves. And if they did notice, they probably thought it was a visitor that looked a bit like me."

"Mr Renton knows it was you. Shoplifting's quite a good way to get yourself noticed."

He shrugged. "I did it for a laugh. Told him it was a bet. That's what I was going to say if anyone else recognised me."

"What about Nora? She knows too."

"That's because she's friends with Mum, but she's all right."

"Other people will notice when you start to change."

He shrugged again.

"So what are you going to do?"

"Don't know yet," he said quietly. "I'm used to being me. I don't want to change into somebody else."

"Everybody changes at puberty," Paula pointed out.

He glared at her. "Not as much as me. If I don't have treatment I'll turn into a girl, and if I want to be more like other boys, I'll have to have treatment too – take extra hormones and stuff to sort out the muscles and the hair." His voice rose until he was almost shouting. "But no matter what they do, I'll still be different. I'll never be a real boy or a real girl."

"Of course, you're right. That was a stupid thing to say. What does your mum think?"

He focused on the river again. "She says it's up to me to decide when I'm ready."

"But you're twelve now, so you're running out of time. I mean with puberty and everything…"

He nodded. "I start high school in Westwick next month and Fran says it would be best if I decide before then, so I can go as Sanders or Sandra." Tears crept forward. "But I don't want anyone mucking about with my body. I don't want them cutting me up and filling me full of drugs."

Paula remembered what Nora had said about his mother's heroin addiction. "Hormones aren't exactly drugs, are they?"

"What do you know?" he asked fiercely. "They're all chemicals."

"Nothing," she admitted. "God, Sanders, this is huge! Most people don't have to make a choice this big in their whole lives."

"I know." He sniffed miserably. "But I do."

He seemed so vulnerable, she wanted to cry. Instead, she put her arm around his shoulders.

"Not today, you don't," she said.

Together they sat and watched the water dancing over the stones, and the little crusts of Sanders' sandwich that had got caught in an eddy, moving first in one direction and then another, but never escaping into open water, until they sank.

Crossed lines

The first thing she noticed was the seagulls. They were everywhere. Circling and jostling and shrieking like something out of Alfred Hitchcock's film *The Birds*.

"What on earth's going on out there?" she exclaimed.

Sanders lunged for the back door. "Bovis," he shouted as he scrambled down the steps.

Paula took in the devastation from the doorway. Potato peelings, old teabags, mouldy orange shells and all sorts of other rotting, unidentifiable things were spread across the grass, path and flowerbeds. Gulls hovered and strutted, picking through the morsels and squabbling over the tastiest. Two fought over the remains of what looked like a black rubbish bag, each flapping its wings and squawking at the top of its lungs in the hope of driving off its rival.

She glanced over the concrete slabs to the wheelie bin. It had been full when she took a bag out after breakfast. Now it lay on its side, lid half open.

"Bovis, where are you?" Sanders called as he ran round the garden.

There was a scrabbling sound from inside the bin and Bovis reversed out with a chicken carcass in her mouth. It was smeared with what looked like a mixture of strawberry yoghurt and tea leaves.

Sanders grabbed her by the collar. "You bad dog," he scolded. "You smell like sick."

Mrs McIntyre shouted from an upstairs window, "Never mind the dog. What about my garden? Yon delinquent animal has turned it into a midden. The next time I look out I want to see it immaculate again."

"I'm really sorry, Mrs McIntyre," Paula said. "It didn't occur to me that Bovis would be able to get into the bin."

"Aye, well, it should have," the old woman said. "That dog is Houdini in a fur coat and it's been digging up my flowerbeds. Now get it all cleared up. And when you've done, phone your father. He wants a word about your birthday."

Mrs McIntyre ducked back inside and the window slammed shut.

Sanders clicked his heels together and saluted. "Yes, sir."

"Sanders," Paula hissed, "don't make it any worse."

Her dad answered on the first ring.

"You must have been sitting on the phone," Paula said.

"I was in the study digging out a back copy of *Cycling Plus* for Ollie."

"Ollie's there?"

"He just popped round to see how your mum and I were. Do you want a word?"

"Not just now," Paula said hurriedly. An email she could have coped with, would have welcomed even, but talking was something else entirely. What if he could hear the deceit in her voice, if he knew just from the tone or the words she chose that she'd been with someone else.

"Are you sure?" her dad tried. "He really…"

She cut him off. "My landlady said you wanted to speak to me about my birthday."

"Yes. I tried your mobile but it seemed to be switched off." His voice was tired.

"Didn't Mum tell you it's broken? That's why I gave her this number."

"Yes, yes, of course she did. I wasn't thinking. Hang on. She's here."

There was the sound of the receiver changing hands and her mum came on the line. "Hello, darling," she said brightly.

She sounded almost like her old self, but Paula knew she was putting on an act for everyone's benefit.

"How are you?" Paula asked.

"We're managing. Ollie's here cheering us up."

"Dad said."

"We were all wondering what you're planning to do for your birthday."

"I hadn't thought," Paula said dully.

Her mum sighed. "Don't leave it too late. It's only ten days away. Do you think you might come down?"

"I don't know, Mum. I doubt it. What's there to celebrate?"

"Well, don't decide yet. Think about it." There was more movement. "Here's Ollie to have a chat."

Paula winced.

"Finally, we speak." His voice was filled with relief. "How are you, babe? I've been missing you like crazy."

"Fine, Ollie, getting by."

"You don't sound fine. You sound like shit. Look, I've got some holiday to take." His voice took on a pleading tone. "Why don't I come up and we can spend a bit of time together?"

"Up?"

"To Scotland."

"How'd you know I'm in Scotland?" Paula demanded.

"Your mum told me."

She twisted the phone flex around her hand. "She shouldn't have done that."

"Don't worry, she didn't say any more. Your dad leapt in before she could divulge the exact details of your whereabouts. Your secret's still safe."

He sounded irritated now and that wasn't like him. Ollie made out that nothing ever annoyed or worried him. When she and Pete were a bundle of nerves before a race, he took it on himself to be the calm one. He would talk on and on about strategies and winning times, always measured, always utterly positive. His actions betrayed his true feelings though, as all the while he would be tapping one foot like a metronome or rubbing away at an imaginary bald spot on the top of his head. She and Pete had long ago realised that inside, Ollie was far more stressed than they ever were, but they knew how important it was for him to maintain the pretence that he was in control.

"Sorry, I'm sorry," she said. "I hate being so secret squirrel. I know it's not fair on you, but I need to keep things simple right now."

"Paula, please, don't push me away."

"I've got to go."

"But..."

The thought of seeing him was too much to contemplate – it was all too messy, too painful.

"Say goodbye to Mum and Dad for me," she said. "My landlady needs to use the phone."

The receiver was back in its cradle before he could respond.

Sanders' choice

Paula switched on the laptop, clicked on Google and typed in *partial androgen insensitivity syndrome.* There were almost 20,000 pages to choose from. She opened the first one and began reading.

Sexual development is governed by a single pair of chromosomes. Partial androgen insensitivity is a carried on the X chromosome.

She scanned her brain for any fragments of information surviving from school biology lessons that might help make sense of this. Xs and Ys. The way we were made had to do with Xs and Ys. She willed something more to emerge from the mental fog. That was it: men have an X and a Y chromosome, and women have two Xs. She allowed herself a brief smile of satisfaction before returning to the page.

Although they may never realise it, some females carry the abnormal gene for PAIS on one of their X chromosomes. This gene affects the chemical receptor in cells which is intended to trigger their response to androgens. Since only one of each pair of chromosomes is passed on to children, half will inherit the faulty gene from a carrier mother. If the child inherits an X chromosome from the father, she will be genetically female and will also be a carrier. But if the sex chromosome from the father is a Y, the child will be genetically male and will suffer from PAIS.

Her head hurt. Paula wanted something even a science dunce like her could understand without having to read it six times. She closed the page and opened several others at random, but they were worse, full of references to karyotypes, probands and covert mutations. She tried another. It was headed *PAIS: your questions answered.* She scanned down to a section entitled *Causes and physical features.*

Partial androgen insensitivity is a rare genetic disorder which results in babies biologically meant to be boys failing to achieve normal male development. This is because their bodies are unable to respond appropriately to male hormones known as androgens. These chemical signals are secreted into the bloodstream by the testicles. Before birth, androgens are responsible for the development of male genitalia and, after birth, for the other physical and psychological characteristics associated with maleness.

At last, an explanation that made sense. She read on.

Babies with PAIS develop testicles which secrete normal quantities of androgens. But, because the androgen receptor is faulty, the cells can't respond normally. As a result, these babies suffer varying degrees of abnormal genital development. Although genetically male, their appearance may be almost identical to normal female genitals or, at the other end of the scale, they may look normally male except that the urethra opens below the tip of the penis.

When they reach puberty, the development of children with PAIS is determined by their level of androgen resistance. They may develop breasts due to the small amount of oestrogen released by the testicles, but there is usually little or no growth of pubic or other bodily hair, as this is triggered by androgens. Nor will they develop facial hair or the muscularity and personality characteristics typical of normal adult males.

Paula felt queasy and light-headed. It was horrifying, alien. Yet it was Sanders' reality. She took several long breaths, opened another page and forced herself to continue reading.

Individuals with the ambiguous genitals characteristic of partial androgen insensitivity were traditionally subjected to "corrective" surgery during infancy. Some hospitals still do this. However, an increasing number of experts now believe that such cosmetic intervention is both unethical and potentially damaging, because it is difficult if not impossible to reverse. More and more, surgery of this type is considered only when essential for the infant's health and well-being.

But surgery is not the same as assigning a child a gender. This is merely an issue of labelling. It is done following genetic and hormonal testing and is generally based on discussions between parents and doctors about which gender is likely to be more suitable for the child as he or she grows up.

Where possible, surgery to make the genitals appear more "normally" male or female is left until the child is old enough to make an informed decision for him or herself.

Everything Sanders had told her was true. The poor kid; it was utterly unfair. No wonder he didn't want to talk about it. Paula shutdown the laptop. Enough. She couldn't take in any more.

Opening the door, she waved Sanders down the hall and towards the kitchen.

"You look like crap," he observed brightly. "What time did you go to bed last night?"

"I was up late reading. Have you considered a career as a diplomat?"

"I hadn't thought about it. D'you think I should? I've always fancied being a novelist or a racing driver. Or maybe an actor. Or I was thinking about a pilot, or..."

She held up a hand to silence him. "Stop right there. Just put the kettle on so I can have some coffee. I'm going for a shower."

He had woken her from a sweaty, restless sleep by tapping on the bedroom window. She'd opened her eyes to see him grinning through a gap in the curtains. The alarm showed half-past ten. She wondered briefly why it hadn't woken her at eight. She had definitely set it when she got into bed. Then she remembered – she had had the dream again, and this time, when she went to follow her younger self through the gap between the garden walls, Paula had been shocked to realise they were not alone.

A man of about her own age, dressed in jeans and a green sweatshirt, stood slouched, hands in pockets, against one side of the alleyway. He looked like a young Bill Thompson. Little Paula had already run past, but when she went to do the same he stepped, smirking, into her path, barring the way.

She tried to dodge round him and he moved again to block her, hands still in his pockets. She could see over his shoulder that little Paula had already disappeared. Even if she could get past, it was too late. Little Paula was gone.

Adult Paula took a step back as if to admit defeat and the man broke into a triumphant grin, revealing his missing front tooth.

It had been three a.m. when she'd switched on the bedside light with a trembling hand. Sitting up, she'd pulled the duvet tightly around her. Why was Bill Thompson so pleased to have stopped her following her younger self?

Unable to get back to sleep, she'd made a cup of tea and tried to concentrate on a novel, but the question kept coming back: what was he doing in her dream? It was after seven when she finally began to nod off. Her last automatic act as sleep reclaimed her was to stretch out and switch off the alarm.

Showered and dressed, Paula returned to the kitchen to find Sanders busily chopping vegetables. "Salad for the picnic," he said, looking up brightly. "It's a long walk to Westwick, even if we get the bus back."

"Assuming we get that far. No Bovis today?" Paula asked, still half asleep.

"At my nan's," Sanders replied, handing her a mug of coffee so strong it could have kept her awake all week.

She dropped a slice of bread into the toaster and sat down at the table. "Is she getting on all right with her new teeth?"

"I think they're a bit sore 'cos she was really grumpy. When I said that guy at the farm was asking after her and Mum, she nearly bit my head off."

Sanders rubbed his forehead, leaving tomato seeds in his fringe. "She said, 'If I hear you've been there again, I'll skelp your arse.' "

"I thought you said she took you there before?"

"I know, but she gets like that sometimes. Mum says she's just crabby and that's where she gets it from. Sometimes she says I talk so much it makes her brain swell and if I don't stop it'll be the death of her."

"Who, your mum or your nan?"

"My nan. Well, both of them."

Paula suppressed a smile. "I know how they feel."

He scowled. "Why are grown ups always cross? Mum says it's because they know their time's running out and they don't want to waste it putting up with things that irritate them."

"I'm sure that's true, but your mum's not that old is she?"

"She is. She's twenty-nine in September." He returned to chopping vegetables and, after a pause, spoke so quietly she almost didn't hear him. "I was thinking I might go to the gala as Sandra."

"What did you say?" she queried.

"The gala – I think they call it a fete in England."

She glanced at him to see if he was joking. He didn't look up, just carried on piling salad ingredients into two Tupperware boxes. She watched his small hands organising cucumber, radishes and tomatoes – they were almost like a girl's, arranging the slices. But putting a salad together was one thing, going to the village fete dressed as a girl was quite another.

"Is that wise, do you think?" she asked. "Won't the whole village be there?" She knew how cruel people could be, children in particular, especially when they were running about hyped up on sugary junk food.

When Sanders didn't respond, she asked, "What does your psychologist think?"

He studied his feet. "I haven't told her. But I've got to try sometime." There was a defiance to his voice that took Paula by surprise. "Whatever I decide, people are gonna be horrible about it, so why not start now and get it over with?"

Paula thought for an awful moment that he was going to cry, but he didn't. He just clipped the lids onto the boxes a little more fiercely than was necessary, and stood there with his arms wrapped round them as if they were the only things left he could depend on.

Flying to the moon

When her mum had announced they were going back to Scotland, to the seaside, for their summer holiday, Paula's excitement had lasted precisely as long as it took for her to add that Pete wasn't coming. They were going to spend a whole three weeks in a house by the beach across the water from where they used to live in Edinburgh, and she could play on the sand and go swimming in the sea every day – without Pete. He was going camping in France with Ollie and his parents.

"Doesn't Pete want to come to the seaside with me?" Paula asked incredulously.

They had never spent longer than a day apart. They sat side-by-side at school and played with the same group of friends. If one fell out with someone, they both did. If one decided apple juice was nicer than orange, that was all they both wanted to drink. If one refused to eat peas or decided Brussels sprouts made them sick, neither would touch them. When one was ill and had to stay at home, whether it was a tummy bug, a sore throat or chickenpox, within hours the other was sweating and writhing in agony. They were like two halves of the same person, utterly unable to function alone. As the "big twin", Paula took it upon herself to tease and scold him, but they never disagreed or fell out like other brothers and sisters. They were Paula and Pete, Pete 'n' Paula. Always had been and always would be.

"Of course he would want to, darling, if Ollie's family hadn't asked him to go away with them," her mum said stroking her hair. "Ollie is Pete's friend. Even twins don't have to spend all their time together. Going on holiday with Ollie doesn't mean Pete doesn't care about you. You know Ollie doesn't have any brothers or sisters. Don't you think it was kind of Pete to agree to go and miss the fun of being with you, just so Ollie could have someone to play with? I think you should be very proud of your brother for having such a good heart. You have all the rest of the year together. You can spare him for a few weeks."

"Pete's my little twin. That's more important than a best friend," Paula raged. Her lip trembled. "He shouldn't be kind to anyone else. I wouldn't go with someone else and leave him on his own. I would ask him to come or I wouldn't go."

Her mum smiled. "Even if you were doing something as exciting as going camping in France, and there wasn't room for another person in the car or the tent?"

Paula shook her head firmly. "Even if I was going to the moon."

"There definitely wouldn't be room for an extra person in a space rocket and you wouldn't want to miss out on that would you?"

"I'd make the driver stay behind."

"I think a rocket has a pilot not a driver, and you wouldn't be able to go anywhere without him."

"Pete could drive."

Her mum hugged her and spoke softly. "You're going to have to manage without him one day. What about when you're grown up and have a boyfriend? You won't want your brother around all the time then."

"I'm never going to have a boyfriend. Pete and me are going to live together. We've agreed."

Her mum smiled again. "I'm going to remind you about that when you're a pair of moody teenagers with spots and greasy hair who can't stand the sight of each other. Anyway, you'll have a great time at the seaside. There'll be lots of other children your age, so you'll have plenty of new friends to play with."

"What about our birthday?"

"We'll celebrate yours in Craskferry and Pete will have his in France. It'll be lots of fun."

Paula sniffed and rubbed her eyes.

"Don't be a baby about it now," her mum chided. "I want you to show your brother and everyone else how grown up you are by not making a fuss. You can do that can't you, darling?"

Defeated, Paula could only nod. She felt very small and frightened at the thought of being without Pete for such a long time, but she desperately wanted to be a big girl and impressing him mattered more than anything.

"That's a good girl. We're all going to have a lovely time."

Paula sat on the beach steps thinking about that day as she looked out across Craskferry Bay, remembering how miserable she had been at the prospect of surviving without Pete for three weeks. She could never have imagined it would one day be a lifetime. She had spent the past week trying not to think about it; distracting herself by reading in the sun or exploring the local coast and countryside on foot or by bus with Sanders. She had kept her promise not to raise the subject of his dilemma and he, in return, had provided his usual stream of cheerful nonsense to divert her from her thoughts.

She jumped when Mrs McIntyre opened the gate behind her.

"There's a man at the front door for you."

"Sorry?" she said startled.

"A man, at the front door."

"Do you know who it is?"

Her landlady turned to walk back up the garden. "He didnae say."

The hall was gloomy after the bright sunshine outside, and Paula was at the door before she could see who was standing on the step.

"Oh, babe, I was beginning to despair of ever seeing you again."

Paula didn't move. "Ollie," she said uncertainly. "How did you find me?"

He looked crestfallen. "It wasn't that difficult once I got here. You can't last more than a couple of days without a newspaper, so I guessed the one person certain to know where you'd be was the newsagent."

"And he told you. He's a very helpful man."

Ollie ignored her sarcastic tone. "Aren't you going to invite me in?"

"Of course." She tried to sound normal, but all she wanted to do was scream.

Scream at her mum for betraying her like this. She knew she didn't want to see Ollie and yet she had gone ahead and told him she was in Craskferry. Scream at Renton for being so free and easy with his customers' addresses. Sanders was right not to like the bloody man. What business did he have telling everyone and anyone people's whereabouts? Scream at Ollie for refusing to take no for an answer, and scream at herself for everything – for pushing him away when he didn't deserve it, for cheating on him with Andy when he certainly didn't deserve that, for not having the grace to give him a proper welcome when he had been so decent about her running away. He was in horrible pain, yet he had driven hundreds of miles simply because he cared about her – and all she felt was irritated. When had she turned into such a bitch?

Paula managed to get something approximating a smile onto her face. "Come in." She searched for something else to say. "Are you hungry?"

"Starving and knackered."

She led him through to the kitchen. "I'll make us some supper then. Pasta all right?"

"Brilliant. I'm so hungry I could eat grass. I brought your favourite." He pulled a bottle of rosé out of his sports bag.

"Oh, Ollie, you're too good to me. I don't deserve you." She gave him a quick hug, pulling away to put the bottle in the fridge before he could reciprocate.

"Nonsense. You..."

"Don't." She shook her head. "Please don't. I won't be able to cope if you're nice to me. I've been so awful to you."

Turning to gather ingredients and utensils, she felt his eyes on her back. "Paula..."

"How was the journey?" she asked before he could say anything more.

He sighed. "The traffic on the A1 was horrible. Every man and his dog was on the road today."

"The weather's been so good everyone wants to get away from London." The weather? Was that the best she could do? She tried again. "You're looking well." Pathetic. They were talking like strangers, but it was all she could manage.

"You look fabulous," Ollie countered.

"Everyone else seems to think I look like a wreck."

"They're all blind. You look really fit and that tan suits you."

"I've been out in the sun a lot."

"Maybe that's what you needed – time to relax. Sometimes it's good to take a break from everything. And your hair's amazing. It's so different, you almost don't look like you anymore."

She met his gaze for the first time since he'd arrived. "I'm not me anymore. I want to be different, someone else."

"Is it helping?" he asked softly.

"Not really. I still feel like shit. I don't know who I am anymore or what's happening to me, and it's got nothing to do with a haircut and some blonde dye." She was virtually shouting at him. "I don't know what I'm going to say or do from one minute to the next."

She waited for a response but he merely nodded.

"Half the time I feel like I'm outside of myself looking in." Her voice was quieter now. "It's like watching a complete stranger."

Ollie held out his arms again. "Come here."

Paula stepped into his embrace and this time she didn't pull away.

He buried his face in her hair. "What are we going to do with you?"

She leant her head against his chest. "I don't know," she murmured. "I just don't know."

A slammer too many

At first Paula and Pete had been just big sister and little brother, born less than a year apart. Then, aged seven and six, thanks to their dad's invention of Pete's extra-special extra summer birthday, they became twins. Part of the reason Paula insisted on being included in the plan was that it would get her an extra birthday that year. As she hoped, she got a second lot of presents in July, and Pete was so pleased to have been promoted from little brother to twin that he didn't point out she had already had plenty in January.

After that, they both had all their cards and presents in July. People who didn't know any better assumed they were real twins, and Paula and Pete rarely corrected them.

The year they had turned five, they were living in Scotland, where being born in the same calendar year meant they started primary one together, so they were always in the same class anyway. They did absolutely everything together: walked to school side by side, sat at neighbouring desks, played with the same friends at break, and spent every evening and weekend in each other's company. They were a unit; they didn't need anyone else. That was why Ollie's arrival in their lives was such a shock for Paula.

On their first day at their new primary school in London, she and Pete sat together as usual. Paula's desk was at the end of the row, so she didn't have another neighbour. She didn't care, as she felt no great need to get to know the other children. Pete was the only person who mattered. But he had an empty desk beside him. For the first few days no one sat there. Then, towards the end of the week, another new boy arrived. The teacher said his name was Ollie and placed him at the empty desk. From that moment onwards, he attached himself to Pete, whispering to him, telling him jokes and helping him with his schoolwork. When their dad bought them their first bikes, Ollie pestered his parents until he got one too and they could all cycle the local streets together.

Whatever she and Pete did, Ollie did too, and she told herself she didn't mind. Pete liked him and that meant it was okay. She had made some friends of her own by now, reluctantly admitting to herself that it was fun to have other girls to share things with, but Pete – and with him Ollie – came first for her. They were The Three Musketeers; their motto was "All for one and one for all".

Her desire to please Pete made her conceal how upset she was when he chose to go to France with Ollie rather than to Craskferry with her, and when they were together again at the end of the three weeks, she quickly forgot what it was like to be without him. Their parents must have realised how deeply the separation affected her though, because from then on until they left school, family holidays were exactly that: Mum and Dad, Paula and Pete.

When they got their first tandem, Ollie and his solo were never far away and soon they were all entering competitions – Pete and Ollie in the male events, Pete and Paula in the mixed. As adults, people often remarked that they could be triplets, and not just because of their matching kit and Pete and Ollie's identical cyclists' build of powerful legs, lean torsos and slim arms. Pete was virtually the same height as Paula, and Ollie was only a couple of centimetres taller. Pete and Ollie even gelled and spiked the top of their short brown hair to match. At first it had annoyed Paula, made her feel as if they were turning into the twins and she was the extra one. But as the wins mounted up, they all agreed it was a lucky cut, and they never changed it. Like it or not, Paula knew that if she didn't want to lose Pete, she had to accept Ollie – there was simply no alternative.

They all went to the same university, waded through mud and warm beer at festivals together in vacations, lived in the same house when they graduated, and then, when Paula and Pete's dad slipped a disc and had to step down from his role as cycling coach, Ollie took that over too. He was a natural, with an instinctive understanding of when to praise and encourage, when to berate or cajole, and that brought the three of them even closer.

They were a good-looking trio with plenty of friends, and though both Pete and Ollie had girlfriends, and Paula had her share of boyfriends, their relationships were never serious. No outsider could claim a permanent place in their gang.

And then, three months before Pete died, things changed forever. It was March, the weekend of Ollie's thirtieth. He and Pete were competing in an event in Manchester and Paula went along to cheer them on. To mark his birthday, Ollie treated them to a night in a swanky boutique hotel instead of the usual nylon carpeted B&B.

The men won their races – there was never any doubt they would – and the three of them hit the town for a double celebration. It was very late when they made it back to the hotel.

"Look," Ollie pointed out delightedly as they crossed the foyer. "The bar's still open. Let's have one for the road."

"Shouldn't that be one for the lift?" Paula queried.

"Good spot. One for the lift then."

"Oh no, this is one fine mess you'll have to get into without me, Laurel and Hardy," Pete said. "My drinking shoes are full. I'll see you in the morning."

He gave them a little wave and headed unsteadily towards the lifts.

Ollie offered Paula his arm. "You would make an old man very happy, Miss Tyndall, if you would accompany him for a final refreshment on this most special of nights."

"Honoured and delighted, sir," she replied and linked her arm into his.

They started off on margaritas but moved on, at Paula's suggestion, to tequila slammers. Looking back, this was where it had started to go wrong. Even after the best part of a bottle of Rioja with dinner, followed by a couple of large vodka tonics, she had felt reasonably in control. The margaritas had made her slightly off balance, reckless even, but without the slammers to wash away what remained of her judgment, it would never have happened, not in a million years.

She remembered competing to see who knew the funniest Englishman, Scotsman and Irishman joke, as they banged the coaster-topped glasses on the bar and knocked back the contents. She could even remember Ollie telling her she had won, but the joke itself was long gone from her memory. She had a feeling it wasn't that funny anyway; the mood they were in, everything seemed hilarious.

By the time the barman suggested Paula and Ollie continue their party elsewhere because he needed to close up, they were the only drinkers left. Arm in arm, they wove their way across the foyer and made it into an empty lift just as the metal doors were shutting. Clinging together for support, they fell back against the side.

"That was a hoot and a half," Paula said. "My lightweight little brother'll kick his own arse when he hears about the sparklingly witty repartee he missed."

"Wittily sparkling," Ollie corrected.

"No, sparklingly witty. That was my sentence and I say it was sparklingly witty." Paula I waved a finger at him. "If you want to correct something, go and find a sentence of your own."

"If you want to be pedantic, go and find a lift of your own," Ollie countered.

She poked him in the chest. "You're the one who's being pedantic. *You* should go and find a lift of *your* own."

Ollie responded by grabbing her around the waist, lifting her off the floor and twirling her round. "I'm sorry, madam, I'm going to have to put you out at the next floor," he said solemnly.

"Put me down, you great moose." Paula pounded her fists on his shoulders in mock fury.

The next minute, she was lying on top of him on the carpet outside the lift.

"What happened?" She sat up and rubbed her elbows.

"I think we reached our floor," Ollie said. "Which way's Pete's room?"

"Not sure. Why?"

"So we can drink his mini-bar dry and tell him what he missed."

"That's an extremely bad idea." She managed to stand up. "You know what he's like if he doesn't get his eight hours."

"Yeah, a bear with piles."

"Come on, we can raid my mini-bar instead."

She held out her hand and helped Ollie to his feet. "Chop, chop, let's go."

The vodka and Coke was the last straw for Paula's bladder, but in the couple of steps to the en-suite something important slipped her mind. After she peed, she decided to brush her teeth. Then she got undressed for bed. It was only when she walked back into the bedroom stark naked that she remembered she wasn't alone.

Ollie was sitting cross legged on the bed. "Hello boys," he said delightedly.

Ignoring him, she walked round to the other side, pulled back the duvet and climbed in.

"Should I get in too?" he asked.

"Go on then," a voice that came out of Paula's mouth said.

Ollie refilled her glass and got up to clear their plates. "It's ages since I've had spaghetti puttanesca. I'd forgotten how good it is."

"It's one of my favourites, but I don't like it as much as carbonara." Paula winced inwardly at the inanity of the remark and drained her wine. She had been chatting about Craskferry and describing the bike rides she had been on, but she wouldn't be able to distract him from more serious topics for much longer.

He sat back down.

"I haven't got anything sweet for pudding but there's brie in the fridge," she suggested, blotting a fleck of parmesan off the table with her fingertip.

Ollie grabbed her hand before she could return it to her lap. Part of her wanted to shake him off and scream the house down, to make him go away forever, so she would never have to reveal the mess inside her head to him; another part wanted to throw her arms around him and never let go, to confess about Andy and beg for his forgiveness, but guilt and confusion silenced and immobilised her.

"It's been awful without you the past couple of weeks," he began, turning her hand over and studying the lines of her palm as he spoke. "Sometimes I didn't know how I was going to cope. I started to think you were blaming me."

Paula found her voice. "Blaming you?" she asked puzzled. "Why would I do that?"

He shook his head. "I don't know. Because I wasn't there to protect him maybe. If I'd been there, it might not have happened."

She looked away. "I'm as much to blame as you – more. I was his big twin. It was my job to keep him safe."

"Paula, he was an adult."

"But he was still my little brother."

"I know. He always hated riding alone the night before a race. One of us should have been with him. Didn't he ask you to go?"

"He knew I was on a deadline for work. You?"

"No. I hadn't spoken to him for a couple of days before..." Ollie's voice trailed off.

"That's not like you."

"I'd been busy too," he said miserably. "I suppose he didn't want to bother me."

Paula reached for his hand and they sat in silence for a while.

Ollie spoke first. "Why did you run away and not return my calls?"

"Don't... I can't... I don't..." The way she felt then, the way she felt now: she couldn't even begin to explain any of it. "I'm just so tired. Shall we go to bed?" she heard herself suggest.

Paula lay as still as she could, trying not to give any sign that she was awake. Even with her eyes closed she could tell it was daylight, but she didn't dare open them and check the time in case the movement woke him. As long as Ollie was asleep, she could pretend it hadn't happened.

It had been easier to have sex than talk, and he had seemed so grateful for what he must have seen as a sign things were getting back to normal, that she had carried on even when a voice inside her was screaming, "Stop! Don't do this – it'll only make things worse." But could things ever be normal again? Could they go back to the way they were? She had slept with him that first night in Manchester simply because he was there. She had been drunk and naked, and he was there. When they woke up the next morning to the sound of someone hammering on the bedroom door, she had been instantly ashamed.

"What the hell's that noise?" Ollie had muttered without opening his eyes.

Paula pulled the duvet over her head.

A voice from the corridor called, "PT, are you in there?"

Christ, it was Pete. She leapt out of the bed and flung herself against the door. She was pretty certain it locked automatically when it closed last night, but what if she was wrong?

"Is it too much to ask to have a shower in peace?" she called through the thin wood. Her throat was so ragged it was amazing any sound came out.

"You're not up yet? It's nearly twelve. We were supposed to check out by eleven and I can't find Ollie. If we don't get packed and out double quick, they'll charge us for another night."

She needed to make him go away. "It's okay, he was here a little while ago. He overslept too. He's just popped out for some air. He said he'd meet us in the foyer. You get your stuff and go down. I won't be long."

"You'd better not be."

She listened as his footsteps retreated down the hall. When she finally turned round, Ollie was sitting up grinning.

He patted the duvet beside him. "Get back over here."

"There's no time for that now." She backed into the en-suite and locked the door.

Paula turned the shower to its coldest setting and stepped under the water, biting her knuckles to stop herself crying out from the shock. She wished she could wash the alcohol out of her system and with it the knowledge that she had just slept with her brother's oldest friend. Her oldest friend. He was virtually her brother too. She might as well have slept with Pete. Hurling herself out of the shower, she made a grab for the toilet bowl.

Ollie tried the door handle. "Are you okay in there? Are you being sick?"

It felt like an age before the retching stopped and she was able to answer. "Sorry, too much booze."

"Open the door and I'll help you clean up."

"No," she replied too quickly. "I'm fine now. Everything's fine. I'll be out in a minute."

What on earth had possessed her to sleep with him? She knew objectively that he was a good looking, funny guy. Several of her girlfriends used to just about foam at the mouth with lust whenever they all went out together, but he hadn't been that interested in them.

His last girlfriend, a teaching colleague of Pete's called Lily, was always desperate to tell anyone who would listen how fabulous he was in bed, and she was devastated when he dumped her after a couple of months. Ollie's relationships never lasted much longer than that. Whenever the girl gave any sign of wanting things to get more serious, he seemed to panic. Within a couple of days, she would be weeping on Paula's shoulder: *It had all been going so well. She had never met anyone like him – handsome, intelligent, witty and kind.*

Paula offered comforting platitudes: it was Ollie's loss, they deserved better, and so on, but she always felt detached. To her, Ollie was family and she just couldn't see what all the fuss was about. Not that the sex had been terrible or anything. From what she could remember – could allow herself to remember – it was fine. No, better than fine. Not amazing, but good enough that if he had been anyone other than Ollie, she would have been pretty pleased to wake up beside him.

He was fully dressed and sitting on the bed, tying his laces when she emerged wrapped in a towel.

He smiled at her. "How are you doing? You look a bit shaky. Are you going to survive the journey?"

"I'll be fine once I've had a couple of gallons of coffee," she lied.

"I'm going to need a few cups too – and a very large fried breakfast. Thank God Pete's driving."

"He'll be wondering where we are." She wished Ollie would hurry up and go.

Finally, he stood up. "I'd better grab my stuff. See you downstairs."

He kissed her quickly on the lips and let himself out into the corridor.

Over breakfast in a greasy spoon and on the drive back to London they both behaved as if nothing untoward had happened. Ollie was the first to be dropped off. The tandem he and Pete raced was stored at his house. Paula stayed in the car while Pete helped him get it off the roof rack. As Pete wheeled the bike up the path, Ollie mouthed through the car window, "Call you later."

She was closing the front door when her mobile rang.

"That was a bit weird, wasn't it," he said.

It felt as if someone had dropped a lead weight into her stomach. She forced herself to speak. "Hi, Ollie. You can say that again."

"We're going to have to tell Pete. It'll be too strange otherwise. Do you want to do it or will I?"

"Do we need to tell him?" Christ, Ollie didn't think it was a one off. "I mean, do you think we really have something we need to tell him?" Ouch, not very tactful.

"Does that mean you don't?" He sounded stung.

If she and Ollie fell out over this, how could he ever coach them or ride with them again, and what would it do to Pete if she destroyed their winning team? She needed to tread carefully. Groaning internally, she said, "I just think we need to talk about it first ourselves. Why don't you come over?"

Back to reality

"Oh no, you're awake. I was planning to surprise you with breakfast in bed." Ollie said as he wrapped his arms around her.

"How about you make it while I go for a quick run instead?" Paula suggested. "My back's a bit stiff. I must have been lying awkwardly. Moving should free it up."

"Okay, but it'll be on the table in exactly thirty minutes, so get a shift on."

As she got out of bed, he leant over and patted her bottom. "Sexy."

She suppressed a shudder.

It was another beautiful, clear-skied day and the beach was already busy with families unfurling windbreaks and setting up deckchairs. Paula walked down to the hard sand, did a few stretches and began jogging gently towards the cliffs, rotating her arms alternately as she went. Loosened up, she increased the pace.

She'd left her iPod on the bedside table and without music to drown out her thoughts, she found herself remembering that Sunday evening after she and Ollie first slept together. It was less than four months ago, but so much had happened since, it felt far longer.

He must have run every red light south of the Thames because he was on her doorstep in less than twenty minutes. She had tried to work out what she could say to end things without hurting his feelings, to protect Pete and Team Tyndall, but her mind remained stubbornly blank.

She'd showed him into the sitting room and bought a couple more minutes by going to the kitchen to make a pot of tea. It didn't do any good. As she laid the tray on the table in front of the sofa, her brain still felt numb.

"This is really embarrassing, isn't it?" he said. "I feel like I'm about fifteen again."

Paula poured the tea. "I'm so mixed up my brain seems to have seized completely."

He was perched on the edge of the sofa clasping and unclasping his hands. "And being monumentally hung-over isn't helping."

She sank into the chair beside him. "I'm never going to get drunk like that again."

Ollie studied the floor. His right foot had started to tap. "Is that the only reason it happened?"

Paula opened her mouth to reply. She wanted to say yes. Drinking too much always made her horny. But was it really that simple? Was the alcohol just an excuse? And an excuse for what exactly?

"I don't know," she admitted. "I really don't."

"So what do we do now?"

"I don't know the answer to that either."

God, she was being utterly useless. Why couldn't she just say that sleeping together had been a mistake? It was all her fault. She didn't know what had come over her. She was really sorry, and could they please pretend it never happened and all those other clichés? If it had been anyone but Ollie, she wouldn't have had any trouble saying it, but if it was anyone but Ollie, she wouldn't have had to.

She took a gulp of tea. "Ow, that was hot."

"I'll get you a glass of water."

"Stay where you are. I'm fine."

"So..."

Paula took a more careful sip.

Ollie exhaled slowly. "I'm not going to pretend I regret what happened last night, because I don't and I'd like it to happen again." He turned to face her. "There, I've said it. So what do you think?"

"I… I don't know. It wasn't something I planned."

"I don't think either of us planned it, but that's not the point, is it?"

"Maybe we just need to take things very slowly and not say anything to Pete until we're sure."

Jesus Christ, what did she just say? Take things slowly and not tell Pete till they were sure? Sure of what?

A smile of relief spread across his face. "Yes, definitely. Good idea."

She stood up. "I don't want to throw you out, but I'm feeling poisoned by all that booze and totally worn out. I need to go and lie in the bath and get an early night."

"Absolutely, no problem." He got to his feet. "I'm so glad we were able to talk things through and that we feel the same way." He wrapped his arms around her and kissed her hair. "This could be the start of something great."

Returning from her run, Paula opened the back door to find Ollie serving up bacon, scrambled eggs and fried bread.

"Perfect timing. Sit yourself down and pour the coffee."

She did as he instructed.

He sat opposite her. "You had two visitors while you were out."

She bit into a piece of fried bread. "Who was that?"

"A bloke with a little white dog turned up a few minutes after you left."

"Really? I don't know a bloke with a white dog."

"He said his name was Terry."

Paula felt herself blush. "Oh, no, Nora's husband. I thought he was a dog."

Ollie paused with a forkful of food in mid-air. "What?"

She shook her head. "Never mind. What did he want?"

"He said he and his wife are having a barbecue tonight and did we want to go."

"We?"

"Is it not okay now to tell people I'm your boyfriend?"

She swallowed, pushing down the scream of "NO!" that was fighting to escape. "Sorry, I didn't mean… Go on."

"That was it. He said they're at number 27. We're to go round at about eight o'clock and take plenty of alcohol."

"You accepted?"

"Why not? He seemed a nice bloke and I thought they must be friends of yours. It sounded like just what you need."

She opened her mouth to demand what right he had to say what she needed, but the look of outrage on her face was enough.

"Sorry, sorry. I'm like a bull in a china shop sometimes. I should have asked you instead of assuming." He took her hands in his. "I just want to make things better for you, to have the old Paula back."

"Ollie…"

He nodded. "I know it's stupid. Things are never going to be the same. I do realise that. I just…" His eyes filled with tears.

"It's okay. I'm sure they are nice people – I know his wife a little. She has a café I've been to a few times."

He leant over and stroked her cheek. "We don't have to stay long. Terry said it would just be a few friends eating burnt sausages and having a laugh. Maybe it'll be good for us both."

She sighed. "Just an hour or so then." It felt as if she was being sucked into a deep, dark hole. "Who was the other visitor?"

"That was a strange one."

"How so?"

"A little girl with blonde bunches and too much eye make-up just appeared at the kitchen door. I don't know how I didn't see her coming up the garden, because I was standing at the window washing last night's dishes."

"Sanders. Probably came down the side path."

"Sanders?"

"It's a diminutive of Sandra," Paula said quickly. "What did she want?"

"She seemed to think you'd made some kind of arrangement to go out for the day."

"Bugger." Paula bit her lip. "I completely forgot."

"When I said you hadn't mentioned it, she handed me that." He pointed to a carrier bag lying on the worktop. "Then she turned tail and scuttled down the garden without another word."

Paula stretched over and checked inside the bag: a box of sandwiches, two bags of crisps and a couple of Mars Bars.

"She'll be furious with me for forgetting." It felt odd referring to Sanders as she. "I'll have to find her and apologise."

"What were you going on a picnic with a kid for anyway?"

"She's sort of adopted me. It's a long story. I'll tell you later." She picked up the cafetière. "More coffee?"

"So why did you just vanish like that?" Ollie turned to look at her. "Couldn't you have talked to me if it was all getting too much?"

She'd wondered how long it would take him to ask the question. They were walking hand-in-hand along the beach beyond the harbour. When he took her hand, her instinct had still been to pull away, but she stopped herself. She breathed deeply, forcing herself to relax into the familiarity of his touch.

"I couldn't. I didn't want to talk – not to anyone. I just had to get away," she said slowly.

She saw herself back in the van with Andy. His remark about her running away had made her question whether she was running from something or to it. She still didn't know. She wondered if he had thought much about her since their night together.

"Can you talk to me now?"

She pushed the image of Andy away and tried to find some words for Ollie. "After the funeral, I…" She stopped walking and looked out into the bay. It was full of yachts. She wished she was on one of them, sailing away from all this – from Ollie and everyone else she knew, from this conversation, these emotions. "Seeing Mum and Dad, seeing you, knowing we were all thinking and feeling the same things made it all too real, too overwhelming. I had to escape, to be somewhere where I was the only one who knew. I thought it would make it more manageable."

"Has it?" he asked tenderly.

"Not really. I'm falling apart."

He put his arm around her and she leant into him.

"But why all the secrecy?" he asked.

"Because Mum and Dad would have tried to talk me out of it. They wouldn't have wanted me to go. I feel bad about leaving them, but they've got each other."

"You could have told me."

She managed a faint smile. "You would have wanted to come with me, and when I said no, you'd just have followed me. You're here now aren't you?"

"Fair point."

As they turned to start walking again, she caught sight of Sanders and Bovis wandering along the edge of the dunes. Sanders was back in his usual uniform of cut-off jeans and a T-shirt. She watched him bend down, pick up a piece of driftwood and throw it for Bovis to retrieve.

"Sanders!" she called.

He didn't appear to hear. She pulled away from Ollie and ran towards him.

Ollie caught up in a few strides. Putting a hand on her shoulder, he tugged her to a halt. "That's not the girl who came round this morning."

"Yes, it is."

"That's a boy."

"I know. I need to speak to him."

"Sanders!" Paula called again.

This time he looked round. When he saw her, he took hold of Bovis's collar and started to trot in the opposite direction.

"Wait, please," she shouted. "I'm sorry."

"You always say that," he yelled without breaking stride.

"Sanders, hang on. Let me talk to you properly. I'm really sorry I forgot we were going out. I want to make it up to you."

"Don't worry about it," he called over his shoulder. "I can manage on my own."

Paula made to follow him, but Ollie held her back. "Leave it. He doesn't want to speak to you."

She raked a hand through her hair. "I always seem to let him down."

"Who is he anyway?"

"He's the girl who came round this morning."

"That's crazy."

"I know." Paula turned and began walking back the way they had come, forcing Ollie to follow her. The wind snapped tendrils of hair across her face.

"And?" he asked.

"I don't want to talk about it just now."

After a few minutes' silence, Ollie said, "Why Craskferry?"

At least that was easy to explain. "It's where we came that summer you and Pete went to France. It was the only time we were apart, the only place with no memories of him. But…" She paused. "That's not the only reason I came."

Paula stopped walking and turned to face the wind once more. Ollie waited for her to continue.

"I think I was meant to. I don't know why yet, but I've been having strange dreams."

"What about?"

"Myself as a little girl, running along the beach here with a kite."

Ollie slid his arm through hers and steered her round so they could carry on walking. "Sounds like maybe your subconscious is trying to take you back to a happier time."

"I thought that at first too, but there's more. I'm there as a grown up, watching myself, you know, as a kid." Paula shook her head. "Sorry, I'm not explaining this well. Things are weird, wrong… menacing." She wrapped her arms around her torso. "First I was drowning in horrible black oil and then there was this man – it was all really creepy."

"I'm not surprised you're having strange dreams. Look what we're going through."

"But you're not dreaming weird stuff."

Ollie gave her arm a squeeze. "Everyone deals with things differently. They're just dreams."

"But they're not," Paula persisted. "They mean something. I know they do."

"Babe, maybe you're just reading things into them because you're upset."

Paula chewed at the ragged edge of a fingernail. "I'm not imagining this because I'm upset, Ollie. Please believe me. They're so vivid. I think there's something about this place – something that happened here maybe – that I need to know, understand, remember… I don't know what. I've no idea what it is or why it matters so much, I just know it does." She was nearly crying now.

He squeezed her arm again. "Okay, babe, okay. Everything's going to be fine."

Sushi and sausages

Ollie suggested they walk back via the Co-op and get some wine for the barbecue, but neither of them had any money. When they got to the flat, Paula asked if he would mind going for the booze on his own. She had to check her work email. It was a lie, but she needed to be alone.

She put on some music and curled up on the sofa. "Pete?" she asked softly. "You wouldn't have been so quick to dismiss my dreams. You understood me. Why can't Ollie? He used to, or at least I thought he did. I know he cares desperately, but sometimes we don't seem to be on the same wavelength at all."

After a few minutes there was a knock on the front door. Ollie, nose to the etched glass, was holding up two carrier bags.

"That was quick," she said, only just concealing her annoyance.

"I got two bottles of South African pinotage and a couple of chilled whites – a chardonnay and a sauvignon blanc – in case you wanted to open one now. It might help get us in the mood for socialising."

She took the bags from him. "Let's crack open the sauvignon."

Nora answered the front door. "Hi, I'm so glad you could come." She kissed Paula on the cheek, politely ignoring the fact that they were half-an-hour late.

"It was really nice of you to ask us," Paula managed. She had put their arrival off as long as she dared. "This is Ollie."

Nora and Ollie shook hands. He held out a carrier containing the two bottles of red and the remaining white. "Alcohol, as instructed."

"Wonderful. Come in and meet everyone."

As she led them through the house and out to the garden, Paula said, "I wish you'd explained Terry was your husband and not another dog. You didn't really tell him what I said, did you?"

Nora grinned. "I couldn't resist it. He thought it was funny."

On the patio, a stocky man of about forty wearing a stripped butcher's apron was turning sausages and vegetable kebabs on a huge gas barbecue.

"Not everyone appreciates my wife's sense of humour," he said, laying down his tongs. He shook Paula's hand. "Terry One, village taxi driver and honorary dog."

Four other people were standing a few feet away, chatting and drinking. Paula recognised the men: Adrian Linton, who owned the greengrocers-cum-health food shop, and the guy from the chippie. She hadn't seen the women before.

Nora said, "I'm sure you know Adrian. No one can stay in Cra'frae for long without finding themselves in his wonderful shop."

Adrian nodded to them both. "Good to see you."

"And this is Felice Beato," Nora went on. "He feeds us all when we want a break from our own cooking."

"I know," Paula said. "We met the day after I arrived."

Felice studied her for a moment. "So we did. I was disappointed you didnae come back for one of my deep-fried Mars Bars." He sounded far less Italian away from the shop.

Nora put her hand on the arm of an Oriental woman standing next to him. "This is Kyoko, Felice's better half. As you're about to discover, she makes the best sushi on the planet, but we don't tell the holidaymakers about that."

Kyoko grinned. "Local sushi for local people. We hide it through the back of the shop – you need a password to buy it."

Adrian leaned forward conspiratorially. "It's whelk, by the way."

Kyoko punched him playfully on the shoulder. "Shhh, whelk's next week's password."

"You'd never make a secret agent, Adrian," the other woman teased.

"This is Carole," Nora said. "Sanders' mum."

Paula struggled to hide her surprise. Sanders had said she was nearly twenty-nine, which would make her not quite seventeen when she had him, but she looked barely that now – and far too healthy to have been a drug addict. She was very slim, with the clear, pale skin and build of a pre-pubescent girl.

"You know Sanders?" she asked.

Paula wasn't sure how to respond. He clearly hadn't mentioned her to his mum. She wondered where he had said he was going all the times they had spent the day together. "We met on the beach. He's a very entertaining boy."

Carole's smile was almost a grimace. "He's certainly that."

"Right then," Nora said. "Who needs a top up? Paula, Ollie, what'll you have? Red or white? Or there's plenty of beer in the fridge."

Kyoko arranged several platters of sushi on a long wrought iron table beside the barbecue, while Nora poured the drinks. They began to eat.

"This is fabulous," Ollie said.

Kyoko grinned. "My talents are wasted on these country bumpkins, but what can I do? They couldn't manage without me."

"Who would cut our hair, for a start?" Carole put in.

"You're a hairdresser?" Paula asked.

Kyoko nodded. "At a salon in Westwick, but in a former life I worked in London. That's where Felice and I met. He came in one day for a haircut, stinking of fried fish. I introduced him to sushi – far less smelly – and the next thing I knew we were married and moving here."

"But why Craskferry?" Ollie asked.

"That's my fault," Felice said. "I wanted to live in Scotland – one o' my grannies was from Glasgow."

"We found an advert for the shop on the internet," Kyoko continued. "And the rest is history."

Her husband tweaked her earlobe. "You love it here."

"Sad but true. I couldn't go back to the big smoke now."

"I've never lived in a city and I know I couldn't do it," Nora observed, helping herself to more tuna. "All that stress and pollution."

"That's not all there is to city life," Ollie countered. "What about the pubs and nightclubs, the art galleries and the theatres?"

"You haven't been to the Steam Packet yet?" Adrian's face was deadpan.

Ollie gave him a puzzled look.

Nora giggled. "It's our local. Actually, it's not bad. KT Tunstall used to play there before she got famous. And if we want art and museums and theatre, Edinburgh's not that far."

"Nora and I were born in Cra'frae," Terry said. "We've never lived anywhere else. We're country bumpkins and proud of it."

"What about you?" Ollie addressed Adrian. "Are you a native?"

"I'm a refugee from Edinburgh," Adrian responded. "As cities go, it's beautiful, but I'd far rather be here."

"And you?" Ollie said to Carole. "Another refugee or a born bumpkin?"

"Bumpkin through and through," Carole replied. "I've always lived here."

Terry got up to check the sausages, and Nora went to get the salad and more drinks. Ollie followed her inside.

"Is this a permanent move for you two, Paula?" Felice asked. "Ollie doesnae sound all that convinced about country life."

"It might be permanent for me. I don't know yet. Ollie's just visiting."

He emerged from the kitchen holding a fresh beer and a basket of garlic bread. "Are you taking my name in vain?" he asked cheerfully.

Before Paula could respond, Felice said, "Paula was just saying she hasnae decided yet if she's staying for good."

"I thought this was just a holiday." Ollie's tone was casual but she saw the shock in his eyes.

"I… I don't know," she said lamely.

No one spoke for a moment. Felice caught Paula's eye as Terry passed round sausages and vegetable kebabs. He whispered "sorry". She smiled weakly.

The conversation moved on. Reaching across the table for some bread, Paula realised that Carole seemed to be watching her. She smiled at her, but the other woman looked away and began chatting to Adrian.

Nora topped up Paula's glass. "Anyone else for more alcohol?" she asked. "Terry, are there any sausages left?"

Ollie drained his beer. "I'll get another, if you don't mind." He stumbled slightly as he stood up. "Time I invested in a smaller pair of feet."

Terry shared out the last of the sausages and kebabs, and they began to talk about holidays.

"Wouldn't it be nice, just once," Kyoko said, "to be able to go away in summer like everyone else?"

"Dream on," Adrian said. "It's holidaymakers who pay our mortgages. We can't go anywhere until they've all gone home."

"What do you do, Carole?" Ollie asked.

"I do a bit of cleaning in one of the big B&Bs."

"Aye," Felice said, "we spend our entire lives feeding holidaymakers, cleaning up after them and driving them around."

"It's not that bad," Kyoko said. "We're off to Naples over Christmas to introduce Mitsuko to Felice's family. Mitsuko's our daughter. She's six months old," she added for Paula and Ollie's benefit. "Then I'm taking her to see my lot in Japan for a couple of weeks in February."

"Do you have kids?" Ollie asked Nora.

"No kids," she said, "just dogs."

"Don't you want any?" he persevered.

Nora looked uncomfortable. "More wine anyone?"

"I said, don't you want them?" Ollie repeated.

"We can't," Terry said. "I'm firing blanks. We've tried everything, IVF, the lot – nothing's worked."

Paula kicked Ollie under the table. "I came here once for my holidays when I was little," she offered. "I was nine."

"You mentioned spending the summer here the day we met," Nora said, obviously glad of the change of subject. "Did you rent a house?"

"We did," Paula said, "but I can't remember where. The only clear memories I have are of being on the beach. Donkey rides, kite flying, that sort of thing."

Ollie went into the kitchen and returned with another beer.

"Excuse me." The metal feet on Carole's chair made a screeching noise on the flagstones as she stood up. "I have to…"

"Use the upstairs one," Nora said. "Downstairs is being temperamental again."

Carole went inside and everyone else carried on chatting.

After a while, Felice noticed that Carole hadn't come back.

"She was looking a bit peaky," Kyoko said. "I hope she's not ill."

Adrian made to get up.

"Stay where you are," Nora said. "I'll see if she's okay."

She returned a couple of minutes later. "There's no sign of her and her jacket's gone."

Near death

"Paula, you're being utterly ridiculous. You just admitted you brought the tandem with you, so you must have been planning to use it, and you told me yesterday about all the trips you've made on your solo." Ollie tugged at the top of his hair, the way he often did when he was frustrated. "I've got a pair of cycling shoes in the car. So, what's the problem? Why can't we go out for a ride? It's what we need to clear our heads."

Paula closed her eyes and tried to think more clearly. She had woken up achy and nauseous from all the wine at the barbecue, and her head was pounding so hard she could barely see. She knew her refusal didn't make sense and she wanted to explain. But how?

"I didn't bring it to ride," she said finally. "I just needed to have it with me."

"But you said you were trying to get away from everything linked with Pete."

"I know it seems contradictory," she floundered, "but a lot of things feel contradictory right now."

"What if we went out on solos then?" he offered. "One of your new friends might have one I could borrow."

"I should really see Sanders. I need to sort things out with him."

"Great, so now you're a self-appointed social worker for a twelve-year-old transvestite."

"He's not a transvestite," Paula snapped. "He's a boy who's trying to make an unbearable decision."

Ollie softened his tone. "Isn't spending time with Sanders just a way to avoid facing up to Pete's death? You can't run away forever. Sooner or later it'll catch up with you."

Paula knew he meant it kindly, but she wanted, needed with every cell in her body to deny what he was saying. "Suddenly you're the expert on dealing with bereavement?"

She hadn't meant to sound so angry. They had both avoided discussing the previous evening, but her annoyance over the way he had been knocking back beers and his insensitive remarks to Nora about not having children was bubbling just under the surface. He would never admit it, but meeting new people made him nervous, and nerves made him drink too much.

Ollie shook his head and looked down at the breakfast table. His right foot started to tap, making the table vibrate slightly.

"Is that what you've been doing – facing up to Pete's death?" She leant in until her face was centimetres from his. "Is that why you wanted us to go to Dan's party the weekend I left? Why you accepted Terry's invitation? I don't call going on with your life as if nothing's happened dealing with it."

Ollie met her gaze. "And you've found a better way? I can tell you're coping really well."

She sat back and folded her arms across her chest. "I'm coping the best I can."

"You're barely holding it together. And when were you going to tell me you're thinking of staying here for good?"

"I'm not."

"You told Felice…"

"I don't know – I might, I might not. I don't know what I'm thinking, okay? What the fuck do you expect?" She rose from the table and began pacing the kitchen. "A hit-and-run driver killed my little brother. You tell me how I'm supposed to feel about that. Go on, why don't you? Tell me what I'm supposed to do."

"He was my best friend. You're not the only one suffering." Ollie spoke quietly. "Pete was the nearest thing I'll ever have to a brother, but I can't bring my own life to a complete halt because he's gone. I have to keep going."

He reached out to her, but she pushed him away and continued pacing.

Ollie sighed. "I go to work each morning and I come home each evening. I go out on my bike and I see our friends. That's my way of getting through it."

"Exactly – your way. Yours not mine."

"Your parents are distraught too, but they're keeping going."

"Mum's so full of pills she rattles, and Dad's drinking whisky like it's going out of fashion. You really think that's keeping going?"

"They're doing their best."

Paula banged her fist on the table. "And so am I. Why can't you accept that and leave me alone?"

"Is everything all right in here?" Mrs McIntyre's head appeared round the kitchen door.

"Everything's fine," Paula barked.

Her landlady withdrew and closed the door.

"Oh, Christ." Paula sat down and rested her forehead on the table. "She must think I'm the tenant from hell."

"Then maybe she'll give you a refund and you can come home," Ollie said.

Paula spoke slowly, emphasising each word. "Did you listen to a thing I just said? I need to be here. I have to do this my way, just as you have to do it yours."

Ollie walked round the table and put his arms around her. "Okay, I hear you. We'll both just do the best we can."

Paula nodded, all the fight drained out of her.

"How about some fresh air?"

She nodded again.

"Let's have a walk on the beach."

She took a long breath. "No, you're right. I was being silly. We should go out on the tandem."

"Only if you're sure."

"I am."

"Let's visit the donkeys," she suggested as they approached the turning for the Thompsons' farm. "They live just along here."

"Whatever you say."

They rode up the gravel track and propped the bike against a wall by the farmhouse.

"I'll see if either Mr Thompson's about."

The door was closed this time, and there was no bell, just a heavy brass knocker in the shape of a ram's head. Paula rapped twice. A dog barked and a male voice yelled at it to shut up.

A few seconds later, Bill Thompson opened the door. "Hello, hen." He smiled at her revealing his missing tooth. "What brings you back so soon?"

"Is it okay to go down and say hello to the donkeys?"

"Aye, no problem. Are you on your own? Did you no' bring your little friend? I was just makin' a pot o' tea – you're welcome to come in for a cup."

Before she could reply, Ollie appeared at her shoulder. "She's not on her own – she brought her big boyfriend." He put a protective arm around her waist. "Got a problem with that? Want to hit on me too?"

"Ollie!" Paula exclaimed.

"I was just offerin' a cup o' tea. I didnae mean anythin' by it," Bill said quickly.

Paula took hold of Ollie's hand. "Come on. We'll skip the donkeys." She turned to Bill. "I'm really sorry, Mr Thompson. My friend misunderstood. He didn't mean to be rude."

"You're all right, hen. No hard feelin's."

When they were riding down the farm road again, Paula said, "What did you have to be like that for?"

"He was a creep."

"He was just being friendly."

"And since when was I just your friend?"

"For God's sake, Ollie. You're completely overreacting."

He swung them into a left turn, down a road she hadn't ridden before.

"Of course, I forgot," he said. "You've got your little friend. Why would you need a boyfriend too?"

"That's not fair!" Her words were drowned out by the roar of a large van pulling out to pass them.

They rounded a corner and found themselves at the top of a steep hill. "Tuck in," Ollie ordered.

Paula brought her chin down almost onto her handlebars, drew her elbows into her sides and pulled her knees in as close as the bike's frame would allow. She closed her eyes and tried to concentrate on the rush of cooling air over the sunburned skin of her arms and legs. As the road began to flatten out, she felt Ollie steer them round a right-hand bend. It seemed to go on forever

"Jesus Christ!" he exclaimed.

She opened her eyes. The road ahead was full of sheep. They were going to crash and be dreadfully injured. Was this what it was like for Pete in the last moments of his life – so far into the zone, lost in that place where there was only him and the bike, that maybe he simply didn't register the red light. And what about the car coming towards him? Did he know in the instant he saw it that he was going to die? Paula felt as if she might pass out.

Ollie braked sharply. Despite their combined weight, the back of the bike bucked up and out across the tarmac. Instinctively, she pulled her shoes out of the cleats holding them to the pedals. She lifted off her seat and felt for the ground with her left foot. They skidded to a halt centimetres from the startled flock.

"That was a close one, PT," Ollie gasped.

"Don't call me that," Paula snapped. "Don't you ever call me that." She clambered off and bent over, hands on knees, as she waited for her heart rate to return to normal.

"Don't be so touchy. There's no harm done." He laid the bike down on the road and looked around. "They must have escaped from one of the fields. There's no sign of a shepherd."

Paula glared at him. "No harm done? We could have been smashed to bits if we'd come off. We could even have been killed."

"Now who's overreacting? We're fine, and so's the tandem."

"No thanks to you. You don't know these roads. You've never been on this bike before and you're not used to riding pilot. You should have been more careful."

"I was riding perfectly carefully."

She righted the tandem and began wheeling it between the startled sheep. "I should never have agreed to this. I want to go home."

"Have it your way."

Cycling back in silence, Paula saw herself and Pete on the tandem. It was the summer they turned sixteen and they were riding the coast-to-coast route from Whitehaven in Cumbria to Sunderland.

She was tugging at the back of her brother's jersey. "Stop, Pete, stop. That girl's hurt."

He shrugged her off. "Don't be soft, PT."

"But we've got to."

"Shut up and dig in."

Still pedalling, she stretched out her right arm and flapped it up and down to indicate to their dad, who was snailing behind them in the car, that she wanted to stop.

He pulled alongside and leant towards the open passenger window. "What's up? You're looking good."

"Paula wants to rescue the girl who toppled into the gutter back there," Pete panted.

"Good grief, Paula," their dad scolded. "Where's your focus? You've got another two miles of this hill. Stop now and you could lose the record."

"You go then," she urged.

"Someone else'll see to her. My job's with you."

"But there isn't anyone else. She might have concussion."

"Christ, Paula," Pete exclaimed. "She's not our responsibility. People that unfit shouldn't be riding the C2C."

"That's right," their dad said. "She's just tired. There'll be another car along any minute. They can help her." He braked and tucked back in behind the tandem.

"Now get your arse into gear," Pete hissed.

Paula drew in a long breath and held it for a second. The centre of her forehead was pounding with blood and fury. *What would make you stop?* she wanted to scream. *If her leg was hanging off? If there was flesh and bone all over the road? Would that be enough?* She scrunched up her eyes and shook her head to dislodge the questions she couldn't afford to answer.

"Stop squirming," Pete ordered. "Are you with me?"

Paula didn't answer.

"Are you with me, PT?" he repeated.

"I'm here," she said in a tight voice.

"Then push. We're going to take this record."

Ollie tapped on the bathroom door. "Are you all right in there? I made you a cup of tea but it's gone cold."

Paula resisted the temptation to yell at him to leave her alone; she knew he was doing his best to smooth things over. "I'll be out in a minute," she called, turning off the shower.

He looked up from his paperback when she came into the sitting room in her dressing gown, a towel wrapped round her head. "Do you want some lunch?"

"I'm not really hungry." She sat down on the sofa and began rubbing her hair.

"There's some kind of fancy dress parade through the village this afternoon. Terry mentioned it last night. He said there'd be stalls and games and all sorts of stuff going on."

"It's gala day," she said without enthusiasm.

"It might be a laugh to go along."

The doorbell saved her from having to reply. Ollie got to his feet.

"I wouldn't bother," Paula said. "It'll be for Mrs McIntyre."

"She went out while you were in the shower, so we'd better answer it." He went into the hall. "It's Sanders," he called from the front door, making no effort to keep the annoyance from his voice.

Paula draped the towel round her neck, pushed her damp hair off her face and went out. Sanders was standing in the vestibule in his shorts and a faded Nirvana T-shirt that was several sizes too big.

"I wanted to talk to you about something before I went to the gala," he said.

At least he wasn't wearing girls' clothes. He must have given up on the idea. "Come on through," she said.

"I'm going to make a sandwich," Ollie said and headed for the kitchen.

Paula sat down and indicated the cushion beside her. "What's up?"

"I'm not staying," Sanders said, picking at a loose thread on the hem of his T-shirt. He glanced in the direction of the kitchen. "Not very friendly, is he?"

"He's all right. Things are just a bit awkward right now."

"Did you see that documentary on Channel 4 last night?"

"Is that what you came to ask? We were at Nora's last night with your mum. We didn't see any telly."

"I know. I thought you might have recorded it."

"I don't have a recorder. Is your mum all right? She dashed off while we were eating."

Sanders shrugged. "One of her migraines. You didn't see the programme then?"

"No, I already told you."

"I wish you'd seen it." He began fiddling with his T-shirt again. "This man in Russia had a penis so tiny that the doctors chopped it off and stitched onto his wrist to keep it alive, and then they made him a new one out of a big chunk of his own arm with plastic rods or something inside it." He spoke rapidly, without looking at her. "It was disgusting. They showed the whole thing and it took ages. After they sewed the new one on, they cut the old one off his wrist and stuck it on the end. It was like Frankenstein, all blood and stitches and raw bits."

"Frankenstein's monster," she corrected gently.

"Right." He was almost whispering now. "It was just hanging there like something in a butcher's shop."

"Are you frightened that's what the doctors will want to do to you?"

He didn't answer.

Paula tried again. "So what happened in the end? Did it all work out for the guy?"

"I don't know," Sanders said. "I was at my nan's and she came in from washing the dishes and made me switch it off."

Ollie walked in carrying two plates of sandwiches. He sat down on the other side of Paula and offered her one. "It's tuna," he said.

She laid the plate on the floor. "I said I wasn't hungry."

"We burned quite a few calories this morning. You need to replace them."

She turned back to Sanders. "I'm sorry. Go on."

"It's not important." He jumped up and ran out into the hall.

Paula went after him. "Wait, please come back and talk to me."

He stopped halfway out the front door. "I haven't got time. I've got to get changed for the parade."

"Maybe this is something you need to talk to your psychologist about."

"I only see her in term time," he said over his shoulder. He sprinted down the path, leapt over the gate and jogged off towards Main Street.

"What was all that about?" Ollie asked, when she returned to the sitting room.

"I didn't find out because you interrupted."

He bit into his sandwich. "These aren't bad." He held out her plate. "You'll feel better if you eat."

"How's a bloody tuna sandwich going to make me feel better about Sanders? I'm supposed to be his friend and I'm being no use whatsoever to him."

"What's he doing coming to you with his problems? Why isn't he talking to his mother?"

"I don't know, he seems to like me – heaven knows why. He took a big risk confiding in me and I've let him down."

Ollie pushed the plate towards her again. "Please, babe, your blood sugar's low."

She took the plate and tilted it until the sandwich slid off onto the floor. Tuna spilled onto the carpet.

"Paula! What did you do that for?"

"It was that or throw it at you."

He took hold of her shoulders. "What's got into you?"

She shoved him away. "Don't touch me. I don't want you to touch me ever again."

"Come on now, calm down. This is silly."

"This is me. This is how I'm feeling, but you think it's silly," she shouted. "You think my dreams are silly. You think it's silly that I didn't want to go to Nora and Terry's or ride the tandem with you. You think it's silly that I care about Sanders and want to help him. Is there anything about me and the way I'm leading my life you don't think is silly?"

He held up his hands in a gesture of conciliation. "Paula, please."

"What? Just tell me, is there anything at all you think I'm getting right? Because if there isn't, I really don't know what you're doing here. Why exactly have we been together the past few months? Why exactly are you here now? Was it just so you could tell me I'm being completely crap about everything and you know better?"

"Please, calm down." He knelt on the carpet in front of her and attempted to look into her eyes, but she turned her head away. "That's not true and you know it."

"Do I? The only thing I know for sure is that I don't want you here any more. I want you to take your things and get out. I don't want you to phone me or email me or try to get in touch in any other way ever again."

Ollie leant back on his haunches. There were tears in his eyes. "Babe, no. I'm so sorry. I didn't mean to upset you. C'mon, we can get through this together. Why don't we both go and pack our stuff and I'll drive us back to London. It's your birthday on Monday. You should be with your family."

Paula felt as if a light bulb had switched on inside her head. "That's why you're here, isn't it? You promised my parents you'd bring me back."

"I told them I'd try."

"Well, thank you all very much. It feels really good to be ganged up on." She pushed back a tendril of damp hair. "It's over, Ollie. It never should have started and now it's over."

"But I love you."

She stood up. "No. You loved Pete and so did I, and that's what this was always about. To you, I was just an extension of him."

Ollie leapt to his feet and grabbed her wrists. "What do you mean by that?"

Paula heard herself speak. "I saw you in the garage."

The words she thought she could never bring herself to say.

It's a boy, you muppet

Three podgy teenage girls in matching pink fairy outfits huddled on the pavement outside Renton's Newsagents. The largest had satin wings that hung at an angle halfway down her back. She dropped an empty crisp packet in the gutter, wiped her chubby fingers on her net tutu and took a swig from a can of Coke.

"Come on," she said to her companions. "I'm no' missing my brother arsin' up the sack race."

Paula followed them along Main Street. Most other people were going in the same direction. Two young men, one dressed as a penguin, the other as a badger, jogged awkwardly past on the opposite pavement. They were carrying a crate of beer between them, costume heads clutched under their free arms.

"Swap you," the largest fairy yelled, waving her can at them.

"You'll have to catch us first," the badger called back. "We're late for the arm wrestling."

"I'll arm wrestle ya," she shouted.

The penguin waved his disembodied head at the girls but he and his companion didn't stop.

The football field was on the far side of the village at the top of a long hill. A banner tied to the railings trumpeted, *Welcome to Craskferry gala games!!!* The smell of fried onions hung in the hot, still air.

A woman stood behind a trestle table at the gate. As the fairies handed over money, she gave them each a ticket and a yellow plastic token. They skipped past, giggling and poking each other with their wands.

Paula bent towards the ticket seller. "I need to find someone – I'm not staying. Can I go in without a ticket?"

"You'll need a ticket, hen. It's £2 for adults, £1 for weans or if you're takin' part, and £2 on top if you're huvin' the hog roast." The woman indicated a card that read *Get roasted*, propped beside a shoebox of tokens.

Paula checked the pockets of her jeans. "I haven't brought any money, and I have to find my friend. Can't I just take a quick look?"

The woman sighed. "You cannae go in without a ticket."

Paula's eyes welled up. "I'll get my purse."

Turning away from the table, she felt a touch on her shoulder. It was Kyoko pushing a baby in a buggy.

"Are you okay?" she asked. "You're very pale."

Paula managed a smile. "I'm fine, just a really bad head. I should learn when to stop. How are you?"

"A bit groggy – Nora and Terry don't do things by halves. Mitsuko and I have come to watch her daddy in the tug-o-war. Goodness knows how he'll get on." Kyoko stroked her daughter's dark hair. "Did you change your mind about going in?"

"I forgot my purse. I'm going back to get it."

"You don't need to do that. I'll treat you. Are you going to the hog roast?"

"Just the games."

Kyoko paid for their tickets and they walked in together. Paula glanced around the packed field. It wasn't going to be easy to find Sanders.

"Not Ollie's kind of thing?" Kyoko asked.

"Sorry, I was miles away."

"The games, didn't Ollie want to come?"

"He had to get back to London."

"That's a shame."

Paula didn't reply.

"People come from all over to Cra'frae games – it's a big event in these parts," Kyoko said. "Did you watch the parade?"

"I missed it. Do you know if Sanders was there?"

"Sanders?" Kyoko thought for a moment. "I think I did see him."

Paula tried to sound casual. "What was he wearing?"

"I don't know. I was in the shop, covering the lunch break." Kyoko bent to lift Mitsuko out of the buggy. "I just saw his head bobbing past the window. He'd done something with his hair though – tied it up in bunches or something. Was he planning to dress up?"

"I think so." Paula scanned the crowd once more, but there was no sign of him. "I'm going to have a walk around."

"Are you not coming to the tug-o-war? Terry and Adrian are in it too." Kyoko checked her watch. "They'll be starting over by the pavilion any minute."

"I'll maybe see you there."

In the distance, Paula caught sight of the penguin disappearing into a large green tent. Without knowing why, she began pushing through the throng towards him. D:Ream's *Things Can Only Get Better* was playing at full volume inside. A hand-written notice on the door flap said *Disco*. She lifted it and went in.

It took a few seconds for her eyes to adjust to the flashing red and blue lights. There were several dozen people dancing, but she couldn't tell if Sanders was one of them. She spotted the bulky silhouette of the penguin standing beside the DJ at the far end of the tent. Walking down the side of the floor towards them, she scrutinised the dancers. There were a few faces she recognised from the village but no Sanders.

The noise and lights were making her dizzy. Edging behind the DJ and the penguin, she made for a thin line of brightness that seemed to indicate another flap at the back of the tent.

She was just about to step outside, when someone blocked her path.

"Well, I never, it's the girl who likes donkeys." It was Bill Thompson. "Not going in for the fancy dress, then?"

He was squeezed into a white three-piece suit that might have looked stylish in a retro way on a younger, slimmer man. He held a thin hand-rolled cigarette, and the smell of cannabis was overwhelming.

He leant close to her ear. "Fancy a dance?"

"No, thank you. I'm looking for someone."

"What about a wee puff o' the naughty stuff then?" He grinned and took a pull on the joint. "You here with your little friend?"

"Have you seen him?" she demanded.

"Sorry." He held out the joint. His fingers were stained yellow with nicotine. "Sure you don't fancy a puff?"

Paula shook her head and pushed past him through the tent flap. The sunlight was dazzling after the gloom inside. She closed her eyes for a couple of seconds. Reopening them, she glanced around – no sign of Sanders. As she weaved through the crowd, she searched for his white blond head, but there were so many people, it was as if they were all trying to impede her. Every time she saw a route through, or caught sight of a figure of roughly the right height and hair colour, the crowd seemed to close in round her.

Her temples were pounding. The colours, smells and sounds of the gala were so churned up inside her head she could no longer tell one from another. All she knew was they were too bright, too strong, too loud, way too loud for her to think clearly. Her hands trembled and her T-shirt was stuck to her back.

"Come on," she told herself. "Get a grip." She hadn't inhaled enough of Bill Thompson's smoke to affect her. It was more likely to be dehydration from the wine combined with delayed shock from her near accident with Ollie. Find Sanders, make sure he's okay and get back to the flat: that was all she needed to do. After that, she could lie down and sleep forever if she wanted.

She drew in a long breath and set off towards the tiny football stand, where a banner strung under the eaves suggested *Make a hog of yourself here.*

Two long queues led to red-clothed tables. Behind them, a pair of men in striped aprons sliced meat from a row of pigs roasting over a pit. A woman in a nylon overall spooned in glistening fried onions before passing them to a colleague to wrap in napkins and hand out in exchange for tokens.

Paula was turning to retrace her steps, satisfied Sanders was not in this part of the field, when a commotion off to the side caught her eye. A group of teenagers were gathered round something on the ground, booing and laughing. A few other people drew closer to see. She went across and peered over the shoulders of a couple of teenage boys. The largest of the trio of plump fairies was kneeling on top of a smaller girl, who was lying on her front with her face in the grass. She had blonde hair tied in bunches.

The other two fairies stood nearby. "What's going on?" Paula asked them.

One shrugged and bit into an oozing pork roll.

"Dunno," the other offered unhelpfully.

"You must have seen what happened," she persisted. "What's your friend doing?"

"It's that weird kid," the girl with the roll said. "Daniella said she was going to kill him."

Paula felt as if she was spinning again. "Kill him?" she echoed.

"Yeah. He called her a fairy elephant." The girl used the back of her hand to wipe a rivulet of pork fat off her chin. "Daniella said she'd be doing the world a favour."

"Sanders," Paula yelled as she pushed between the teenage boys.

Daniella had rolled him over and knelt on his chest. He looked tiny pinned beneath her vast pink bulk. The heavy girl held him by the ears and banged his head off the ground. His face was a blur of mascara.

"Now who's the fucking fairy, you pervert?" she roared.

The crowd stood mesmerised by the bizarre scene taking place in front of them.

Paula lunged forward, but nothing happened. Had she merely imagined moving? She tried again. Still nothing. It was just like in her dream. She opened her mouth to call for help, but no words came out.

Sanders raised a fist and punched Daniella square on the nose. The girl bellowed like a wounded animal and tumbled off him. Blood oozed down her face and onto the front of her dress. He was on top of her immediately, pummelling her torso with both fists. The teenage boys clapped and cheered.

"Get off me, you little fucker," Daniella yelled as she rolled him over again and grabbed his throat.

"Oot ma road!" a voice from behind Paula ordered. "That's ma wee sister gettin' belted."

Daniella's brother stepped into the circle. He wore a large yellow rosette that said, *Sack Race: 1st*. He made a grab for the back of Daniella's dress but her wings came away in his huge hand. Hurling them to the ground, he tried again, this time lifting her out of the way and dropping her onto the grass as if she were a bag of shopping.

He seized Sanders by his T-shirt and pulled him to his feet. "Right, ye wee shite."

"Get him, Fraser," Daniella urged. "Get that skirt off him and pull his knickers down."

"Eh?" Fraser paused and glanced over to his sister for clarification.

"It's a boy, you muppet."

"A boy?" He looked at Sanders. "Is it?"

Sanders glared silently back, his muddy, make-up streaked face expressionless, an almost imperceptible tremor in his bottom lip the only chink in his defiance.

In what seemed like a single movement, Fraser ripped his skirt and pants to his ankles.

Sanders stood ringed by the other spectators, naked from the waist down. His eyes met Paula's, yet their focus seemed to go far deeper, as if he could see right inside her, all the way to the curiosity she was trying to keep hidden, curiosity he was challenging her to deny.

Paula fixed her gaze straight ahead and urged herself not to look down no matter what.

"Girlie, girlie, poofter, freak," someone chanted.

"Poofter, weirdo, freak…" The crowd picked up the call.

"What the fuck…" called a boy standing next to Paula.

"That's just no' right," his pal exclaimed.

"Is that a boy or a girl?"

The question hung in the air.

"That's Carole McCormack's lad," a young female voice said.

"The junkie? No wonder then."

"Girlie, girlie, poofter, freak," the chant continued.

"Is that really a boy?" another voice asked.

"Well, it's no' a girl."

"But that cannae be his willy."

"Stop staring at the poor laddie," an elderly female voice ordered. "You shouldnae all be staring."

"You're starin' yourself, missus," a young male voice called out.

Paula felt Sanders watching her as, of their own accord, her eyes travelled down his body. His penis was a lump of flesh no bigger than a raspberry, a miniature nub of a thing.

She forced her eyes back to his face and opened her mouth, praying for something to come out.

"Sanders." It was barely a whisper.

For a fraction of a second he drew his focus back to meet her gaze, then everything went dark.

She opened her eyes to find Kyoko and Felice crouching beside her on the grass. "Paula, can you hear me?"

Kyoko patted her cheek. "Are you all right?"

"I think I must have tripped," Paula said.

"It looked to me like you fainted," Felice corrected.

"I…" Paula sat up.

"What?" he asked.

She shook her head. "I don't feel too good."

Kyoko held out a bottle of water. "Drink some of this. You've probably had too much sun."

She took a sip. "Where's Sanders? Is he okay?"

"I was just coming to break it up. He ran off," Felice said. "Have some more water."

Paula turned her head away and threw up on the grass. Mitsuko started to cry.

A note in the night

Paula sat bolt upright and switched on the bedside light. There was a gentle crunching sound as if someone was tiptoeing down the shell path. She crept to the window, lifted a corner of the curtain and peeked out in time to see a figure closing the gate and turning down Shore Road. It was 4.45am. Mrs McIntyre wouldn't be going out at this time of the morning. And the figure was too small to be her landlady.

She wondered if it might be Sanders, so she pulled on her dressing gown and went into the hall. Snapping on the light, she opened the inner door. A white envelope lay on the vestibule mat. One word was written on it in a large, childish hand: *Paula.* Inside, a sheet of lined paper contained a single sentence:

Stay away from Sanders or I'll tell the police you molested him.

Paula stared at the paper, brain frozen by the enormity of those few words. Her body took in an involuntary gulp of air and she realised she had been holding her breath. The sudden movement shook her out of the paralysis and she began to shiver uncontrollably. Still clutching the note, she wrapped her arms around her torso and felt goose-pimples through her sleeves. Tea, she needed tea.

Sitting at the kitchen table, she tried to make sense of the coursing emotions. There was shock and guilt for standing and watching along with the others, for not going to his aid as she should have done. She also felt anger. How could Sanders make such a dreadful threat? She hadn't given him the support he was looking for, but this… this was too much. Every time she tried to understand it, her brain seized, unable to get past the fact that a boy she cared about, had thought of as a friend, had done something so horrible to punish her. Had she really let him down so badly that he could hate her this much, that she could deserve such a mean threat? Spreading a rumour like that could ruin a life. Yet she had seen him deliver the note with her own eyes.

Paula felt as if she would never be warm again. She thought fondly of the bath back in her own flat, imagined herself lying up to her neck in steaming bubbles. Somehow a shower didn't have the same allure. She checked the clock above the cooker: almost 6.45. She had been sitting there for two hours. Getting stiffly to her feet, she refilled the kettle.

Paula put the fresh mug of tea on the bedside table, climbed into bed and, pulling the duvet tightly around her, hugged her knees to her chest. Closing her eyes, she waited for sleep to claim her, but the note wouldn't leave her. A pain in her temples made her feel queasy, and her legs ached from hips to toes. Every fibre felt exhausted, yet she could not imagine being more wide awake.

Still shivering, she sat up and took a sip of cold tea. She needed to get up and do something, but what? She could go and confront Sanders, but what if he carried out his threat? If he was angry enough to write it, maybe he could do it. And then what? She was a stranger, an incomer. What if the police believed him? Even if they didn't, they would have to make a show of investigating. She couldn't stay in Craskferry after that. She would have to go back to London, and if word of what had happened followed her there...

Her head pounded so hard she could barely see straight, let alone think. She needed air. She pulled on her running things and, without bothering to brush her teeth or comb her hair, let herself out the back gate.

The sky was flat and heavy with the prospect of rain, and the beach deserted apart from half-a-dozen seagulls down by the water's edge. Their mood appeared every bit as disturbed as her own. She watched as they circled and landed only to take off again almost instantly, flapping desperately against the mocking pull of the gusty wind. It bullied and toyed with them, tugging their ruffled bodies backwards or casting them from side to side until, tiring of its game, they dropped back onto the sand, where they paced, dazed and squawking, and the process began again.

Paula turned and began jogging towards the cliffs, the wind hurling handfuls of stinging sand against her calves. Picking up her pace, she tried to outrun it, but it would not be beaten. It swirled, drying the sweat on her arms and legs almost before it had a chance to form and snapping tendrils of hair across her cheeks. Turning when she reached the cliffs, she faced its full force. Leaning into it and drawing on every bit of strength, she fought her way back along the beach. Every step seemed slower than the last. By the time she reached the post with the red and white lifebelt that marked the start of Shore Road, she was virtually going backwards. She walked a bit further then sat down on a set of steps to catch her breath.

"You must be exhausted."

She twisted round to find Nora standing with Terry Two peering through her legs.

"The wind's so loud I didn't hear you open the gate," Paula gasped. "I didn't realise these were your steps."

"I was watching from upstairs as you battled along the beach. You don't like to give up, do you?"

Paula pushed her hair off her face. "I like to do things my way."

Nora nodded down at the terrier. "I was going to take the wee fella out for a wander but he's not looking too keen."

"He's seen what's been happening to those seagulls."

"Definitely a day for small dogs to stay indoors." Nora gazed heavenwards. "It's going to bucket any minute."

As if in response to her prediction, a trio of fat raindrops landed on the step beside Paula.

"I think it's time for a bacon sandwich," Nora said. "D'you fancy one?"

Paula's instinct was to say no. The very idea of making conversation was exhausting, but the prospect of going back to the flat and Sanders' note was worse. She stood up. "That would be great."

She watched from a stool at the breakfast bar as Nora fried bacon. "Terry One not about?" she asked.

"He's gone to Edinburgh Airport to pick up Mary Renton – Frank the newsagent's mum – she's been visiting her sister in Australia."

"That's a good fare."

Nora flipped a rasher and patted it down in the sputtering fat. "You wouldn't get him out of bed at this hour on a Sunday for anything less."

The rain was streaking down the window panes and it was so dark Nora had to put on the light.

"You wouldn't think it was July," Paula observed glumly.

"What you need is my special hot chocolate," Nora said.

By the time she joined Paula at the breakfast bar with two bacon sandwiches and a couple of mugs of hot chocolate, the warmth of the kitchen had thawed her chill.

Paula cast around for something to say. "Have you spoken to Carole? I gather she was coming down with a migraine on Friday night."

"Aye, she phoned yesterday morning to apologise for disappearing. They come on quite suddenly and she said she just needed to get home." Nora lifted the top off her sandwich and added a generous squeeze of tomato ketchup. She reassembled it and took a large bite.

"Migraines are horrible. My mum gets them and she sees flashing lights and all sorts," Paula said. "The tablets don't really help – she just has to go to bed until it passes."

Nora blew on her chocolate. "I reckon it's a legacy of the drugs with Carole. You can't abuse yourself like that without long-term effects."

"You said she was taking heroin?"

"Mostly, I think."

"That's serious. For how long?"

"Long enough. By the time she got pregnant she was well and truly hooked."

Paula felt herself shiver again. She wrapped both hands round her mug, trying to draw the warmth from it. "She looks far too young to be Sanders' mum."

"I know. She was just short of seventeen, but getting pregnant saved her. When she found out, she stopped just like that – cold turkey."

"It must have nearly killed her."

Nora smiled. "She's a lot tougher than she looks, our Carole. Having Sanders was the making of her. It hasn't been easy though. For a long time she believed the drugs caused his problems."

"I thought it was a genetic disorder."

"It is, but when Carole's gets herself convinced about something, that's that."

Paula wondered if she should say anything to Nora about Sanders' note or what happened at the gala. She would surely have mentioned his humiliation by now if she had heard. Maybe it would help to talk about it all, and surely Nora knew him well enough not to be taken in by his accusation.

"Something weird happened earlier…" she began.

Nora's mobile trilled. She checked the screen. "It's Carole. I'd better answer it."

Nora listened for a long time. "You're certain? And you've called the police? Okay, I'm coming now." She hung up. "Sorry, Paula, I've got to get round to Carole's. Sanders has vanished."

The trials of Bovis

Coming back from Nora's, Paula struggled along the sand, shoulders hunched against the diagonal rain. The back gate was banging so hard it looked as if it was about to fly off its hinges and go bowling across the beach. She winkled her keys out of the pocket of her shorts, took the steps two at a time and grabbed for the handle, but the wind was too quick for her. Whipping it beyond her reach, she was left clutching at thin air. She stumbled, banging her shin hard against the wooden frame. Swearing under her breath, she tried again. This time she caught the gate and locked it behind her. Limping up the path, she scanned the first-floor windows but there was no sign of Mrs McIntyre. She must be out or she would have dealt with the gate herself.

The wheelie bin had blown over and a rubbish bag stuck out. A seagull tore at the black plastic.

She lunged at the bird. "Get out of there, you horrible thing."

It squawked, nonchalantly lifted its wings and let the wind carry it away. The bin was far heavier than Paula expected and she struggled to right it. The wheels bounced slightly as they settled back onto the concrete slab. As she turned away, she heard a small scraping sound, as if something shifted in one of the bags. Again, it came, quite faint, more of a scrabbling than a scraping.

The seagull watched from the wall. "If one of your mates is in there, I'll kick its feathery arse," she warned.

The gull looked on as she opened the lid and pulled out the stinking bag it had been pecking. She leant in and fished for another bag, dumping it on the paving beside the first one. She eyed the gull. "Don't even consider it."

Paula reached in again but it was fur, not plastic, that met her fingers.

"What the hell…" She peered into the bin and saw Bovis curled up in the bottom. She tilted the bin forwards. "Come on, you rascal, out."

The dog didn't so much as raise her head.

"Out now!" she ordered. No response. "It's me, Paula," she tried more gently. "Come on, I'm not cross. I just want you out of there."

Still no movement. She laid the bin on its front and reached in for Bovis's collar. The greyhound gave an almost inaudible whimper as Paula dragged her out onto the concrete. She lay motionless where she landed, eyes closed.

Paula crouched down and stroked her head. "What's wrong? Are you ill?"

Bovis's eyes flicked open then shut again as if to confirm this.

"I'm going to have a feel and see if I can work out what's up. Will you let me do that?"

Paula ran her hands over Bovis's thin body. The dog barely seemed to be breathing. She flinched slightly as Paula touched one of her back legs, and when Paula slid her fingers underneath her chest she felt something moist and warm. She withdrew her hand: blood.

She sprinted inside and grabbed a bath towel from the shower room and wrapped Bovis up as gently as she could. Sliding her arms under the inert bundle, she struggled to her feet. Staggering slightly, she made it up the steps and into the kitchen. She shoved the door shut with her hip and carried Bovis to the sitting room. Plugging in Mrs McIntyre's phone, she called directory enquiries. The nearest vet was in Westwick. She rang the out-of-hours emergency number. It took ten rings to get an answer.

The woman sounded as if she had just woken up. Paula explained what had happened.

"Can you bring her in right away?" the vet asked.

"I haven't got a car and the local taxi driver's away."

"I'll come and get her then. It'll be quicker than trying to raise a cab from here."

Paula sat on the floor cradling Bovis's head until the vet arrived. The plump woman in a tartan windcheater knelt beside the dog and peeled back the towel.

"Oh, you poor thing, you've been in the wars," she said softly, as she began to examine her. "Is she yours?"

"No, she belongs to a friend. I was... looking after her. How bad is she?"

"She's got a broken leg and ribs. Hit by a car most likely."

"Will she make it?" Paula's voice was barely a croak.

"It depends how much damage has been done internally, but I'm afraid you'd better prepare yourself for the worst."

Paula swallowed back tears. "Please do absolutely everything you can, and send me the bill. I'll pay whatever it costs..."

After the vet left with Bovis, Paula undressed and got into bed.

"Can we swap places, just for a little while, Arthur?" she whispered to the threadbare stuffed dormouse lying on the pillow next to her. "I don't think I can take much more of this."

As the people turned to stare, an acid sickness rose in Paula's throat, threatening to choke off her breath. She had thought everything was all right – and again she was wrong. The clouds, the seaweed, the oil were gone. The beach was packed with people: parents, children, grandparents, reading paperbacks, doing crosswords, paddling and building sandcastles in the sunshine. She stood at the bottom of Mrs McIntyre's steps, watching as the latest arrivals tapped in their windbreaks and unpacked their picnics.

Everything looked fine.

But it wasn't.

First a child, a little boy, turned to point. "Look at her," he called to his family. "Look at that funny lady."

Paula glanced down. She was wearing the blue pinafore of her childhood. The hem of the skirt barely reached the top of her thighs and its appliquéd pocket sat, bulging with shells, just beneath her breasts. On her feet were huge clown-sized versions of the fuchsia plastic sandals her younger self had worn, a string from the kite tied to one of the T-bar straps.

As she crouched to undo it, more voices joined the chorus.

"Is she a little girl or a grown up?"

"She's got purple ribbons in her hair."

"What's she doing dressed like that?"

"Is she crazy?"

"Maybe she's a mad person."

"She must be. She must be a crazy lady."

Louder and closer the voices came as Paula struggled with the knot, their looming shadows making it difficult to see what she was doing. At last, she freed the kite. She lifted her head and froze. Everyone was Bill Thompson. Adults, children, men and women – their voices, sizes and clothes were all different, but every single one had the face of Bill Thompson.

Despite the hot sunshine, goose pimples covered her arms. "This isn't happening," she said aloud. "It's not real."

She closed her eyes and opened them again, but nothing had changed.

They moved nearer. "She was watching the children," one said.

"Staring," another said.

"She's one of those perverts." The Bill Thompson who spoke now had the body of a massively overweight woman, squeezed into a tight scoop necked T-shirt and denim mini.

"You're a pervert," the woman repeated. Her breath stank of cigarettes.

Paula edged backwards. "I'm not. I don't know what you're talking about. I wasn't watching anyone."

The bottom step dug into her calves and she threw out her arms to steady herself, letting go of the kite.

The woman grabbed her by the wrist. "Don't lie. We know what you were doing."

Paula shook her off. "I'm not lying."

"We know all about you," a skinny, bent old man standing beside her said.

"Admit it," a thick set man at the back shouted. "You had sex with your brother."

A scrawny woman near the front nodded. "She did. She fucked her brother."

"That's not true. I didn't." Paula looked for an escape route, but the crowd was too closely packed.

"Liar, liar," chanted a small boy. "Dress is on fire."

The others joined in. "Liar, liar, dress is on fire."

Paula felt the heat around her legs before she saw the flames. They leapt up from the sand as if someone had lit a ring of gas jets.

"Liar, liar, dress is on fire." The Bill Thompsons shuffled back as the fire rose higher.

She smelt the hairs on her legs singeing, felt the skin on shins and hands beginning to blister as she stamped and beat at the flames that encircled her.

"Paula, I'm here."

Every head swung round at the sound of the girl's voice. Little Paula stood at the water's edge, the tandem lying on the sand at her feet.

She waved. "Hurry up!" The crowd surged towards her as she struggled to right the heavy bike.

Paula threw herself through the ring of fire and sprinted down the beach, but one of the men got there before her. He lifted little Paula onto the back seat of the bike. As he swung himself into the pilot's position, the sleeve of his green sweatshirt was pushed up to reveal part of a tattoo. It was a pair of work boots resting on either side of an upturned bucket.

The man began pedalling across the sand towards the gap in the wall that marked the end of the alley. His and little Paula's combined weight should have made it impossible to travel over the soft surface, but the tandem moved as easily as if it was on tarmac.

Paula tried to follow them but her vast clown feet refused to move.

"Come back," she cried hopelessly.

"Toodle-oo," Bill Thompson shouted as he waved over his shoulder. "See you later."

Clinging to her handlebars, feet dangling above the pedals, little Paula twisted round. "Promise you'll find me," she called. "Promise…"

The crowd was gathering once more, drawing round Paula, muttering as they nudged closer. The only gap lay behind her. Testing her feet again, she found the sand had released them from its grip. She drew in a huge breath, closed her eyes and let herself fall back into the clear water.

The freezing, burning shock as the sea took possession of her charred skin, numbing her brain and flooding her wounds with salt, was so extreme it wiped out all fear for herself and concern for little Paula. Only the pain remained.

But as the water covered her face, instinct took over. Pushing herself up from the gritty bottom, she staggered to her feet. She stood doubled over at the water's edge, arms wrapped around heaving ribs, blind to everything but the searing redness inside her own eyelids.

By the time she was able to straighten up and open her eyes, the crowd were gone. Every single adult and child had vanished, leaving Paula alone among the half-eaten picnics and jaunty striped windbreaks.

At first she didn't remember the dream. She showered, dressed and gathered up the damp Sunday papers from where they lay on the vestibule tiles. After making a large pot of coffee, she spread out the various newspaper sections on the kitchen table. *Scotland on Sunday* had a front-page lead about a thirteen-year-old boy from Inverness who had been missing for three days. A search party led by his father and uncle had pulled his battered body out of the Caledonian Canal. She threw the paper on the floor and began flicking through the *Sunday Herald*. The lead on page three was about the increase in cases of cruelty to animals.

"Christ, isn't there any good news?" She swept the rest of the papers onto the lino, knocking her mug with them. Miraculously, it didn't break, but coffee splashed halfway across the room.

As she bent down to mop it up with the cloth from the sink, the image of little Paula being carried away on the tandem by Bill Thompson came back to her. Her temples began to throb. Closing her eyes, she rested back on her haunches.

"What was all that about, Pete?" she asked quietly. "You're gone. I pushed Ollie away, messed things up big style with Andy. Sanders left that note and vanished, and Bovis..." She swallowed. "And now even Bill Thompson's getting in on the act. What's going on? Am I going mad?"

She looked up to the ceiling. "Should I pack my things and go back south, like Ollie and Mum and Dad want? Or should I stay and try to make some sense of it all? Please tell me what I should do."

She rested her pounding head in her hands and waited, but no answer came. She checked the clock. Almost six. She needed to eat but there was no food in the house.

Paula could see Kyoko through the huge plate glass window of Felice's Fish Bar, arranging bottles of brown sauce and ketchup on a shelf behind the counter.

She turned at the sound of the door opening. "Hi there, how are you?"

Paula managed a smile. "Hungry."

"That's easily fixed. What can I get you?"

"Fish supper, please."

Kyoko shovelled chips into a cardboard tray and laid a large piece of battered fish on top. "Salt 'n' sauce?"

"Just salt. Did you hear about Sanders running away?"

"I did." Kyoko wrapped the parcel. "Everyone's been out looking but there's no news."

Walking back along Main Street, Paula was drawn towards the welcoming lights of the Co-op.

"You'll need to hurry up. I'm closing," the assistant said sourly. Instead of the usual young man behind the counter, it was a short, bony woman of about fifty with a tight, unnaturally black perm and sparkling white dentures. The deep lines of a lifetime's smoking converged on her mouth. A badge above her right breast said, "Agnes. Happy to help."

Paula would normally have taken time to select a Californian white grenache, a South African pinotage or maybe a shiraz from Australia or Chile. Instead she grabbed three bottles of inexpensive red from the nearest shelf.

"Anything else?" Agnes demanded.

"No, thank you."

She rang up Paula's purchases. "£13.77."

Paula handed over her card.

"You're Paula Tyndall?" Agnes was holding the card by the corner, as if it was toxic.

"I am."

"Put your pin in then."

Alone

"Happy birthday, Pete. Happy birthday, Paula." Paula reached for the tumbler of wine on the bedside table and took a long slug, even though it was only eleven in the morning. "Ooh, vintage vinegar. Shall we open the curtains and see what the day has to offer?" She considered this. "No, let's stay as we are for now. Much easier on the eyes, especially when you're as old as we are."

Last night's clothes lay in a heap on the end of the bed along with the wrapping from her fish and chips. An empty wine bottle had tumbled onto its side. She ran a hand through her tangled hair. "That armpit's not the freshest. What do you think, Arthur? Shall I get up and have a shower, feed the washing machine and go and buy myself the ingredients for a nutritious brunch?" She poked him in the stomach. "Or shall I have another drink and maybe a little snooze?"

She cupped a hand to the ear nearest to him. "What's that you say? I need vitamins? But red wine's full of them. Well, minerals or something. Don't look at me like that. You're not my mother."

Shoving the elderly toy under the pillow next to her, she drained the bottle on the bedside table into her glass. "Now where's that iPod? We need some music to suit the mood of the day." She dozed off to Duffy singing *Mercy*.

At first, Paula thought the sound that had woken her came from the iPod.

There it was again. Someone was knocking on the door. "Miss Tyndall? Paula?" called Mrs McIntyre. "Your parents are on the telephone. They want to wish you a happy birthday."

"Shit." Paula stuffed the corner of the duvet into her mouth.

"I ken you're in there."

Paula lay very still and prayed her landlady wouldn't come in.

"Have it your way, you selfish lassie." Footsteps retreated up the stairs.

Paula lay back on the pillow. "God, Pete, how have I managed to make such a mess of everything? It's our thirtieth birthday and I'm alone and drunk."

"Is everything all right?" Mrs McIntyre was back.

Paula leapt out of bed and threw herself against the door with a thump.

Her landlady turned the handle, but Paula's weight was enough to keep her out.

"Go away," she half shouted, half sobbed. "There's nobody here. Leave me alone."

The pressure was gone instantly. Paula listened as the old woman padded back upstairs. She shoved a pile of ironing from the chair and wedged it under the door handle. Back in bed, she felt for the supermarket carrier bag and pulled out another bottle of wine.

She gulped down a glassful, dropped the empty tumbler onto the rug and slid under the duvet. Pulling it tight around her neck, she closed her eyes. But sleep wouldn't come. She took deep breaths, held them for as long as she could, then exhaled slowly. She tried to focus on her feet, to imagine the tension draining out of the tips of her toes, but the more she willed herself to relax, the tenser she became. Paula rolled onto her side, made her hands into fists and thrust them under the pillow. Breathe, slow and deep, that was the key. Persevere; let the breath carry the tension away. But it was no use: the slower she breathed, the faster her heart seemed to beat, and all the while it felt as if it was getting bigger. Bigger and bigger, swelling up to fill her entire body. Even her skull was beating, huge and pulsating, as if it could explode at any second.

The only thing that gave her some small comfort was the ancient pink cotton pyjamas she was wearing. A gift from Pete on their 21st birthday, they were dotted with little lilac teddies, his idea of a joke. *A mature gift for a mature woman*, he had written on the card. He gave her them the night of the party. It was the first time she had tried tequila slammers and they just about drank the students' union bar dry. She and Pete, Ollie, Jen and a handful of others ended up in the park – she had no idea how they got there or why they thought it was a good idea. Miraculously, she still had the carrier bag containing the pyjamas. She changed into them behind a bush, and danced barefoot round the park singing *The Teddy Bears' Picnic* until she slipped on the dewy grass and twisted her ankle. She was too drunk to feel any pain but it gave way when she tried to put weight on it, and Pete and Ollie had to carry her to a bench. They drank more tequila until they all fell asleep. They were woken up and thrown out just after dawn by a passing policeman, who couldn't conceal his amusement at her bizarre outfit.

The next time Paula encountered the police was almost nine years later and she was wearing the same pyjamas. She was asleep on the sofa of her flat in London when the doorbell rang. It was after midnight and the *West Wing* DVD she had been watching had come to an end. She knew as soon as she saw the two officers – a man and a woman, both younger than her – that something was desperately wrong. Her first thought was her parents: they were on holiday in Florida and not due home for another five days. Perhaps they had been mugged and hurt. Maybe one of them had had a heart attack. Half-a-dozen awful scenarios flashed through her mind instantaneously, but none concerned Pete. She asked what had happened, but they were intent on ushering her back inside. Trying to avoid a scene on the doorstep, she thought afterwards.

Their precise words vanished from her memory as soon as they said them. There had been an accident, and Pete was dead. That was basically what they were there to tell her. One of them said something about difficultly finding who was next of kin, taking some time to track her down. She managed to explain that her parents were away, her mouth forming the words without any input from her frozen brain.

There was some discussion about contacting them and it was agreed she would wait to call until after she had identified the body. Identified the body. Of her dead brother. Pete. Her little twin. It was unthinkable.

So she didn't think, didn't imagine. The woman officer mentioned tea, offered to make some, but Paula shook her head. She got dressed, putting on the first pair of jeans and top that came to hand, and they drove her to the hospital.

She followed them through long, antiseptic corridors, eyes half closed against the fluorescent glare, her body numb, as if she was floating slightly above the ground instead of walking on it. If one of them had taken out their truncheon and hit her over the head, or some stray psychopath had jumped from a side ward and thrust a knife into her, she wouldn't have felt it. She would merely have sunk to her knees and welcomed the oblivion.

They showed her into a room and the door closed behind her. A bald man with a neatly clipped ginger beard and a white coat stepped forward and murmured a few words. He indicated a shape under a sheet. She was to look and confirm they had got it right: she understood that was her task.

In that split second before she let her eyes rest on him, she did manage one coherent thought: what if she said no, that they had got it wrong and it wasn't him? If she could make them believe her, then, it wouldn't be him. Pete wouldn't be dead and everything would go back to the way it was. She could go home, put her pyjamas back on and return to watching DVDs. In the morning, they would meet for the race, just as they had planned. They would ride and they would win.

The man asked her a question. "Does your brother have any distinguishing marks?" he repeated. "Maybe a scar or a tattoo?"

A tattoo. This was her chance to prove it truly wasn't Pete. Paula pulled the left leg of her jeans up a few centimetres to reveal the delicate P&P monogram on her ankle. "There – same as mine."

The man nodded and moved down to the end of the sheet. He raised the corner. The cycling shoe was a larger version of a pair Paula had herself. She frowned at the horrible coincidence.

The man pointed to something now, a bluish shape above the ankle bone. A tattoo exactly like hers.

Paula shook her head and turned away. "No, that isn't it."

"Please," he urged, "could you look again?"

"I said that's not it." Her voice was shrill.

"We need you to make the identification."

"Why can't I see his face?" she demanded.

"It's better this way," the man said gently.

"I want to see." She seized the top of the sheet and pulled it back. It wasn't Pete. It was a thing, a monster, lying there. Not even human. Its head was the size of a pumpkin. A pumpkin so swollen and infected with purple and black rot that it could burst at any moment. It really wasn't him.

She smiled as she turned to the man, who stood a respectful distance away. "It isn't…" she began.

He walked over and placed a hand on her upper arm, pulling the sheet back into place with his free hand. "Please, we need you to identify him."

"But..." Paula felt her smile fade.

"Would you like to get some air and come back a bit later?"

The mobile phone in the pocket of her jeans rang, startling them both. She took it out and checked the screen. It was her dad calling from Florida. He probably wanted to wish them good luck for the race or share some silly story. He never could get to grips with the time differences when he was abroad.

Paula rejected the call and returned the phone to her pocket. She looked at the man. "Yes," she heard herself say. "That's my brother, Pete Tyndall."

It didn't matter that she knew it wasn't really him. Pete wasn't dead. It was just something she had to say in order to get out of the hospital.

The policewoman drove her home. She offered to come in for a while but Paula said no. She wanted to be on her own to make the call, which was simply another task she had to perform before things could get back to normal.

The conversation, first with her dad and then her mum, was like the one with the police: her brain simply refused to retain it. It was over in a few minutes. She said what needed to be said and all she could remember was the sound of her mum screaming.

Paula put the phone down and laid her hands in her lap. She studied them for a while, not sure what to do next. The male officer had suggested calling a friend, but that would mean explaining to someone else what had happened – what the police and the hospital had said happened – and what would be the point of that, since it wasn't true? Her mum and dad would be back tomorrow. Talk could wait until then.

When no other plan came to her, she got up and went through to the bedroom. She undressed and put her pyjamas back on. Then she went into the kitchen and opened the bottle of wine that was chilling in the fridge ready to celebrate their victory in tomorrow's race. She took the bottle and a glass and returned to the sitting room, climbed back onto the sofa, retrieved the DVD remote from the floor and pressed play.

Burying Pete

Her parents wanted her to stay with them until the funeral, but Paula refused. She knew that to survive she had to keep away for as long as possible. One of them rang every few hours. She couldn't tell if it was because they needed to reassure themselves that at least she was still there, or if they thought they were helping, but she always got off the phone as quickly as she could. Just the sound of their voices brought that grotesque image from the hospital back into her mind. Sometimes she let it ring, but she forced herself to answer often enough to prevent them turning up at her door in a state of panic.

Her dad was mostly calm and practical, discussing transport arrangements and who they still needed to inform. Every now and then his voice wavered as if it might be about to crack and he would bring the call to an abrupt end. Other times it was slurred. Her mum veered between manic activity, seeking Paula's opinion on everything and anything, and all-out hysteria. Should they ask for donations to Pete's favourite charity, whatever that was? What music would he have wanted in the church? Should they have wine, or just sherry and whisky, at the tea, and what kind of sandwiches – Pete always liked egg, didn't he, but would people expect smoked salmon?

Paula fobbed her off with noncommittal answers and waited for the next bout of sobbing. She felt detached from the preparations, as if they were for a party she wasn't invited to. She understood that Pete was not around, but she couldn't use the word dead. That would have meant accepting that the horribly distorted creature in the hospital was actually him, and that she could not – would not – do. He was not present, that was all. She had seen the tattoo of their initials on the ankle of that hideous thing, but she told herself it was an illusion, a sick trick played by her own subconscious. Pete wasn't dead, how could it be otherwise?

They had got their tattoos on a whim after they won their first national title, an endurance record that had stood for ten years. The event was in Nottingham, a city they hadn't been to before. Ollie had needed to get back to London to make an appearance at his uncle's retirement party. She and Pete were wandering around light-headed with victory and hunger, looking for somewhere to get a decent pizza or plate of pasta, when they stumbled on the tattoo parlour. They had had a couple of beers but they were sober enough to know what they were doing.

It was Pete's idea to get a permanent reminder of their success.

"What about it?" he asked as they stood gazing at the window full of photographs.

"You're kidding," she replied, always the more cautious of the two.

He grinned. "Come on, PT. Show me you're not chicken."

When he held the door open, she found herself stepping inside. The tattooist was a skinny woman with long white hair and weird pink eyes.

When Pete said he wanted a version of the five rings worn by Olympic athletes using bicycle wheels, she sucked her teeth. "That's fine for you," she said, folding long thin arms across her chest. "But you can't expect her to spend the rest of her life with a bit of machinery on her bicep. What you want is something personal but attractive and discreet."

"What about our names then?" Pete suggested.

The tattooist shook her head. "What happens when one of you gets serious with someone else? How's it going to look wearing another bloke or girl's name? I don't ever recommend names for couples now, everyone breaks up so quick."

"We won't," Pete said stoutly. "We're twins. We'll be together forever."

The woman snorted.

"She's got a point, Pete," Paula put in. "What if we just had our initials, maybe on our ankles, so they would show above our socks when we're riding?"

"PT, you're a genius," Pete exclaimed. "We'll have P&P, like it's our crest, so anyone who's watching can see we mean business."

"P&P it is then," the tattooist said.

Within a few days of her parents' return from Florida, Paula knew she wasn't going to the funeral. She understood they were relying on her to be there, but her own need was far more compelling. She didn't tell them, of course. They would have gone on at her until she was forced to relent. She simply wasn't going to turn up. When they realised she wasn't coming, it would be too late to do anything about it.

It was Ollie who spoiled her plan. She had been avoiding him, feeling no more able to cope with him than with her parents. After the first couple of calls, she stopped picking up when she saw his name on the phone, but he soon got wise to what she was doing and started ringing from other people's. That was when she stopped answering any calls apart from her parents', and he began emailing instead, pouring out his grief. She answered the first few – one-line replies that took no account of his feelings, because she couldn't afford to – and when they kept coming she started hitting delete without opening them.

She had known it wouldn't be long before he was on the doorstep, and she told herself she could deal with it, but when he did come round, the sight of him was too much to bear.

She opened the door a few centimetres. "I'm sorry, I can't see you right now. I can't do this," she said.

"Do this?"

"You know, everything."

"You make it sound like there's a choice," he said incredulously. "You can't just decide Pete's not dead."

"Please go. I've got work I need to do."

"Fine, so be it."

He turned away and she closed the door.

She didn't hear from him again until the night before the funeral. He had called a couple of times during the day. The phone showed other people's numbers, but when she listened to the messages, it was him begging her to get in touch. She deleted them.

The doorbell rang at just after nine o'clock. She opened it without thinking.

"You're not coming, are you?" he said.

It was raining heavily but he wasn't wearing a coat.

"You're soaking," Paula observed flatly.

"Can I come in?" He was shivering.

She hesitated.

"Please. I won't stay long."

She stepped back to allow him into the hall.

"Answer the question."

"Tea, coffee? Or there's beer."

"Paula," he almost yelled, "you've got to stop this. Are you coming to the funeral?"

"Tea then."

He grabbed her by the shoulders. "For Christ's sake, you're behaving like you're armour plated. Why can't you accept what's happened?"

"Because I can't, and you're right, I'm not coming."

He wrapped his arms around her rigid body. "Well, I'm here to tell you that you are. We're going to pack a bag and you're going to your parents. Your dad'll be here any minute."

"Ollie! How could you?"

"I had to. Your mum and dad need you to be there. Deny Pete's dead if you want to, but you still have to go. If he isn't dead, where's the harm? Think of it as humouring the old folk."

Her dad drove her home and Ollie arrived to eat breakfast with them next morning. The only time he let her out of his sight was when she went to the loo, and even then he hovered outside the bathroom door. He took hold of her arm as they left the house and didn't let go until they were outside the church.

Everyone was there: friends, relatives, colleagues from the school where Pete taught, his pupils, the entire cycling club and plenty of other people Paula didn't recognise. Her dad and Ollie spoke and Pete's head of department gave a reading. Her dad had asked her to say something but she refused. She heard people speak but it was all so much buzzing in her head.

After the service, lots of people kissed or hugged her, others just shook her hand or patted her arm, all made some kind remark or other, but she heard no-one.

She walked with her parents and Ollie to the graveside. There were more words and slowly, very slowly the coffin was lowered. Paula tried to focus on the wooden casket sinking into the ground in front of her. And then someone began screaming "no, no, no" over and over again.

Ollie caught her under the arms as her legs buckled and pulled her back from the edge of the grave.

"It's okay. I've got you," he said, stroking her hair. "Shh, shh, quiet now."

In the days immediately after the funeral, Paula somehow managed to continue functioning. She understood now that Pete wasn't coming back, but she refused to let herself feel it. If she could keep all feeling, all emotion frozen and stay away from anyone whose grief might disturb her equilibrium, she could get through. She knew instinctively it was the only way.

She worked and ate and, providing she had a couple of glasses of wine before bed, she slept on and off. She didn't venture out other than to do research that wasn't possible over the internet and to buy food, and she didn't answer the phone or go to the door when the bell rang.

And then she had that dream about the little girl. The first time she had it, she didn't think much of it. She was trying not to think about anything other than work, which was piling up. Even though she was putting in far longer hours than normal, she didn't seem to be making much progress. After the second dream, she couldn't get it out of her head. She had never had the same dream before and it seemed odd that it should happen now. Then it came again and again.

It was a Wednesday night, almost three weeks after the police arrived at her door, and she was sitting with a large glass of wine, flicking through some old Sunday supplements before she put them out for recycling, when she came across the feature on Scottish seaside towns. She recognised the wide panorama of the opening spread immediately. It was the beach from her dream. The caption said it was Craskferry. The name was familiar but, at first, she couldn't think why.

She studied the picture again, focusing on the sweep of sand and the red stone harbour, and suddenly she remembered: it was where they went for the holiday she spent without Pete. Puzzled, she continued to stare at the picture. Why was she dreaming about Craskferry?

Draining her glass, she bagged up the papers for recycling and went to bed. But she couldn't get the photograph out of her head, and when she finally fell asleep, she had exactly the same dream.

She woke the next morning knowing what she had to do. She pulled on her dressing gown, fired up the laptop and did a search for property to rent in Craskferry. Rachel Fanshawe's name came up straightaway. It wasn't even nine o'clock when Paula phoned the letting agent's number and left a message.

Unravelling

The light glowed red inside her eyelids. Her temples were pounding, neck muscles knotted tight and something dug into her cheek. Lifting her head a little, she felt hard plastic. One eye opened a fraction to see the corner of her laptop keyboard. It was the morning after her and Pete's extra-special extra summer birthday, and she had fallen asleep at the desk – in Mrs McIntyre's rental flat, in Craskferry. She opened the other eye and immediately regretted it. The room rotated, or maybe it was her. Something moved. Her eyes snapped shut and she swallowed back the nausea. Why had she ever thought it was a good idea to get out of bed?

Footsteps.

"Pete? Is that you?" she asked uncertainly.

They stopped but there was no answer.

"Pete?" She sat up. Every muscle hurt. "Pete, where are you? I need to talk to you."

Silence. She tried to stand but her legs folded like pipe cleaners.

"Please, don't leave me, Pete." Tears obscured her vision. "I need you. I need you now. I was always there for you. I always did what you wanted, didn't I? Remember when you broke Granny Crabtree's kitchen window with the football? I took the rap, didn't I? And at Halloween when you dyed Sonia Matheson's poodle green. I said it was me and got grounded for a fortnight."

She wiped her eyes and nose on her arm. "You let me take the blame. Never once said it wasn't my fault." Her voice rose. "So why can't you be here for me now? Don't you owe me that? Can't you see I'm falling apart? I'm having weird dreams. I've fucked up with Ollie and made a complete fool of myself with Andy, and Sanders hates me and now he's missing, and Bovis is going to die…" Paula slumped sobbing onto the desk.

A blatter of rain on the study window roused her. The light had faded to grey. Shivering, she straightened up. The skin on her face was tight, her head aching worse than ever.

Gripping the edge of the desk, she managed to haul herself upright. She edged sideways and transferred one hand to the end of a bookcase. Shuffling a bit further, the other moved to join it. Slowly, reaching hand over hand, she made it to the doorway between study and sitting room. She looked around for something else to hold onto, but there was only the sofa and it was too far away. Sinking to her knees, she crawled across the carpet and stuck her head out into the hall. Certain the coast was clear, she scuttled across the lino and shouldered open the bedroom door.

Sitting back on her haunches, she tried to make sense of what she saw. All the discarded clothes were gone and there was a different duvet cover on the bed. She crawled over and peered underneath. The empty wine bottles and chip wrappings had vanished.

"Come on, let's get you up." Arms encircled her from behind and, with surprising strength, eased her onto the bed and laid her down.

"Pete?"

"Paula, he's gone."

"What?" She turned to the voice.

Her landlady knelt beside her. "I phoned your mother and she told me. Paula, your brother's passed away."

"No!" Paula shook her head so fiercely it made her feel sick. "He hasn't."

"Aye, darling, he has." Mrs McIntyre stroked her forehead. "I couldnae let go o' my man, Gordon, after he died. I used to see and hear him all the time, but it passes."

"No," Paula wailed. "I can't be without him." She took a great gulp of air. "Can't, can't…"

"You have to let go."

"But… I'll… die… too," she sobbed.

"You willnae. You're stronger than you know."

Paula looked at her landlady. "That's just it. I didn't know."

"Didnae know what?"

"That he was dead," she said desperately. "He's my little twin. I should have known, should have felt it somehow, but I didn't. I ate dinner, had a bath, watched a DVD, and it didn't feel any different from any other night of my life." She gave another huge, choking sob. "I didn't know until the police came."

"And you think that makes you a bad sister?"

Paula nodded miserably. "I shouldn't have let him go out on his own before a big race. He wasn't thinking straight. It was my job to look after him – I promised I'd protect him."

"It was an accident," Mrs McIntyre said softly. "You're no' to blame."

Paula tried to respond but she was no longer able.

Mrs McIntyre sat down on the edge of the bed and put her arms around her. "That's it, you let it all out."

When Paula could cry no more, her landlady brought a damp towel and wiped her face. She made sweet tea and held the mug while Paula drank it.

"Could you manage a bit o' toast?"

Paula shook her head.

"When did you last eat?"

She looked at the clock. It was almost eight o'clock. "Is it morning or evening?"

"Evening."

"Is there any news of Sanders and Bovis?"

"That wee lad and his dog?"

"Yes, he ran away and Bovis is hurt – the vet's got her, but she might not live. Please phone her, and call Nora along the road – she'll know about Sanders." Paula started to sob again.

"I'll find out."

Mrs McIntyre returned ten minutes later. "You can stop worrying. The wee lad turned up at home late on Sunday, cold and drookit but no harm done. Said he spent the night in a cave."

"I should have been able to help him, but I didn't." Paula tugged at the front of her hair. "He wanted my help and I wasn't there for him."

"You arenae responsible for Sanders. He has a family o' his own." Mrs McIntyre eased Paula's hand down onto the duvet. "You'll have that hair out by the roots."

"What about Bovis?"

"She's lost a leg but the vet says she's going to make it."

"Oh, my God! If I'd helped Sanders he wouldn't have run away and Bovis wouldn't have been left behind. And, I don't know…" Paula slumped back on the pillows. "I don't know anything anymore. I don't know anything. I can't be with people. I can't be on my own. My head's a mess and I can't make sense of it. I'm dreaming stuff, remembering fragments, but none of it makes any sense at all. I think I'm losing my mind."

"You're no' losing your mind." Mrs McIntyre smoothed Paula's hair back into place. "It's grief. In time your mind will settle and you'll get on with your life, but you cannae rush it. You just have to live with it. You breathe and you eat and you sleep and the time passes. You think about the person you've lost and the time passes."

"But half the time I can't remember." Paula said in a small voice. "There's so much I want to remember but I can't and I'm frightened… I'm frightened that before long I won't be able to remember. I won't remember what it was like when we were little or when we rode together, that I'll forget his face and the way he spoke, the sound of his voice… everything. It'll all just fade away as if he never existed."

"Oh no, darling, that willnae happen. Trust me, you'll see." The old woman stood up. "I'm going to make some more tea and I want you to have a slice o' toast."

After she had eaten, Paula fell into a doze. She was woken by Mrs McIntyre. "There's a phone call for you."

She pulled the duvet around her neck. "Who is it?"

"Don't look so worried. It's only your young man. Come on now, let's get you through to the phone."

Mrs McIntyre helped her out of bed and, with her arm around Paula's waist, steered her through to the study. She handed her the receiver and left, closing the sitting room door firmly behind her.

"Andy?" Paula was amazed by the eagerness of her own response.

"Who's Andy?" Ollie's voice.

When Paula didn't answer, he tried again, "I said, who's Andy?"

"I said Sandy," she replied desperately. "Short for Sanders."

"Oh. Thanks for the warm welcome. It would be nice if just once you could be pleased to hear from me."

"Sorry." She sank down onto the desk chair.

"Paula, we're all really worried about you. Your mum and dad wanted to get in the car and come up – I had a hell of a job to stop them.

"Thank you – I couldn't face…" She felt herself crying again.

"I know, but you can't go on like this. You really can't."

"But what is it you want me to do? You tell me off when I don't show any emotion, and when I let it out you're not happy either. Aren't you pleased that I'm grieving?"

"It's not the grieving I'm worried about."

"What's that supposed to mean?"

"Your landlady told your parents you'd been drinking."

"She what? How dare she?" Acid burned in her throat. "It's none of her business."

"Hold on a minute. You're living in her house and she's worried about you. Of course it's her business. She called them because she didn't know what else to do. You have to let us help you."

"And you think you can just wave your magic wand and make everything all right? Well, you can fuck right off, Ollie. Do you hear me? I said fuck off!"

"There's no need to be nasty."

"Isn't there?" she yelled. "I think nasty's about all we've got left."

"Suit yourself. I'm going to hang up now, Paula, unless you tell me not to. Okay? Do you hear me?"

Without waiting to see if he would carry out his threat, Paula banged the receiver back in its cradle.

The sitting room door opened. "I owe you an apology," Mrs McIntyre said. "I shouldnae have called them."

Paula just stared at her.

"I made a mistake."

"You did," she said flatly.

In the garage

Strange how the details stayed so clear. After sixteen years packed away under layers of experience and incident, when Paula closed her eyes, she could almost smell her own teenage skin, feel it burning as she watched the scene unfold.

The bottle-green paint on the window ledge was blistered, long strips of it peeled back by sun and rain to reveal wood the colour of old bones. She pressed her cheek into the corner of the frame, gritty with dead flies and exhaust fumes, terrified they would see her, but unable to carry on up the path now that some deep, instinctive part of her knew.

She could tell they had been smoking. An open packet of Benson & Hedges, a pack of Rizla papers and a book of matches with a pale blue cover lay on the old kitchen table that had become their dad's workbench, and even through the thick glass, milky with cobwebs, she could smell the cannabis. She could smell it now, more than a decade and a half later.

On the concrete floor, the open lid of the big metal toolbox revealed trays of tiny, nameless items. The tandem sat on its stand, a spanner and an oily rag abandoned beside it.

Pete sat on the edge of the table, the toes of his once white trainers dangling above the dust. His hands rested on the thighs of his jeans. He was grinning. The air was filled with smoke and creosote and traffic noise. A police siren. The shouts of small boys cavorting along the street. And, loudest of all, the buzzing, crackling white noise that came from Paula's own brain, making it impossible for her to catch any ghost of Pete and Ollie's banter that might seep through the glass.

Ollie bent down, wiped his hands on the rag and dropped it back on the floor. He turned to Pete and said something. Pete's lips moved in response and they both laughed. It was like watching a silent movie without the subtitles, the racket of the outside world fading away to let the sounds inside her head take the place of a piano score.

Paula watched as Pete handed Ollie the remains of the joint. He held it between thumb and forefinger and took a drag. Gripping his chest, he staggered back and, in slow motion, crumpled to the ground, cigarette still between the fingers of his right hand. She counted her heartbeats as he lay motionless: one… two... three. Pete frowned, his mouth forming words of concern as he bent forward. Suddenly, Ollie stretched himself out, rolled onto his back, took another long pull on the joint and sat up. They were laughing again.

He stood and passed it to Pete, who took a last drag and dropped the butt onto the concrete. Ollie ground it out with the heel of his trainer. Pete held the smoke in his mouth, cheeks puffed out like a hamster. Ollie leant towards him. Paula held her breath too and counted the beats once more: one… two… He placed his hands on the edge of the table, thumbs millimetres from the outside of Pete's denim covered thighs and leant in a little further. Pete exhaled in his face and then it happened: they were kissing. Three… four…

For a second, the next couple of beats, she couldn't be sure if it was real or merely a crazy illusion formed from all the static in her own head. Then they shifted slightly, the back of Ollie's head no longer obscured Pete's face. She thought they would part now. That it would be over. Surely they'd had long enough to emerge from their weed trance, to spring apart in horror and disbelief at their own inexplicable actions. Seven… eight… nine… But they didn't. Ten… eleven… They shifted again. Paula closed her eyes and took a long breath. It would be over now. Ended. Safe to look.

She opened her eyes. Ollie's hands were on Pete's forearms. Twelve… thirteen… One moved to hold Pete's head, fingers twisting in his hair. Fourteen… fifteen… sixteen… Breathe, she told herself, keep breathing. She could see the tendons, see the veins pulsing in the back of Ollie's hand – how could she see, remember such detail; surely it wasn't possible at that angle, over such distance and time – as he pulled Pete closer, held him there. Lips against lips.

So she breathed and counted. Thirty… fifty… eighty-three… ninety-one… The sound of car tyres on gravel. A door clicking open. Mum and Dad's voices. One hundred. Ollie let go. Paula turned away and walked up the path to the back door.

Home truths

Paula ate the breakfast of bacon and egg that Mrs McIntyre brought her. After her landlady removed the tray, she ran her a bath in her bathroom upstairs. It wasn't until Paula lay back in the warm bubbles that she realised just how sore she was. Everything, from the roots of her hair all the way down to her toenails, ached as if her whole body had a hangover. She stretched out and let the water soak away physical pain, until the bubbles were gone and the bath was cold. She was drying herself on the vast rough towel Mrs McIntyre had laid out when the doorbell rang. After a few moments there was a tap on the door.

"There's someone to see you," Mrs McIntyre said.

"Who is it?" Paula asked.

"The other one."

"What?"

"The other young man."

Paula pulled the towel around her and opened the door. "Andy?"

She looked down the stairs. He was waiting in the vestibule, staring at his feet.

"Hello," she called uncertainly.

He looked up and took a step forward. "Hello, Paula."

"Put this on." Mrs McIntyre held out a fuchsia pink candlewick dressing gown.

Paula stepped back into the bathroom and swapped her towel for the dressing gown. She took the stairs two at a time.

"That's a very attractive garment."

She shook her head. "I don't know why I'm so pleased to see you. I really shouldn't be."

"I'm just glad that you are."

She led him into the sitting room and they sat on the sofa.

"So why are you here?" she asked.

"Mrs McIntyre tracked me down in the Yellow Pages. She was very enigmatic. She said something odd about having called the wrong one and that my presence was required urgently."

"Oh." Paula couldn't hide her disappointment.

"I wanted to apologise, too, though. I shouldn't have stormed off like that."

"I deserved a chance to explain."

"I know. I don't know what came over me." He examined his fingernails. "I was jealous, I suppose. I'm so glad she phoned. I didn't want to leave things the way they were. It's not my style to sleep with someone and run."

Paula smiled. "I'm glad to hear it." She leant towards Andy, fingers outstretched. At that moment, a movement outside the window caught her eye. A white car skidded to a halt on the loose gravel by the gate. A huge bunch of pink and white flowers leapt out and sprinted towards the door, and behind them came the very last person she had expected, or wanted, to see.

"Oh Christ," she began, but Ollie was already in the hall and striding into sitting room. When he saw Andy, he let the flowers drop to the floor.

"I'm Ollie. Ollie Matraszek. Paula's boyfriend," he said, far too loudly for the small room. "And I'm guessing you must be Andy."

Andy stood up. "Andy Parker."

"Andy Parker." Ollie seemed to be rolling the words around his mouth. "I get the feeling, Andy Parker, that Paula may have failed to mention our relationship to you."

"She did mention it, but..." Andy's voice was steady, but when he glanced over at Paula, she could see the shock and pain in his eyes.

"Well, then, I think you'd better go."

"Maybe I had."

"Good decision." Ollie stepped back to let him pass.

Andy turned on the threshold. "Goodbye, Paula. I'm sorry it turned out this way."

She got to her feet. She knew she was supposed to respond, but what could she say? The air between the three of them was so heavy with words spoken and unspoken, all tangled up in a mess of past and present, of anger, need and so many other things she couldn't name, that she could barely pull a breath into her lungs. She wanted to elbow past Andy and run out into the street. To get away from both of them, to find oxygen and space and clarity.

So she offered the only words that stood out clearly. "I'm sorry too."

Andy stepped into the hall and pulled the door shut behind him.

Ollie lowered himself onto the sofa. "Just when you think things can't get any worse." He cocked his head expectantly. "So… Sandy? Andy?"

Paula found herself staring at the print above the fireplace. A thatched cottage surrounded by a garden of lupins, foxgloves and sweetpeas, one corner dappled with mould where a tide of seaside dampness had crept under the glass. "So," she echoed.

This was her cue to join him on the faded chintz, to confess the terrible wrong she had done him and be contrite. To let him shout and then negotiate for his forgiveness. To draw a straight black line under everything, unequivocal and final. Then she would pack up her things, stow Andy away in the box marked *Memories: no longer needed* along with Pete and everything else from the past, return to London with Ollie and get on with the rest of their lives. It was the opening she had been looking for, the one that really could lead to space and clarity.

She sat down and, with her gaze on the hideous swirling carpet, waited a few seconds for the sentences to assemble. She opened her mouth and the first of them came out.

"I saw what you did in the garage."

Her head jerked up at the shock of her own words and their eyes met. The last time she had said it, he had stormed out of the room, gathered his belongings and set off back to London without a single word. And now she had brought it up again. Ollie looked baffled. He had returned to patch things up. This wasn't the right script and they both knew it.

"What did you say?"

The words came out again. "I saw what you did."

"And? Are you trying to tell me that justifies whatever you've been up to here?" He was incredulous. "If that's what you're saying, you're even crazier than I thought."

This – she – was crazy. That much was obvious, and she needed to fix it before she blew her chance. "No, not at all. I don't know what made me say that."

"Well, since you did, maybe it's time we addressed it."

Paula put her hands over her face. "No, please. We don't need to. It's in the past. Why do we have to go back there?"

"I don't know, Paula. You tell me." He took hold of her wrists and pulled her hands into her lap so he could look into her eyes, but she turned away.

"What exactly is it you think I did?" he persisted. "There was no I. It was we, us, Pete and me."

"No!" She hauled her hands free and covered her ears. She was desperate to get up and run but her legs wouldn't co-operate.

"Tell me," he demanded. "What did you actually see? We kissed, and you can't bear it. Your precious little twin and me, together, with no place for you. It's been gnawing away at you ever since."

"No, no, no, no…" she chanted but Ollie would not be drowned out.

"Pete and I kissed. Or, if we're being strictly accurate, Pete kissed me. In that moment, he wanted me. He wanted me in a way you and he could never share. All you could do was look in through the window, and what made it even worse was that you knew we could see you. We knew you were there and it didn't stop us."

"Liar," Paula shrieked. "You didn't see me. Pete didn't kiss you. You kissed him. It was all you. I saw you pull him towards you."

"Oh, Paula." Ollie's voice was strangely quiet now. "You know that's not right. You must have wondered why his girlfriends never lasted. Why a good-looking bloke like him made it to nearly thirty without a serious relationship. Have you never thought what he was hiding?"

"I'll tell you who's doing the hiding," she yelled. "You! I saw your hands on him, your fingers in his hair, but he didn't want you. Not like that. He never wanted you, and that's the only reason you wanted me – because I was the nearest you could get to him."

"That's not true. What happened between you and me has nothing to do with Pete. How could you think that? You're the only one I ever felt that way about. Pete saw you that day because he was facing the window, but he didn't stop because he didn't want to. He initiated it.

You've twisted it all round in your head, remembered it the way you want it to be. I had my back to you and that means it was his hands you saw, not mine. His hands in my hair, but you can't bear to remember that because you think it should have been you he was kissing. That's why I could never be good enough for you, because I wasn't Pete. But you know what, nothing more ever happened between us. And shall I tell you why? Because I didn't want it to. Pete did, but I didn't."

"How dare you," Paula screamed. "How dare you tell such lies?"

"Because they're not lies. Every word is true and you know it. Pete kissed me. He kissed me, not you, and you've been eaten up with jealousy ever since. We never stood a chance you and me." Ollie got to his feet. "How could we? I wasn't Pete."

I wasn't Pete... I wasn't Pete... The words played over and over in Paula's head, drowning out the sounds of the front door slamming and Ollie's car screeching away.

Voicemail

A clear plastic sandwich bag lay on the doormat. Inside was a mobile phone. Paula picked up the bag and turned it over in her hands. It looked like her old phone, the one she had hurled into the sea, but it couldn't be. She took it back to the sofa, where she had been curled up for most of the day. Mrs McIntyre had found her there a couple of hours after Ollie left, shivering and sobbing. Her landlady made her a cup of sugary tea and tucked her up with a tartan rug and a hot water bottle. The warmth had drawn her back down into the blissful freedom of a dreamless sleep. Woken by the sound of something dropping through the letterbox and urgently aware she needed to pee, she staggered out into the hall in the fading light, legs stiff as an old woman's. The bag caught her eye as she returned to her refuge.

Paula switched on the standard lamp and gathered the rug back around her. She opened the bag and took out the phone and a small square of lined paper. The note was written in purple felt pen. It said, "Thought U might want this." She didn't recognise the writing.

She pressed the on button and the phone beeped into life. A scroll through the contacts proved the impossible: it was hers. And it was fully charged and working. How could this be? She had heard it drop into the sea with her own ears.

A crunching noise on the shell path outside the window startled her, and she looked up to see Sanders peering through the gap under the net curtain. She held up the phone and mouthed questioningly, "You?"

He nodded.

When she let him in, he pointed at the pink candlewick dressing gown. "Stylish."

"Never mind that. Are you okay?"

He shrugged. "S'pose."

"Mrs McIntyre said you slept in a cave. Your mum must've been frantic."

"When I went home she yelled and cried a lot."

"I bet she did. So what on earth were you doing with my phone?"

"Long story." He stared at his trainers, which were shedding sand on the vestibule tiles. "I'll tell you another time."

"You'll tell me now." Paula pulled him into the sitting room.

"Please don't be cross," he whimpered, sinking down onto the carpet. He wrapped his thin arms around his torso. "Bovis is really sick."

She knelt beside him. "Oh, Sanders, I know. I'm sorry."

He leant against her as tears dribbled down his cheeks.

Paula gave him a handful of tissues from the box Mrs McIntyre had left. She put her arm round his shoulders. "How's she doing?"

"Mum thinks she escaped from the garden to look for me when I didn't come home on Saturday. The vet says she was probably hit by a car near here and she looked for somewhere familiar to hide." He took a gulping breath. "Paula, the vet had to cut off her back leg. Bovis has got three legs and it's my fault because I ran off and everyone was panicking and she must have realised something was wrong and she wanted to help find me…"

Paula hugged his shallow chest to her. "Shh now. It's not your fault. It was an accident. Terrible things happen sometimes." She gazed over his head to the window and the rapidly darkening street.

When his tears eventually subsided, she said, "Pete and I had a neighbour with a Dalmatian when we were little. He was called Doobry and he was stone deaf."

Sanders blew his nose. "That's a silly name."

"It was. Doobry ran into the road one day and got knocked down by a van. He lost a leg but, you know, it was amazing how quickly he adjusted. He just got on with life. Animals are very good like that. You'll be surprised how fast Bovis recovers."

He looked up at her. "Do you think so?"

"I know so. She's going to be fine." He didn't need to know that Paula had never had a neighbour with a three-legged dog called Doobry or anything else.

"I don't want her to hate me."

"She'll never hate you." Paula breathed back more tears of her own. "Bovis loves you more than you'll ever know."

She passed him some more tissues and he dried his face.

"Now tell me something honestly. Did you write me another note, on the night of the gala?"

"No."

"You're sure."

"Aye. Why?"

Paula shook her head. "It doesn't matter. It's nothing."

"I'm sorry about the phone. I shoulda given it back before."

"Where did you find it? I threw it in the sea. It shouldn't be working."

"It didn't go in. I made the splash."

She let go of him and sat back against the sofa. "You were there, watching me? Spying on me?"

He nodded miserably. "I was sitting on the other side of the rocks. I saw you come and sit down with your chips. I was worried about you. You seemed so sad, so I watched for a bit. You were checking your messages and then you started talking to yourself and threw the phone. It landed beside me. I thought if I listened to it I'd find out what was wrong, so I splashed in a rock pool to make you think it'd gone in the water."

"I see you've kept it charged."

"Mum's charger fits it."

"So have you been listening to my voicemail?"

He looked sheepish. "I thought I'd better in case there was anything important. That Ollie called a couple of times, said, 'please call me, I love you', stuff like that."

"And you didn't think to tell me?"

"I reckoned if he loved you, you'd already know he wanted to speak to you, so I deleted them. Well, except the text asking where you were. I answered that one before I realised who it was."

"Sanders! I was blaming my poor mum for telling him I was in Craskferry." Paula's head felt as if it was clamped in a giant vice. She massaged her temples with her fingertips.

"I said I was sorry."

She sighed. "Why give the phone back now?"

"Some bloke called Andy just left a message. It sounded important – I saved it for you." He got to his feet. "Mum'll be wondering where I am."

When he had gone, Paula dialled 121. The recorded voice said she had two saved messages. She closed her eyes and waited for the first one to begin.

"Hiya, babe." It felt like a lifetime and no time at all since she had heard Pete's voice. It seemed to fill her, as if it was coming from somewhere way down inside her own chest. She mouthed the words along with him. "You all set for tomorrow morning? We're gonna be great. They won't see us for dust. Don't forget you said you'd get more High5 for the bottles. I'm just going for a quick blast on the solo. Call me when you get this."

She resaved it and, shivering again, reached behind her for Mrs McIntyre's rug. The second message began.

"It's Andy. God, Paula, I don't know whether I'm coming or going with Ollie turning up like that." The pause was so long she thought he had hung up. Then he spoke again. "I probably shouldn't be phoning you, but I'm going to make one last try. I thought we had something. If you think it's worth talking about, call me. If you disagree, just delete this. I'm staying with my friends in Edinburgh tonight and heading back to London in the morning. I won't call again." He paused again. "That's it, I suppose. Take care."

"End of messages," the recorded voice intoned. "To return this call press five."

Paula paused, her thumb hovering over the number five.

Letting go

Her mother smoothed a wrinkle out of the folded T-shirt and added it to the stack on Pete's bed. Paula watched as she touched each of the other piles – sweatshirts, pants, socks, shorts and trousers – checking them off a mental list. "There," she said, "that's everything."

"What about a hankie?" Paula said.

"He can use paper ones, like he always does."

Paula pursed her lips. "He should have a spotty one."

"What on earth for?" Her mum returned an unwanted T-shirt to a drawer. "He's not going to catch a cold in France in summer."

"But he might need to run away and come and find us," Paula explained gravely. "He needs a spotty hankie to wrap his things in and tie to a stick. That's what people do when they run away."

Her mum sat on the bed and patted the duvet beside her. "Sit down for a minute." She put an arm round Paula. "Remember when we talked about this before, and I said that Pete isn't going on holiday with Ollie because he doesn't want to be with you? He loves you, but Ollie's his friend and it's okay to go away with him."

Paula gnawed a fingernail and didn't say anything. She hated Pete for agreeing to go to France with Ollie. He was her little twin and he should always want to be with her. He couldn't possibly want to be with Ollie more than her. Ollie must have made him do it. That was the only answer – it was all Ollie's fault, and she would never forgive him for it.

"Pete isn't going to stop loving you just because he doesn't see you for three weeks," her mum continued. "We'll miss him, and he'll miss us sometimes, but we're all going to have a lovely time, and nobody's going to run away." She gave Paula a squeeze. "Okay?"

Silence.

"Okay, Paula? Look." Her mum opened a drawer and brought out a parcel wrapped in Happy Birthday paper. "Pete got an early birthday present for you. I don't think he'd mind if you have it now."

Paula stared at the package.

"Go on, open it."

She didn't move.

"I'll do it then." Her mum tore the paper off. It was a stuffed toy. It looked like a rat. "See, it's a dormouse. He chose it himself."

Paula took the animal and hurled it across the bed, knocking neatly folded clothes onto the floor.

"Paula!"

"I hate you and I hate Ollie. I hope he dies in stinky France and never comes home." She ran across the landing into her own room, slammed the door and flung herself onto the bed.

Ollie and his parents arrived early the next morning. Paula watched from the porch as Pete climbed into the back of the Volvo next to his friend. Mrs Matraszek twisted round in her seat and said something to the boys. They all laughed. As Pete replied, Ollie looked over at Paula. His expression was just the same as the day the headmaster announced at school assembly that he had collected more money than anyone else for the orphans in Africa. Mr Matraszek stowed Pete's bag among the camping gear in the back, returned to the driver's seat and started the engine. Pete and Ollie waved with both hands. Pete and Ollie. Ollie and Pete. Before that moment it had always been Pete and Paula, Paula and Pete, but Ollie had spoiled it and things would never be the same again.

"I hate you," Paula mouthed as the car pulled out of the drive onto the main road.

She took her muesli and coffee to the kitchen doorstep and ate while watching a pair of sparrows argue over Mrs McIntyre's bird feeder. They flapped and chirruped until the smaller one fled over the wall into the next garden. The victor returned to the feeder but was soon chased away by a plump starling. When the starling finished with the seeds that had fallen into the flowerbed, it turned its attention to the lawn, cocking its head inquiringly for the sound of worms as it hopped back and forth. The smaller sparrow, which had been waiting on top of the wall, swooped back down to the feeder and resumed its meal. Placing the empty bowl on the step beside her, Paula stretched out her legs and wiggled her bare toes on the warm concrete. She took a sip of coffee.

"Don't giggle, wiggle," she said quietly.

"What was that?"

Her chest tightened and she swung round. Andy was standing by the sink. She stood up and dusted a stray oat flake off her shorts. "Nothing, just something silly I was remembering." She struggled to keep her voice casual. "I didn't hear the bell."

"I met Mrs McIntyre on her way out."

Paula stepped back into the kitchen. The lino was cool under her feet.

Andy took a step towards her.

She thought for a second about kissing him. "Coffee?" She pointed to the cafetière on the worktop. "It's still hot."

"No, I'm fine." He raised an eyebrow expectantly.

"We need to talk."

"We do."

Neither of them spoke as Paula retrieved her mug and bowl from the doorstep. She felt his eyes on her as she rinsed and dried them and emptied out the coffee pot.

"How about a drive?" he suggested eventually. "We could go up the coast and look for seals."

She laid the dish towel on the worktop. "I'll get some shoes."

Paula leant back against the headrest and examined the van's interior. The cigarette packet she had noticed in the footwell the night they drove to Scotland had been replaced by an empty sandwich container and a broken cassette box.

Andy watched her finger the slight tear in the seam of her seat, the scratch on the rear-view mirror, the scuff mark on the front of the glovebox. "Nothing's changed," he said.

"It has," she said. "It's all different."

They drove most of the way along the coast road towards St Andrews in silence. Paula pretended to be absorbed by the countryside and the succession of pretty fishing villages they passed through, but she was thinking about Pete and Ollie and Sanders and Andy. So much had happened in the past few weeks and she was only just starting to make sense of it all. She wound down her window and drew in a lungful of the salty breeze. She had been mad to think she could outrun her grief or the mess she had got into with Ollie. Trying to escape and getting involved with Andy had only made things more complicated. But she was sure of one thing now: it was time to untangle it all.

Andy turned off the road at a sign saying Nature Reserve and parked the van. They walked across the broad dunes to the beach.

Pale, unblemished sand stretched out in a wide curve in both directions and ran down to a white-edged sea that seemed to fill the entire horizon.

"Wow," Paula said. "This is beautiful."

The only other people were dots in the distance.

"It's so empty compared to the beach at Craskferry."

"Most of the tourists don't venture this far," Andy said. "My parents used to bring me here when I was a child. Dad and I would spend days building whole cities of sandcastles."

"You came for holidays? You never said."

"It didn't seem important. My mum's parents lived in St Andrews, so we spent a lot of time up here." He pointed to the left. "Let's go this way."

"So how come you've ended up driving a white van?" Paula asked as they walked. "You don't exactly seem the type."

He grinned. "What type is that? Fat, bigoted road hog? Dodgy, unreliable layabout? Is there a particular type I should be?"

"Sorry, I just meant…" She shook her head. "I don't know what I meant."

"It's okay, I was only teasing." He squeezed her hand. "I didn't always drive a van. I used to be a trader in the City – I started as an office junior straight from school and spent eight years climbing the greasy pole. By the time the financial crash came in 2008, I was living in a penthouse in the Docklands, driving a Porsche, working fourteen-hour days and going on exotic holidays three or four times a year…"

"Blimey, I can hardly picture it. Driving a van seems much more you than that."

"I know. I was all but burnt out, and then everything started to go crazy – banks failed, the markets tumbled. Everyone I knew was panicking about what was going to happen to them. They had so much debt, were under so much pressure to perform, to keep up appearances, but it was all built on an illusion – nothing but smoke and mirrors, you know? We were running at top speed just to stand still. Suddenly, it all seemed really pointless, so I handed in my notice, sold my flat for a knockdown price, and went travelling to clear my head. I've always loved driving, and I wanted to be my own boss, so when I came back, I bought the van and, well, the rest's history, as they say."

"And you're happy doing what you do now?"

"I'm happy. I'm in control of my own life and it's built on something real. It feels honest, and that's what matters."

"Honest, yes." Paula stopped walking and gazed out to sea. A huge oil tanker was gliding along the join between water and sky. "Honesty's a good thing, isn't it? To be truthful with yourself and with others."

Andy put his arm around her waist. "I think so."

She sighed. "All right then. I'd like to be honest too. Can we start again? Go right back to the beginning, so I can explain everything?"

"If that's what you want."

"It is."

They sat down on a large flat rock.

After a long silence, Paula said, "Ollie and I go back a very long way and maybe we'll be friends again one day." She turned to face Andy. "Or maybe we won't. What I can tell you is that he isn't my boyfriend."

"He seemed to think he was."

"I'm so sorry about all that. We were together for a while, but it wasn't right for me. Too much history." She dug the toes of her trainers into the sand. "I let it drag on because I was too cowardly to finish it, even hid it from Pete – it was awful, so wrong. Ollie was part of what I was running away from. I should have explained to you before, but I was trying to ignore it. Just hoping it… he… would go away."

"I didn't give you a chance to explain."

Paula smiled ruefully. "Anyway, it's definitely over now."

"Because of what happened between us?"

"Because of what happened between him and me. We said some stuff that needed to be said. Ollie made some pretty hard accusations. He was wrong, but what he said made me think. I realised I'd always been jealous of his friendship with Pete. I pretended to myself that it was fine – we were the Three Musketeers – but I resented it. I'd always resented it."

Andy considered this for a few seconds. "None of us likes to admit to difficult feelings. We hate to see ourselves as the baddie, the selfish one, the mean one. But it's human to feel that stuff. At least you've admitted it."

"I suppose so. Thank you."

"For what?"

"For listening and understanding."

"So what about us? I mean, is there an us?"

"Do you want there to be?" she asked tentatively. "I've mucked you around pretty badly."

"I'm willing to give it another try if you are." He stood up and held out his hand. "Shall we see if we can find those seals?"

Paula got to her feet. "Let's."

They walked on for a bit without talking, then Andy said, "I didn't think *thanx* was your style."

She gave him a quizzical glance.

"You know, spelt with an x. After I left the voicemail, I got a text back just saying "*thanx*".

Paula smiled. "It was Sanders, a kid I'm friends with. He had my phone."

Andy pointed along the sand. "Look what's over there."

"I can't see anything apart from sand and rocks."

"Look again. Those rocks are moving."

She squinted in the direction he had indicated. One end of the shiny grey mass was shifting slightly. "They're seals!" she said excitedly. "I thought they'd be out in the water."

"They like to bask on the beach. Come on, let's take a closer look." He pulled her along the sand.

"I wonder if Sanders has been here. It might cheer him up."

"Sorry?"

"I was just thinking out loud. He's having a pretty tough time of it." She hesitated. "He's a rather unusual boy, and unusual doesn't always go down well. Something dreadful happened to him at the village gala day."

"We could bring him, if you like. I don't have to be back in London for a few days."

Paula thought for a moment. "No, I've got a better idea."

Don't giggle, wiggle

"Wiggle your toes," their dad yelled across the gap between his solo and the tandem. "Are you wiggling?"

Pete's head bobbed as he failed to suppress a snort of laughter.

"Yes, Dad, I'm wiggling," Paula called from the seat behind.

"Pete, what about you? Are you wiggling?" their dad repeated. "You've got to wiggle as you pedal."

"I'm wiggling too." Another snort.

Paula chortled. "We're both wiggling, Dad."

"That's good. If you don't keep your toes relaxed, you can't articulate your feet and ankles properly, and if you don't articulate your feet and ankles…"

"The muscles in your legs can't work properly," Paula and Pete chanted in unison, "and if your leg muscles can't work, you can't win the race."

"Exactly," their dad said. "So wiggle."

"Your toe bone connected to your foot bone," Pete sang under his breath. "Your foot bone connected to your ankle bone…"

"Stop it." Paula poked her brother in the ribs. "Don't make me laugh."

She was turning the pedals effortlessly despite the climb and she knew she could go on forever if they asked her to. Pete stretched a hand behind him and pinched her wrist. She slapped his hand away and gave him another poke. The tandem wobbled.

"Dem bones, dem bones, dem dry bones," Pete sang just loud enough for her to hear.

Paula tittered.

Their dad swung his bike in closer. "What are you two up to?"

"Nothing, Dad," Paula said.

Pete sniggered.

"Guys, guys." Their dad smiled. "Don't giggle, wiggle."

The three of them began to laugh. Pete started singing again, "Your ankle bone connected to your leg bone. Your leg bone connected to…"

Paula and their dad joined in. "…your knee bone. Your knee bone connected to your thigh bone."

By the time they reached the flat at the end of the long ascent, they were singing at the top of their voices. At a sign for a viewpoint, their dad indicated right and pulled across the tree-lined road. Pete and Paula followed him into the parking place. An ice-cream van sat at the far end. In a car beside it, a couple of elderly ladies in brightly patterned summer dresses were eating cones.

"Who's for a 99?" their dad asked, extracting a £10 note from the pocket of his shorts.

Paula hopped off the tandem and plucked the note out of his hand. "I'll get them."

She skipped over to the van. Her legs felt light, her muscles as fresh as when she got up that morning. As the man scooped and wrapped, she glanced into the parked car. The woman in the passenger seat had a small black and white dog on her knee. Her companion held her cone out, and it slurped up the remaining ice-cream before crunching greedily into the wafer. The woman in the passenger seat winked at Paula.

Pete and their dad had propped the bikes against a low wall and were sitting on a bench, gazing out across the valley.

"Shove up." Paula plonked herself down between them and handed out the cones.

They rested their feet on the wall as they ate. The late afternoon sun was warm on the bare skin of Paula's arms and legs. She smiled at Pete. He had ice-cream running down his chin and a thin smudge of chain oil on his cheek. He grinned back. It was two days after their thirteenth birthday, and she had never been happier than in that moment, slumped between her dad and brother, eating a large strawberry cone with a flake jammed in the top. She licked a pink drip off the back of her hand. It tasted of sugar and salt and dust and heat.

Their dad demolished the last of his cone and checked his watch. He wiped his hands on his shorts and stood up. "Best hit the road, if we're going to be home in time for tea."

They climbed back on the bikes and turned out onto the road.

At the start of the twisting descent, their dad bent low over his handlebars and called over his shoulder, "Last one to the bottom's a hairy kipper."

"Come on, PT. Let's show him." Pete crouched down and Paula followed suit. Within a couple of pedal turns they were haring downhill, squealing and whooping as loudly as their lungs would let them.

Paula's cry woke them both. Andy rolled over in the darkness and wrapped his arms around her rigid, sweaty body. He stoked her hair until she began to relax.

"Was it a nightmare?" he asked.

She pressed herself against him. "I was on my own on the back of the tandem. There was no one on the front seat, and I was hurtling down this long, winding hill. I couldn't reach the brakes to stop the bike, so I was trying to steer it by leaning, but it was getting faster and faster – far too fast to jump off. I could see all these donkeys milling around in the road at the bottom and I knew I was going to hit them. I was so scared I was going to hurt them. Next thing I was lying in the gutter. The donkeys were gone and the little girl with the kite was standing over me, but she didn't look right. She had a black eye and her face was different. She wasn't me anymore."

Andy stretched across to switch on the bedside lamp. "That's horrible." He thought for a moment. "You said 'the' little girl. Have you dreamt about her before?"

Paula sat up and hugged her knees through the duvet. "The dreams started after Pete died. I haven't had one for a few nights and I thought maybe they'd stopped. The girl's me when I was small and she's always holding a kite." She put a hand in the air to demonstrate.

"I thought you were left-handed."

"I am," Paula said.

"You held up your right hand."

"So I did." She looked at her hand. "But that's the one I use in the dream. Isn't that odd?"

Andy rubbed his chin. "What did you mean when you said 'she wasn't me anymore'?"

"She used to look like me but I didn't recognise her this time." Paula paused. "No, that's not quite right. I'll tell you who she looked like – Sanders. I don't mean she was him – it wasn't exactly his face. Just a bit like it around the nose and eyes."

"So who's Minnie?"

"Minnie?"

"That's the name you shouted out."

"Really?" Paula said. "I've no idea."

Andy swung his legs out of the bed. "Shall I make us a cup of tea?"

"What time is it?"

He glanced at his watch. "Half-past four."

"Please. I'm wide awake now."

He grinned at her as he pulled on his underpants and T-shirt. "That sounds promising. Back in a minute."

It had started to rain, large drops splattering against the open window. Paula got up and closed it. She climbed back into bed and tried to empty her mind of images of donkeys and tandems and kites.

As she drank her tea, she gazed idly at the heavy curtains. Huge orange and gold flowers with long green stems danced across the cream background like something from a sixties acid trip. The colours were all wrong, but the simple curving shape of the flowers reminded her of something. The dress! The embroidered pocket of the flowerpot dress she had loved so much. Why hadn't she noticed that before?

Suddenly she said, "We played together the summer I came here."

"What?" Andy placed his mug on the bedside table.

"Minnie and me. We met on the beach. She was a year or so younger than me, I think. We used to collect shells and look for crabs and build sandcastles..." Paula's eyes were bright. "And she had a kite. It was red and green, just like in my dream. I can remember her flying it. I must have seen her nearly every day."

"So it wasn't you at all."

"I suppose not." She ran her hands through her sleep tangled hair. "But why have I been dreaming about Minnie? What does it mean?"

"Does it have to mean anything?"

"I don't know. Maybe, maybe not."

"It could just be a whole load of memory fragments coming to the surface and getting mixed up. Our minds are like that, especially when we're under stress. All sorts of weird stuff bubbles up. You've had a terrible time the past couple of months. Not long after I started in the City, I had a really chaotic manager who put us all under ridiculous pressure. I began having bizarre dreams – my manager prancing about wearing reindeer antlers, being followed everywhere by an eight-foot-high coffee cup, colleagues dancing round a maypole with me balancing on the top – deeply strange. But when he finally got the sack, they stopped. Maybe yours will in time too."

She sighed. "Perhaps I am making too much of it all."

Andy peered into her mug. "Are you finished with that tea?"

Paula smiled. "I certainly am." She reached over the side of the bed and put it on the floor.

Penguin rescue

Sanders was thrilled when Paula suggested a trip to Edinburgh Zoo to visit Nils Olav, the celebrity penguin. Andy took them in the van. On the journey, Sanders regaled them with his entire repertoire of penguin jokes and by the time they reached the outskirts of the city had moved on to elephants.

"Definitely certain sure you don't want to come with us, Andy?" he asked as they pulled up outside the zoo.

"No, really, it's fine," Andy said evenly. "I'm going to see my friends and I'll be back for you at four."

When they emerged from the ticket office, Sanders took Paula's hand and began hauling her up the hill. She had wondered if she would recognise the place from her childhood visits with Pete, but nothing looked familiar.

"Come on," he urged. "The penguin parade's not till two, so we'll start with the snakes and then the capybaras."

"The capywhats?"

"Capybaras, stupid. They're brilliant." He tugged her hand. "Come on, you'll see."

When they got to the capybara enclosure, a man and woman dressed in business suits were standing by the fence. The woman gestured at the small wooden hut inside and said something Paula didn't catch. The man, who was eating a sandwich, read a plaque attached to the wire mesh.

"They're the world's biggest rodents, native to South America," he announced.

Sanders stopped beside him. "I told you I knew where we were going," he said triumphantly.

"That's what you said when you took us back to the reptile house for the third time before I spotted you were reading the map upside down," Paula pointed out.

On their final visit, Sanders had spent the best part of ten minutes interrogating a keeper about the habits of the komodo dragon, before she managed to drag him away.

Paula surveyed the empty pen. "So where are the capywhatsits?"

"Capybaras." He pointed to the hut. "In there, I think."

Next to them, a woman spoke harshly to her companion. "I don't care what they are, it's not on. I'm not having the firm's name associated with them."

"They're only rodents." The man took a bite of his sandwich.

"It's vibrating. The whole flaming house is moving. When they said they were just big guinea pigs, I thought, you know, something this size." The woman held her hands, one clutching a briefcase, about a foot apart. "Cuddly, cute. Not giant bloody sex maniacs."

The man put his case down on the path. He sighed and leant against the fence. "They're just bonking. All animals bonk."

"They don't have to do it in broad daylight. Look, look at it moving," the woman raged. "I can see their bums from here."

"Where?" The man freed a fragment of sandwich from between his front teeth with a fingernail. "I can't see anything."

"There, in the doorway. There's two big hairy arses going up and down. They're bonking their bloody brains out. This is supposed to be a zoo not a fucking sex show."

The man turned to Paula and, glancing at Sanders, mouthed "sorry".

Paula smiled and mouthed back, "It's okay."

"They're called Itchy and Scratchy," Sanders said, "and they have a very high sex drive. They can't help it. It's what capybaras do – eat and sleep and bonk. I read about them on the internet."

The woman stared at him.

"I like them because of their faces," he added. "They have very long top lips and big teeth and tiny little ears."

She turned back to her companion. "Well, I don't care what the partners voted for, I'm not spending the firm's money sponsoring one of those..."

"But you'd get a special plaque," Sanders interrupted. "Next to that one. They put your name on it and the name of the animal you've chosen so everyone knows who's paying for its dinner and stuff."

The woman shook her head. "I'm going to look at the lions. You know where you are with lions."

Paula checked her watch. "I think it's time for lunch."

They found the self-service café. Sanders loaded his tray with a plate of fish and chips, and Paula took a baked potato with cheese. They carried their food to a table by the window.

Sanders peered at the map. "Over there's the red river hog and that way's the bush dog." He speared a chip with his fork. "And the penguins are beyond that."

"What's a red river hog?" Paula asked.

"They're really good. They're kind of bristly with red hair and white tufty bits and they live in groups called sounders and do snout boxing."

Paula swallowed a mouthful of potato. "Snout boxing?"

"They push at each other with their noses." Sanders made a butting motion with his head. "We should see them next. If they're awake – they sleep most of the day."

"Are there any animals you don't know about?" she asked.

"Only the really boring ones." He stuffed more chips into his mouth. "They're mostly much more interesting than people."

Paula sipped her glass of water. "Nicer too. I'm really sorry about what happened at the gala."

Sanders shrugged and dipped a piece of fish in a pool of ketchup. He stared out of the window as he chewed.

She tried again. "I wish I could have done something to stop it. I wanted to kill those kids."

He carried on looking out of the window and didn't reply.

"They were worse than animals," Paula said.

Sanders took another forkful of fish. His eyes were wet with tears.

"Let's go and see those red hogs when we've finished," she said.

Two of the strange whiskery beasts were crunching apples and chunks of cabbage by the fence of their enclosure. Sanders knelt beside them. "See the long whiskers and the tufts on their ears? If another animal threatens them, they shake their heads so all the extra hair makes them seem really big and it frightens them away."

"Maybe we could all do with some extra tufts," Paula said.

"Aye, mibby."

They arrived at the penguin pools with ten minutes to spare before the parade, so they bought ice-creams from a kiosk and sat eating them on a bench.

"There he is!" Sanders pointed to a giant metal penguin. "There's the statue of Sir Nils Olav."

A youth with an empty pushchair plonked himself beside them. He gave a loud sniff which turned into a snort, and began playing a game on his mobile phone. After a couple of minutes, a ginger haired girl of about four trotted into view on the tarmac path that ran around the pools. She went up to the statue and gave it a determined poke in the chest. When her finger met solid metal instead of feathers, her face crumpled and she began to howl.

The youth glanced up. "Whit's wrang noo?"

She pointed shakily at the statue and spluttered between wails, "Yon bad burd bit me."

"Stupid wee cow," he exclaimed. "It's no' a real penguin."

"That's Sir Nils Olav," Sanders offered. "He's a celebrity."

Paula shot him a warning glance but he ignored her.

"He used to be a wing commander in the Norwegian army, but they promoted him to colonel-in-chief."

The youth turned to Sanders, squinting in the bright sunshine. "Aye, an' ah'm Wayne Rooney."

"Not everyone's as interested in that kind of stuff as you are," Paula said.

Sanders made a face.

Grabbing his charge under the arms, the youth heaved her into the grimy pushchair. "Belt up, Britney, or ah'll tell yer ma y'were cryin' like a bairn," he threatened.

He extracted a dummy from the pocket of his jeans and rammed it into her mouth, but as soon as he went back to his game, she spat it onto the path and continued bawling.

"Yer ma said she'd skelp ye if ye didnae dae as ah telt ye," he warned without looking up. "So shut the fuck up, wid ye?"

The crying got louder.

The youth laid his phone on the bench and retrieved the dummy, wiping it on the sleeve of his hoodie before shoving it back in her mouth.

Britney spat it out again. This time he left it lying where it landed. "Can ye no' dae that?" he said crossly. "The burds'll be oot soon."

The wailing stopped. "Can ah get ma birthday present then?" the girl asked.

"Aye, ye can. Here's yer ma noo."

A teenage girl in denim micro shorts sat down on the arm of the bench beside the youth. She had the same ginger hair as the child. "Call themsel'es a shop," she complained. "They dinae sell fags."

She leant across her partner to Paula. "Got a fag, missus?"

Paula shook her head. "I don't smoke."

"Lucky you," Britney's mum replied sarcastically.

Sanders tugged at the sleeve of Paula's T-shirt. "Come on, we need to stand up or we won't see."

They joined the crowd that was gathering along the edges of the path. On the other side of the fence, the penguins were massing. A keeper unlocked the gate and held it open as half-a-dozen of the biggest birds, the ones jostling for pole position, spilled out onto the tarmac. They flapped and looked around as if surprised to find themselves on the outside, even though the parade was a daily occurrence. A couple of dozen more wandered out and, led by another keeper, they set off at a sedate waddle along the path.

"I can't believe they let us get this close to the birds," Paula said.

"It's brilliant, isn't it?" Sanders said. "Which one do you think is Sir Nils Olav?"

"I don't know. They all look the same to me."

"They probably think that about us." He bit the bottom off his cone and sucked out the ice-cream. "Y'know, that we all look the same. I bet he's the one in front."

"I'd be surprised if they give us any thought at all," she said. "Tell me again, which are the king penguins?"

"They're the tall ones – only emperor penguins are bigger, but they don't have any here." He pointed to a huddle of smaller birds with white stripes across the tops of their heads that made them look as if they were wearing headphones. "Those are gentoos, and the cross looking ones at the back with the funny eyebrows are crested rockhoppers."

"Yon's the one! Yon big one!" Britney had escaped from the pushchair and was jumping up and down in the middle of the path, pointing at the lead penguin, which was bearing down on her with surprising speed.

Her mum appeared at Paula's shoulder. "Frankie," she yelled through the crowd. "C'mon an dae somethin'."

Paula gave an involuntary cry as the youth elbowed past her, catching her ankle with one of the pushchair's wheels. He pulled a crocheted blanket from the tray under the chair and bent down, but instead of scooping Britney up and out of harm's way, he threw it over the leading penguin and made a lunge for the bird. The keepers were too quick for him though, and before he could pick it up, two of them grabbed him by the arms. A third lifted the blanket from the startled bird and ushered it and its companions back towards the gate of the enclosure.

Britney started to howl again.

"Y'fuckin' eejit," her mother yelled at the would-be kidnapper, as the keepers led him away. "When ah said we'd get her a penguin, ah meant wan o' they stuffed yins in the shop, no' a real yin."

She shoved Britney into the tiny pushchair, snapped the harness shut and raced after them.

"I don't know what the world's coming to," a plump grey-haired woman standing beside Paula declared. "Edinburgh used to be such a refined place."

A middle-aged American man on her other side observed, "I had no idea a penguin parade could be so exciting."

Paula turned to Sanders. He was watching open-mouthed, eyes like saucers.

"That was Nils Olav," he whispered. "That ned tried to steal Nils Olav. I hope he goes to prison for ever and ever." His lip was quivering.

"Sadly, I think it's unlikely," Paula said. She put her arm around his shoulders. "The keepers were never going to let anything bad happen to Nils Olav. They were looking out for him all the time."

Sanders sniffed.

"When you've got people who care for you, no matter how bad things might seem for a while, they always turn out all right in the end." Paula felt her eyes welling up. "Don't you think that's true?"

"I s'pose," he conceded.

She blew her nose. "Now why don't we go back to the café? I need a coffee to steady my nerves."

"Can I get some chocolate cake?" he asked in a small voice.

"I'm sure that could be arranged."

"Okay, then we can find the elephants. They're not as good as penguins, but they're all right, and your nerves'll be safe, 'cos they're too big to steal. You know, I've got more elephant jokes I didn't tell you yet."

"Oh good," Paula said weakly. "Coffee and cake it is, then elephants with jokes."

Minnie

Andy put the carrier bags down on the kitchen table. He took two bottles of rosé out of one and stood them in the fridge.

Paula stirred a pan of tomato sauce. "Perfect timing," she said. "I'm just about ready to serve."

Andy stood behind her and massaged her shoulders. "Smells good."

"Feels good."

He let go. "That's enough of that then."

"Meanie."

"There's a present here for you."

She turned round. "You got me a present?"

"Afraid not, unless you count the wine." He handed her the other carrier bag. "It was on the doorstep."

Inside the bag was a tattered *Oor Wullie* annual. A note taped to the front said in familiar purple felt pen, *Thanx for the zoo. There's somethin interestin inside.*

"It's from Sanders." Paula said. "He was telling me about *Oor Wullie* a while ago. He's this little boy who's always getting into scrapes. He said he'd got a load of annuals."

"My grandparents gave me a couple when I was a kid. They were a hoot. He raced around in a go-cart made from a wooden crate and was always breaking windows with his catapult and getting into trouble with PC Murdoch."

"Sanders said he thought I'd like him. I think he kind of identifies with him."

"That makes sense. Glass of wine?"

"Yes, please. I'll drain the pasta." She was tipping the water into the sink when it came to her. Bill Thompson's tattoo in her dream: the work boots, the bucket – it was *Oor Wullie.* Goose pimples rose on her arms as she spooned pasta and sauce onto their plates. The image was so vivid that she thought about it as they ate.

"So what do you think?" Andy was looking at her intently.

She took a gulp of wine. "About what?"

"Your last meal on earth. What would you rather have: French, Italian or Indian?"

She regarded him blankly. "I don't know, it depends…"

He smiled. "It doesn't matter. You were in a world of your own."

"I know. Sorry." She dropped her fork into the remains of her pasta. "I'm not very hungry."

They took the annual and the rest of their wine down the garden to the beach steps. The tide was high, forcing the evening strollers to pick their way along a narrow band of sand. The rocks where Sanders had hidden the night she threw away her phone were completely covered.

Paula rested her head on Andy's shoulder. "Pete would have liked it here. He was terrible at unwinding – always dashing about, stressing about his lesson plans, his class's exam results, our training – really driven, but I think he could have relaxed here."

They sat in silence for a while, sipping wine. Andy flicked through the annual and Paula gazed out to sea.

Eventually she said, "Whatever he did, he needed to be the best. Coming second just didn't cut it. He got that from Dad. Right from our first race, he was determined to win. I enjoyed being there, being part of it, being with him, but the winning never really mattered to me – I'm more like Mum in that. I loved seeing Pete happy though, his enthusiasm, the glow it gave him. That made all the effort worth it."

Andy closed the annual and began to stroke her hair as she spoke. There were tears in her eyes.

"You should have seen his bedroom when he was a teenager – dirty dishes, smelly socks, chocolate wrappers – a complete tip, but there was never a speck of dust on the shelf where he kept our trophies. He wouldn't let anyone else touch them, not even me. He kept a special blue cloth in his underwear drawer and he used to polish them every Saturday morning when we got back from training. He was the same when he got his own flat – stacks of homework assignments, newspapers, magazines, mess everywhere. The only housework he ever seemed to do was polishing his trophies."

"Did you never think of taking the cycling further? Going for the national team or something?" Andy asked.

"It was never really an option."

Paula looked out across the sea, the flat water a slatey grey in the fading light. When they were still in their teens, they had discussed taking their racing to the next stage, but there were hardly any national events for tandems, let alone mixed ones. Most high level racing was on solo bikes. She had tried time and again to persuade Pete to go it alone. Everyone said he had the potential to make the England squad. Ollie did his best to convince him to try, said they would go for it together, but it was no use. Pete refused to even attempt it unless Paula went for a place in the women's team. He must have known she would never do it; that all she wanted was to cycle with him. Yet he insisted: they would do it together or not at all. That was why Pete never rode for his country. It was her fault.

The muscles in her chest tightened. If only she had made a bit of effort, just pretended she was serious about a national place, he would have done it. He would have made the grade. There was no doubt about that. But she hadn't wanted it for herself, and that had stopped him reaching the very top. It was down to her selfishness. The more they won on the tandem, the less Pete raced alone. Whenever she asked why, the answer was always the same: we're twins, we're a team. Before long, his solo was just for training when they couldn't get together. They were Team Tyndall and there was no room for anything else, no possibility of individual success. It was almost as if she and Pete were two halves of the same person, as if she represented the feminine half of him – the part he couldn't own himself.

Her ribs had become a straightjacket. Her lungs were filling with concrete. Pete could have been a famous sportsman if it wasn't for her. An Olympic medallist. A celebrity. Her breath caught in her throat; there was nowhere for it to go. She looked down at her hands gripping the glass. The nails and the ends of her fingers were turning white. What else had he missed out on because of her? What might he have achieved? What kind of life might he have had? The voices and laughter of the evening strollers were far away now; the sound of the sea lapping on the pebbled shore a distant whisper. The outline of her hands was blurring.

"Breathe. C'mon Paula, breathe." Pete's voice was urgent in her head. "Long, deep breaths; let the air in, really fill your lungs. That's it, good girl."

"Are you all right?" Andy asked.

She willed her muscles to relax. "Yeah, I'm okay. I'm fine." She rolled the stem of the glass between her palms. "Pete was gay, you know." The words were out before they had a chance to register in her brain. "We never discussed it but I'm pretty certain he was. Isn't it awful that we never discussed something so important?"

"Did he have a partner?"

"I don't think so. He had a few girlfriends over the years but they never lasted. I told myself it was because he hadn't met the right person, but that wasn't it at all. They were just camouflage. I think he was afraid I wouldn't approve."

"Why would he think that?"

"Something happened a long time ago, something I saw. He knew I'd seen him. He saw my face. But…" She looked pleadingly at Andy. "It was a shock, that's all – such a shock that for a long time I misremembered what I'd seen. It was just so unexpected. I wouldn't have disapproved of him being with a man, though. I just wanted him to be happy."

"I'm sure he knew that."

"Did he? It's so sad that he never got the chance to be with someone he really cared about."

A tendril of hair fell across Paula's eyes.

Andy tucked it behind her ear. "He had you."

"It's not the same though, is it?"

After a long pause, Paula said, "He would definitely have liked it here. The quiet roads, the countryside, the beach, the people. Sanders would have made him laugh."

"Why didn't he come here with you when you were children?"

"He went to France with Ollie's family. I was so angry with him for abandoning me," she said quietly. "I was determined to be completely miserable, but then one day on the beach I made friends with Minnie."

"Was she on holiday too?"

Paula thought for a moment. "No, she was local. She lived with her mum in a flat just off Main Street. Down a little alleyway. Isn't that funny? I can remember where she stayed. Tall, white buildings in a courtyard. But I've no recollection of the house we rented."

"That's memory for you," Andy said.

She wiped her eyes with the back of her hand and looked at him. "I've been thinking about the dreams. You know, I still believe there's a reason for them. The little girl – Minnie – seems to want to talk to me but we never do. The dream's different every time, but that part doesn't change. Now there's Bill Thompson, who used to look after the donkeys on the beach – I think he wants to harm her in some way. And she's got a black eye. It really doesn't feel like random memories. It means something, something important. I just don't know what." She sighed. "Does that sound mad?"

"It doesn't sound mad at all. If it feels significant to you, then it is."

Paula shivered. "It's getting chilly."

He took off his fleece and put it round her shoulders.

She kissed his cheek. "Thank you, kind sir. Oh, there's the Terrys." She waved to Nora's husband, who was walking towards them along the sand strip with Terry Two trotting at his heels.

He waved back. "Hi, Paula. How're you doing?"

She smiled. "Getting by."

She introduced the men and they shook hands. "Any update on Bovis?" she asked.

"Aye, I bumped into the vet in Adrian's shop this morning. Bovis is doing really well. She's a tough old thing."

Terry checked his watch. "I'd better get the wee fella home. I've got a pick up at Westwick station in twenty-five minutes."

"Say hi to Nora for me," Paula said.

"Will do." He scooped the terrier up under his arm and strode off towards his gate.

Andy began flicking through the annual again. Suddenly, he stopped turning pages. "I don't believe it," he said.

"What?"

"Did you write in this earlier?"

"Write in it? No, why?"

He held out the open book. "Sanders said there was something interesting." At the bottom of the left-hand page someone had scrawled in a childish hand, *Paula Tyndall was here. 1992.*

"Bloody hell. It looks like my writing when I was a kid. How could I have written in Sanders' book in 1992?"

Andy turned to the frontispiece. "That's how. Look." An adult had written, "This book belongs to Minnie Clapperton."

Paula's hand flew to her mouth. "Oh my God. Clapperton. That was her name. Minnie Clapperton. What is Sanders doing with her annual?"

"He probably found it in a charity shop."

"I suppose. That's where he gets half his clothes. But isn't that a weird coincidence?"

"It is a bit. You're still shivering." He stood up. "A walk will warm you up."

They were passing the Co-op when Paula stopped. "There! It was that alley over there. That's where Minnie lived." She took Andy's hand. "Come on."

She pulled him across the road and down the narrow gap between the buildings. It opened out into a cobbled courtyard lined with flat-fronted, white-harled tenements each with three storeys.

"These look old," Andy observed. "They could be eighteenth century."

Paula glanced around. "It was upstairs, but I'm not sure which one. They all look the same." She had been invited for tea one day, trailing back from the beach tired and sandy-legged with Minnie and her mother. They propped their spades against their buckets and took off their shoes on the landing outside the front door. The doormat was rough on her bare soles and the hall smelled like cabbage. She and Minnie sat on high stools at the kitchen counter, feet dangling, and her mother gave them slices of pie filled with mince and gravy. There was lettuce too, but no dressing like at home, and the plates and tea cups were pale green. Minnie's mother sprinkled salt on the lettuce, which made it gritty on her tongue.

Andy read the names over the bells beside the nearest door. "There's no Clapperton here."

"They probably moved on years ago."

"There's no harm looking." He checked the next building. "Bingo! Agnes Clapperton lives on the first floor. That could be Minnie's mum. Do you want to ring?"

Paula went over. "I don't know. I need to think about it. I feel like I've heard the name before though."

He squeezed her hand. "Why don't we go back to the flat and open the other bottle of wine?"

As they turned to go, Paula spotted a familiar shape in the gloom of the alley. "Sanders, is that you?" she called.

He emerged into the courtyard. "Hiya Paula, hiya Andy. Did you like the annual? Wasn't that funny about your name?"

"Where did you get it?" she asked urgently.

"It was Mum's."

"Do you know where she got it?"

Sanders shrugged. "Dunno. A shop, I suppose, or maybe it was a present from my nan. I've got to go – she's at work and she wants her cardi." He took a key out of his pocket and walked over to the door Paula and Andy had been looking at.

"Your nan's not Agnes Clapperton is she?" Andy said.

Sanders turned round. "Aye, why d'you want to know?"

"I remember now," Paula interrupted. "Bill Thompson said that was her name. This is getting way too strange."

"Does your mum have a sister called Minnie?" Andy asked Sanders.

"She doesn't have any sisters. Anyway, her name's Minnie."

"Don't tell stories, Sanders," Paula snapped. "Her name's Carole."

"I'm not telling stories," he replied indignantly. "It's Carole now, but it used to be Minnie. She changed it when she had me. She said she couldn't be a mum called Minnie." He grinned. "Geddit, Minnie-mum – minimum."

"Be serious for a minute. Your mum used to be Minnie Clapperton?" Paula checked.

"Yes, but Carole's her real name. No one ever used it because she was so little, like Minnie Mouse. But then she wanted to be more grown up so she stopped being Minnie. She hasn't been called Clapperton since she was ten. That's when Nan got married again, to Denzil McCormack." He leaned towards them conspiratorially. "Mum says he ran off with a barmaid from the Steam Packet on her twelfth birthday and broke Nan's heart. Nan didn't change their name back in case he got sick of the barmaid and came home, but he never did. They live in Glenrothes now with six Rottweilers, and Nan's gone back to Clapperton."

Paula clutched her head. "Your mum, Carole McCormack, was Minnie Clapperton? All this time I've been dreaming about your mum."

She was sitting at the kitchen table in her running clothes eating an apple when Andy came through. She had woken early, slipped out of bed while he was still asleep, dressed and tiptoed out to take her usual route along the sand to the cliffs.

After the warm fug of skin and sweat and sex in the bedroom, the air had been fresh and cleansing in her lungs, making her breathing easy. But inside her head, the chaos was worse than ever. Images from the dreams jostled for space as she ran: Minnie on the tandem with Bill Thompson, Minnie disappearing into the alleyway, Minnie with a black eye.

"Focus." It was Pete's voice again. "Concentrate. Stay on the balls of your feet. Stay light, stay in the now."

"Stay in the now," Paula repeated aloud. "Stay in the now."

Soon there was only the familiar slap and suck of trainers on damp sand, the spring and stretch of muscles, and the cries of the gulls circling above. Soon she was out-running them all: Pete, Minnie, Bill Thompson. She was on her own, her mind free and clear, her thoughts her own once more. That was when she realised. By the time she was back at the steps, she knew exactly what the dreams meant. No wonder Sanders' nan was cross when he told her they had seen Bill Thompson on their visit to the donkeys.

"Shall I do you some eggs?" she offered as Andy filled the kettle.

"No thanks. I'll just have coffee and cereal. I need to get on the road."

"But you'll be back up next weekend?"

He wrapped his arms around her. "Sooner if I can palm off a couple of bookings. What are you planning for today? Are you going to bury your nose in the papers?" He pointed to *Scotland on Sunday* and the *Sunday Herald* lying on the table.

"I'm going to see Minnie," she said.

Two little girls

Carole peered round the front door, revealing the make-up stained collar of a white towelling dressing gown. Her hair was tangled and her eyes smudged with old mascara. She looked even paler than she had at Nora and Terry's.

"I wondered when you'd turn up," she said sourly.

"Can I come in? I need to talk to you," Paula said.

"I don't think so. I'm not interested in what you've got to say."

Carole moved to close the door, but Paula stuck her foot in the gap. "Please."

"Didn't you hear me? I said I'm not interested. Now shift."

"I heard you, but I'm not moving till you let me in. I'll stand here all day if I have to."

"Fine, have it your way. I'm not providing a floorshow for the neighbours." Carole stepped back and opened the door fully. "Kitchen's through there. Make some coffee while I get dressed. I cannae do this without caffeine."

The small kitchen was clean but untidy, with dishes, open cereal packets and magazines cluttering the work surfaces. A patch of brown vinyl flooring had worn away in front of the back door, revealing the concrete underneath. It reminded Paula of being in Pete's flat. She filled the kettle and went through the cupboards until she found a jar of instant coffee and a set of mugs decorated with cartoon kittens playing with balls of wool.

A page from a 2011 Brad Pitt calendar was taped to the fridge. Someone – probably Sanders – had blacked out half his teeth and drawn a bikini top on his naked chest. On the varnished pine table, a note in Sanders' writing balanced against a bottle of orange squash said, *Gone to Nans back 4 lunch.*

Paula was putting milk in her coffee when Carole reappeared dressed in jeans and a T-shirt with the slogan *Keep staring – I might do a trick.* Her sandy hair was scraped back in an elastic band, and she wore purple and white striped socks but no shoes. She looked like a slightly older version of Sanders.

Paula held up the milk bottle.

Carole nodded and sat down. She retrieved a packet of John Player Specials and a plastic lighter from under a dog-eared copy of *Hello*. "I'm surprised it's taken you this long to come round."

Paula carried their mugs over and sat opposite her. "I only just realised."

Carole's hands shook as she lit her cigarette. She lifted a pile of ironing to reveal the sugar bowl, and added two heaped spoonfuls to her coffee. "Sanders said he told you everything."

"Sanders?"

"That's why you're here, isn't it?" She drew on her cigarette and regarded Paula through the smoke. "To tell me what a crap mum I am? How his problems are all my fault? He's always making friends with visitors. Before I know it, I'm getting a lecture on how I've fucked his life up." She took a mouthful of coffee. A vein pulsed in her temple. "Well, let me tell you, Paula, you don't know what it's been like for Sanders and me. You've no idea. But, whatever." She waved her hands in a gesture of dismissal. "You don't care about that."

"But..." Paula began.

"Just hang on. You can have your say in a minute, if it makes you feel better. It won't bother me. I've heard it all before. The only difference is it's usually kids he pals about with, not grown ups. Next thing Mum and Dad are on the doorstep telling me I shouldnae let him run around at all hours on his own, that he's leading their little angels astray, talking nonsense, telling lies..." She shook her head and took a couple of quick puffs. "But why shouldn't I let him? He won't come to any harm round here, and so what if he talks rubbish half the time? It doesn't matter. It's just Sanders. They don't know about him. They don't know what it's like not being able to make friends with the local kids because he doesnae want them to find out." She looked hard at Paula. "But he trusted you. He told you everything."

Paula nodded. "He did."

"You probably know I was a drug addict. Everybody does," Carole went on, hardly pausing for breath. "But that isn't what caused his condition. Of course, I blamed myself. I thought it was a punishment. I cried every day for months. But you cannae cry forever; you have to get on."

She blotted up some stray sugar grains with her finger and dropped them into her coffee. "No one knows why PAIS happens. And yes, when Sanders was born I could have decided who he should be. Mibby it would have made things easier for him, but would it have made him happier? I don't know. What if I'd got it wrong?" She gazed past Paula to the curtain-less window and the overgrown garden beyond. "In the old days, that's what the doctors did – chose them a sex and let them live with it – but that's not how they do it now. Most doctors let kids like Sanders make their own choice, and I was happy with that."

Carole leant forward. "There's enough people wanting to tell you how to behave, what to think. That's why I give Sanders his freedom. Most people think he's just a strange kid. Some know there's something a bit different, but only a handful know exactly what it is." She took another gulp of coffee. "At least, that's how it was until the gala. His life's going to get even harder now, poor little bugger."

She stubbed her cigarette out on a saucer as if she was crushing the life out of a particularly loathsome insect. "It was going to anyway. He's got to choose soon, but it's his decision. I won't interfere and I won't let anyone else…"

"My God," Paula said. She felt suddenly queasy. "You wrote that note. You were trying to warn me off."

Carole stared at her. "What note?"

"The one that was put through my door threatening to tell the police I'd molested him. I thought it was Sanders then I realised it wasn't his writing."

"What are you talking about?" Carole lit another cigarette. "I don't care what you think about me, but Sanders likes you and you've been kind to him. I'd never make a threat like that."

Paula sipped her coffee. It was tepid and bitter. "But who else could have written it?"

Carole shrugged. "There's no shortage of evil people around."

"Anyway, I didn't come to talk about Sanders or the note, and I'm not here to criticise the decisions you made or the way you've brought him up. That's none of my business."

Carole frowned. "What is it then? Why are you here?"

"You really don't know? I thought that's why you left Nora and Terry's."

"What are you on about? I had a migraine."

"I know, but after I remembered everything, I thought it was an excuse. You were staring and scowling at me. I assumed you knew who I was."

Carole stared at her. "An excuse for what? What do you mean I knew who you were? I wasn't scowling at anybody; my head was sore. I didn't know you from Adam. Sanders didn't tell me he was friends with you until after he ran away."

"You honestly don't remember me? You don't remember us playing together?" Paula asked urgently. She leant forward, the table top sticky against the bare skin of her forearms. "The summer I came here when we were little. Minnie, you must remember."

Carole sat back in her seat. "No one's called me Minnie for yonks." She searched Paula's face. "We were friends? I played with loads of visitors when I was a lassie."

"It was 1992. I was on holiday with my mum and dad. You had a red and green kite that we used to fly on the dunes…"

"You were the big girl I built amazing sandcastles with?" Carole interrupted. She was smiling now, revealing a slight chip in one of her bottom teeth. "Your dad helped us. We covered them in shells and seaweed, and made moats with water and driftwood drawbridges, and we flew my kite and went for rides on the donkeys." She considered for a moment. "Didn't you have a brother that was somewhere else?"

Paula nodded.

"That was you? That's weird."

"I know. Pete, my brother, was camping with a friend in France." She paused to give the words time to marshal themselves. "He died recently."

Carole's smile froze. She took Paula's hand. Her touch was warm. "I'm so sorry. How…"

"He had an accident on his bike," Paula said quietly.

"That's terrible." Carole looked thoughtful for a moment then stood up. "I think I've got a picture."

Paula surveyed the kitchen as she listened to the other woman moving about upstairs. A hand-made card was taped to the fridge below Brad Pitt. Sanders had written *HApPY BIRTHDAY MuM* around the edges, each of the widely spread letters in a different colour of felt pen. In the centre was a drawing of a woman carrying several shopping bags. She appeared to be tapping one foot impatiently. A speech bubble coming out of her mouth said, *Your eatin me out of house an home!!!* There were more of his drawings and paintings stuck on the wall above the table. A surprisingly sophisticated landscape with a steam train seemed quite recent, but the rest looked as if they had been there for years. There were crudely painted houses on yellowing paper with curling edges, splodgy cats and dogs, and an enormous lilac elephant wearing red high-heeled sandals.

Carole returned with a dusty shoebox. Pushing aside the papers and other junk on the table, she tipped it up. A lifetime of faded memories spilled onto the unwiped surface: photos, newspaper clippings, greetings cards. Picking up a handful of pictures, she began sorting through them. She held out a glossy close-up of herself looking no older than Sanders. Her eyes were red and swollen and she was clutching a tiny wrinkled baby swathed in a pale green blanket. Sanders' eyes were tightly shut. "That's the day after he was born."

She offered Paula another. "First day at school." Sanders was grinning, hands on hips, as he showed off his oversized blazer and voluminous shorts. A Mutant Ninja Turtle rucksack was propped against one stick-thin leg.

Tears welled under Paula's eyelids. "He looks so small and vulnerable," she said, wiping them away with the back of her hand.

Carole continued to rummage. "There!" She held up a square print that had been torn in half and taped back together. "That's you and me, isn't it?"

Two girls, one several centimetres taller than the other, stood beaming beside a sprawling complex of sandcastles. They were both clutching plastic spades. Paula was wearing the flowerpot dress. The kite lay on the sand by Carole's bare feet and behind them, in the distance, a group of donkeys waited patiently for riders.

Paula took the photograph from Carole and studied it. It was her dreams, her past made concrete. Hard evidence that she hadn't imagined it all. She had actually been here. The memories that had been surfacing were based on something real.

"I can hardly believe it," she managed. "There we are." She placed the picture on the table in front of her but didn't take her eyes off it.

"There we are," Carole confirmed.

"I've been having dreams. There's a little girl – the dress, the kite are just the same. I thought she was me, but it was actually you."

"You've been dreaming about me?"

"Over and over, and I've finally worked out what it means. In the last dreams, you had a black eye."

"A black eye?" Carole turned her gaze back to the neglected garden as she thought about this. Suddenly, her hand flew up to her face. "Oh, my goodness, I remember."

"That's what I wanted to talk to you about." Paula reached out and briefly touched her hand. "I let you down badly and I wanted to apologise."

"Oh, my goodness." Carole repeated. She turned to Paula. "My mum was so angry."

"She was having a relationship with Bill Thompson, the donkey man, wasn't she?" Paula said quickly. "She wanted you to call him Uncle Bill, but you wouldn't. You told me you hated him. Then the day before we were leaving, you asked if you could come home with me. You said you could be my sister, but I said no, I already had a brother. You cried. You cried so much." She leant over the table and clasped Carole's small hands in her own. "You were trying to tell me something, weren't you? About Bill. That he was hurting you. That's why I dreamt about you with the black eye. You needed help and you came to me because I was the big girl, but I didn't understand. Minnie, I'm so, so sorry. I let you down. I left you there with him. It's no wonder you started taking drugs. It's all my fault because I didn't help you."

Carole stared at her. "No," she said eventually. "No, that's not what happened." She pulled her hands out of Paula's grasp. "That's not what happened at all. I… You… You're the girl who caused all the trouble."

"What? What on earth do you mean?"

She ran a finger down the join on the photograph. "That's why it's torn in half – Mum ripped it up. I saved the bits, taped them back together and hid it where she wouldn't find it. I always kept it, in spite of what happened, because you were my friend. You were my friend."

Paula felt as if she was going to be sick. "Carole, please tell me what you're talking about."

"One day when we were playing..." She paused to light another cigarette. "I cannae believe how clearly this is coming back. We were digging a hole. We were up to our knees, really digging, sand going everywhere. You said we had to hurry, that you were really cross with your brother for going away without you. We were going to dig all the way to France and you were going to climb down and find him – and you were going to drag him back. That's exactly what you said: *drag him back*."

"I said that?"

"You did, and the black eye was nothing to do with Bill Thompson. I didn't much like him, but he never hurt me. I think he dumped Mum not long after, went off and got a job on the rigs or something."

Paula's tongue felt dry and thick. She swallowed some of the disgusting coffee to moisten it. "Are you sure? You could be suppressing the memory."

"Certain. I know who gave me that black eye – it was you!" She leant across the table. "You did it just before you left. I asked to come home with you – you're right about that. I reminded you what you'd said about being angry with your brother. I said if I was your sister, I'd never go away and leave you. I kept begging you to let me be your sister. You got really cross. You said you were a twin and you didn't need a stupid sister. That's when you punched me. You sent me flying and I hit my head on a stone. I was knocked unconscious and there was blood all over the place. You were wearing that dress." Carole tapped the photo with a bitten fingernail. "It was the last thing I saw before I blacked out. They took me to Westwick in an ambulance. Mum was raging. She wanted to call the police but Bill said it wasnae worth the bother. They kept me in overnight and did loads of tests. At first I wouldn't say anything to anyone, just sat there staring about. Then when I started talking again I kept asking, 'Have I missed him? Did he give my presents to someone else because I was bad?' When Mum asked what I was on about, I said Santa. I thought it was Christmas time and I'd missed him because of being in hospital. She says it was weeks before everything came back to me. She was beside herself – convinced I'd got brain damage. She wouldnae let me out the house on my own the rest of the summer."

"No! That can't be right. That's awful." Paula's head was pounding. She rested it in her hands, fingers icy against the heat of her forehead. "You must have misremembered."

The kitchen door opened. Paula glanced up. Sanders and the bad-tempered woman from the Co-op came in.

"Look, Nan, Paula's here," he said to the woman. He turned to Paula. "Have you come for lunch? This is my nan, but you can call her Agnes."

"What are you doing here?" Agnes demanded.

"Mum!" Carole said. "Don't be so unfriendly."

"You dinnae ken who she is. I knew when Sanders told me about her before the gala. Never forget a name, me." Agnes pointed a red-nailed finger at Paula. "You're the hooligan that assaulted my girl. She's no' been right in the head since. I thought I told you to stay away."

"What do you mean 'no' right in the head'?" Carole snapped. "There's nothing wrong with my head."

"Y'ken exactly what I mean. Y'd never o' taken all they drugs if it wasnae for her scramblin' yer brains."

"That's complete, crap, Mum. The drugs were nothing to do with Paula. I took them because I was a stupid wee girl, God help me."

"Y'were never the same after she attacked you."

"Mum, shut up." Carole turned to Paula. "Ignore her, she's talking out of her arse."

"You wrote the note?" Paula whispered incredulously to Agnes.

"She thought it was Bill Thompson that hit me," Carole said.

"I thought that's why you were annoyed when Sanders said he'd met him at the farm," Paula put in.

Agnes snorted. "Billy Thompson wouldnae hurt a fly. I was annoyed because the bastard went and dumped me when he got a sniff o' a job offshore. As for the note…"

"What note?" Sanders asked. "What's everyone so cross about? Shall I make a pot of tea?"

"Wheesht you, we don't need tea," Agnes snapped. She turned her attention back to Paula. "I certainly did write it. You're a hooligan. You ruined my girl's life, and I dinnae want you near any o' my family."

"Don't be so daft, Mum," Carole said. "It was nothing – a falling out between two kids more than twenty years ago. No more than that. She came to make up."

"What's twenty years ago?" Sanders interjected.

Paula opened her mouth and closed it again without saying anything.

"Not now, Sands," Carole said. She looked at her mother. "If I don't bear a grudge, why should you?"

"That's as mibby," Agnes said, "but no one hurts my family and gets away wi' it. You needed six stitches. They shaved half the hair off the back o' your head and you cried for two days."

"What are you all talking about?" Sanders demanded.

"Go upstairs," Agnes said. "This is nothing to do wi' you."

Carole caught hold of his arm. "Stay where you are. It's a fuss about nothing."

Paula got to her feet. "I'm the one who should go," she said. "I really am sorry, Carole. I don't know how I could have got it so wrong."

Feelings

Paula took up her usual position on the steps leading down to the beach. The tide was out and a group of children played cricket on the wet sand. An unsteady toddler clung to his mother's hand as they made their way to the water's edge. He stamped his bare feet up and down in the shallow foam and waved his free arm gleefully. The young woman bent down and, taking hold of his plump torso, swung him round on a level with her face. She kissed his pink cheeks and she set him back down on the sand. When he held up his arms to be lifted again, she knelt and, giggling, hugged him to her.

Paula reached into the pocket of her shorts and fished out her phone. She dialled her parents' number.

Her mum answered on the third ring. She sounded slightly brighter than in their previous conversations. "Paula? It's good to hear your voice. I'm so sorry we didn't get to talk on your birthday. How are you? Mrs McIntyre said you were doing much better."

Paula ignored the fact that her parents had been talking to her landlady behind her back. "I'm fine, Mum. How are you and Dad?"

"Your birthday – yours and Pete's," her mum corrected herself, "was difficult, but we got through it and we're still here, taking it one day at a time, as they say."

"I know, me too. I wanted to ask you something. The summer we came here, do you remember a little girl I played with?"

She thought for a second. "Of course, a tiny thing. She was called something like Millie. A very sweet girl."

"It was Minnie." Paula took a deep breath. "Do you remember what happened?"

"What happened?" her mum asked carefully.

"Just before we left to come home, did I do something?"

"Well…" Her mum hesitated. "It wasn't really anything. You didn't mean any harm, but you were quite a bit bigger than her… As I say, it really wasn't anything."

"It's okay, Mum, you don't need to protect me. I know what it was. I gave her a black eye and knocked her out. She needed stitches after she fell and hit her head. I just wanted to know how you remembered it."

Paula could hear her mum breathing. Eventually she said, "You did hit her, but you didn't intend to hurt her. It was completely out of character. She said something about Pete and you lashed out – a childish reflex."

Paula's throat constricted. "I told her I was angry with him for going to France, and she said she would be my sister and take his place." Her voice was little more than a whisper. "She kept saying it and in the end I punched her. I could have done her serious harm."

"But you didn't mean it," her mum interjected quickly.

"But I started it. I said I didn't want to be a twin anymore."

"You were nine years old and you loved your brother. No one ever doubted how much you loved him. It's just one of those things children say." Her mum sounded close to tears. "You must believe me, Paula, you are not responsible for what happened to Pete."

Paula slumped over until her elbows rested on her knees. She propped her head up on one hand, exhausted to her very bones. "I've been having dreams," she said slowly, "about the summer we spent here. There's a little girl on the beach. At first, I thought she was me. Then I remembered about Minnie. I knew I'd let her down, but when I tried to work out how, I got it completely wrong. I made up this elaborate fantasy about her being abused by her mum's boyfriend. But I was the one who'd hit her. Mum, I feel like such an idiot."

"You're not an idiot, darling. Sometimes it's much easier to misremember than to face the truth. With what you've been going through, it's no wonder a memory like that surfaced, but you've got to stop giving yourself such a hard time."

Paula made a small sobbing sound. A tear dripped onto the bare skin of her knee.

"Listen to me," her mum said gently. "Pete's death was nothing to do with you."

"But if I'd been with him."

"You weren't. Pete was an adult, responsible for his own actions. Your dad and I might as well say what if we'd not moved to Scotland when you were little. You wouldn't have started school there and been put in the same class. If we'd stayed in England, you'd have started before Pete and been in separate years. Maybe your relationship would have developed differently. Maybe you wouldn't have wanted to be twins and to ride together. You wouldn't have been going in for that race and he wouldn't have been out training the night before, and so on, and so on. It's a ridiculous line of thinking. You can see that, can't you?"

"I know, but I can't help wondering if somehow, maybe what he did was deliberate."

"Deliberate?" There was shock in her mum's voice.

"I think Pete was gay and couldn't come to terms with it. That he thought if he came out, if I knew… oh, I don't know. I don't know what I'm trying to say."

"Darling, Pete may or may not have been gay – your dad and I have wondered about it – but your brother did not deliberately put himself in the path of that car. He wasn't depressed, he wasn't even unhappy. He loved his life, his cycling, his job and, above all, he loved you. You have nothing whatsoever to feel guilty about."

Paula closed her eyes. On the cine screen of her imagination, she was nine years old again, barefoot and dressed in the blue and white flowerpot dress. She and Pete were sprinting side-by-side down the sand. She was carrying a red plastic bucket and he had a bamboo handled shrimp net. They waded out until they were knee deep in the icy white foam. Laughing, Pete pulled her round and they ran together through the shallows towards the paddling pool by the harbour. If only he'd been in Craskferry with her that summer, instead of in France. But if he had been there, she wouldn't have made friends with Minnie, wouldn't have had the dreams that drew her back, and if she hadn't come back, she would never have met Andy or Sanders. Her life would have turned out entirely differently.

"Darling, are you still there?"

"I know it's not my fault," Paula said so quietly she could have been talking to herself, "but it's hard. I miss him so much. Every day, all the time. I wonder what he would have thought about things, what he would have said about the people I've met up here, the friends I've made. And I do feel guilty, because I'm meeting new people and getting on with my life, and he can't do the same. I think I've met someone special, Mum, but Pete'll never get that chance now. And, you know, sometimes I forget he's dead and I wonder where he is and what he's up to. Then suddenly I remember." She raked a hand through her wind-blown hair. "It's awful."

"Yes, it is," her mum said.

"It's so hard, so very hard."

Back in the saddle

Paula wrapped the chicken sandwiches in foil. The cake was cooling and the icing was ready in a bowl. She tested the temperature of the sponges with a fingertip. Still too hot to ice. She washed and peeled a couple of carrots and grated them into a plastic box, tossing in some pine nuts, sesame seeds and raisins. She poured on oil and a little vinegar, added mustard, salt and pepper, and mixed everything together with a fork.

She knew she didn't have to make this much effort. He would have been perfectly happy with a ham roll and a bag of crisps, but she needed to be doing something.

It was barely six when she had woken, and lying in bed, unable to get back to sleep, she had begun planning the picnic as a way of squeezing out the certain knowledge that this trip was a very bad idea indeed.

The thought was still there as she showered and dressed and ate a slice of toast and marmalade, and she knew that if she didn't fill the mental space with something practical, she would talk herself out of it.

She was waiting on Adrian Linton's doorstep when he arrived to open the shop at nine o'clock, silently reciting the list of ingredients she needed, like a mantra to push negative thoughts out of her head. Once everything was bought, she told herself, it would be too late to back out, but even as she beat together butter and eggs for the cake, and sifted flour and cocoa powder, the voice of her fear was urging her not to go through with it.

Glancing out of the window, she saw the tandem leaning against the side of the shed, badgering and bullying her. Closing her eyes, Paula shifted her focus away from the mess of ingredients and implements surrounding her on the kitchen surfaces to the mess inside her head. Ignoring it wasn't working, so she would try something else.

It's another betrayal, the voice was saying. Look what happened the last time you did this: you almost ended up in hospital. Why can't you leave well alone? You really don't have to do it.

"I hear you," she said out loud. "I acknowledge what you're saying, but I'm doing it anyway. I need to do it."

She opened her eyes, wiped her carroty hands on a dish towel and gave the sponge layers another gentle prod. Reassured that they were cool enough, she smoothed on the icing and decorated the top with Smarties. Without bothering to tidy up, she packed everything into a pannier and filled the water bottles.

Paula went outside and unscrewed the back set of pedals – her pedals – which, like the pair on the front, were little more than clips for the cleats built into the soles of cycling shoes. She replaced them with ordinary box ones which would make it possible to ride in trainers, and lowered the back seat as far as it would go.

As she was pushing the bike down the front path, she had a feeling she was being watched again. Turning, she saw Mrs McIntyre standing at an upstairs window. Her landlady smiled and briefly raised a hand in a cross between a wave and a salute. Paula returned the gesture.

Sanders opened the front door as she was balancing the tandem against his hedge. He was wearing lime green knee-length shorts, a pink Scissor Sisters T-shirt and black slip-on sand shoes. "We're not going on the bus?" he asked delightedly.

"We're not."

"Really?" He was grinning from ear to ear. "We're going on the tandem?"

"Are you ready?"

He did a little dance, waving his arms in the air. "We're absolutely ready, ready, ready."

"We?"

He nodded at Bovis, who was standing on the little square of lawn, watching them. "Her and me, of course."

"You're kidding."

He looked wounded. "She can run beside us."

"Sanders, she's only got one back leg."

"It's not her fault she's disabled and it's illegal to discriminate against her because of it." He bit into the corner of a fingernail. "Anyway, she's still pretty fast."

Paula took off her helmet and rubbed her forehead. Her skull felt as if it was too tight for her brain, and it was beginning to pound. "She's a greyhound, for goodness sake, and she loves you. She'll do anything to please you, and if that means running like buggery, she'll do it for a hundred metres – then collapse in the gutter and fall asleep. That's what greyhounds do. So unless she can balance on the crossbar for the rest of the way, she stays here."

"She mibby could."

Paula shook her head. Why hadn't she listened to that voice? This was a very bad idea indeed.

"Sanders, that was a joke. Even if she could keep up, it would be far too dangerous to have her running along the road." She handed him a helmet. "Now put that on and get yourself onto that saddle before I change my mind. I need to see if you can reach the pedals."

"Two seconds." He led Bovis inside and re-emerged wearing a small rucksack.

Paula held the bike steady while he climbed onto the back seat. If he wasn't tall enough to pedal, it would give her a way out. Unfortunately, his legs were longer than she had realised. His position wasn't ideal – it would put too much strain on his knees if they were trying to race – but it would do for the speed and distance they would be travelling.

"Okay," she said. "Are you sure you're ready for this? You're the stoker and your job is to supply the power."

He made a whimpering noise. "How much power?"

"Enough to get our combined weight up hills. If you're having second thoughts, we can still catch the bus."

"No." He said resolutely. "I want to."

"Fine. All you have to do is pedal as hard as you can when I tell you to, and don't stop until I say. If I say 'easy', you ease off a bit, but you don't stop pedalling. Try not to lean to one side or the other, and don't make any other sudden moves or do anything to distract me. Oh, and you're responsible for directions. You know how to get there, don't you?"

"Of course I know how to get there."

"Right then." She swung her right leg over the bar and clicked her shoe into the pedal. The real question was whether she was ready for this. But it really was too late to think about that. "We're off."

The bike gave a single wobble before Paula got it under control and then they were heading down the road. Her legs felt as if the bones had melted away, leaving her with nothing more than willpower to turn the pedals. She gripped the handlebars so tightly to stop the shaking in her arms sending them off course that she could see every vein and tendon in her rapidly whitening hands. Apart from that awful trip with Ollie, she had never ridden a tandem without Pete, and it felt utterly alien to be on the front with all the responsibility it entailed. They had cycled together for seventeen years, yet she had only ever sat on the pilot's seat to steady the bike and hold the lever while her brother tinkered with the back brake.

"We're stopping at the junction up ahead," she called over her shoulder. "Be ready to put your left foot down."

They came to a halt just short of the line. Flicking her heel out to unclip her shoe so she could rest it on the tarmac – an action that normally required no conscious effort – felt like a major triumph of mind over matter.

"This is awesome. Did you see those pensioners staring at us?" Sanders asked breathlessly. "They nearly swallowed their false teeth. We're kings of the road, superheroes on two wheels – we have the power to go anywhere we want."

"How do you think up all that nonsense?" Paula felt herself smiling despite her nervousness about this trip.

"It's easy. How am I doing?"

"Not too bad for a first attempt. Don't let your concentration wander though; you're sitting on almost five grand's worth of bike."

The weight behind her shifted as he slid off the seat. "Fuck me, five grand!"

"Sanders, don't use that word. You're irritating enough without that too. Now get back on. I can hear a car behind us. Which way are we going?"

They passed Nora and Terry walking Terry Two as they rode up the long hill out of the village to the main road. Nora stuck her fingers in her mouth and wolf whistled, and she and Terry both waved. The bike gave such a shudder to the left as Sanders let go of his handlebars and swung round to respond, that Paula thought they were going to end up in the ditch with their feet in the air.

"Eyes front," she yelled as she fought to get them running straight again. "Do that again and I'm dumping you right here and riding home on my own."

"Sorry."

They had a bit of a struggle getting going again at a couple of uphill junctions, and they took a wrong turn when Sanders got his left and right mixed up, but he soon realised his mistake, and overall Paula was surprised how well they were riding together. He enjoyed it too. Every time they went downhill he squealed with delight, and when she glanced down she could see he was taking his feet off the pedals.

She knew exactly how he felt. Riding with Pete had always meant freedom to her as, with blind awareness, she handed over all control and responsibility, leaving nothing to do but pedal and experience the ride. There was no sensation like the joy of the moment when they found that effortless, rolling gear that meant they were working with the bike instead of fighting against it. There was nothing to match the gasping, burning triumph of beating a steep hill, or the surging, dipping, weaving, whooshing exhilaration of a descent that carried them, panting and goose pimpled through the sweat, back onto the flat.

Now the passenger was in the driving seat. Sanders had chosen their destination, but she was in charge of everything else: when to slow down or speed up, when to change gear, when to brake. And it was all right. The shaking was subsiding. Arms, legs and brain were rising to the challenge and doing what they were supposed to do. She was the pilot, she was in control, and, most amazing of all, she was enjoying the ride too. There was enough power in there, stored up inside her, to do all those things and be able to taste the warm, salt air. She could turn the pedals, steer the bike and smell the fresh breath of the trees. She could see the gulls circling, and feel the hairs on her arms and legs rising in the same breeze that was carrying them aloft.

Eventually, she said, "We'll go even faster if you keep your feet where they're supposed to be and tuck your elbows and knees in."

"Aye, aye captain," Sanders replied.

They reached the turning for the bay in just under an hour – a far slower pace than she was used to – but the important thing was that they made it without injury to themselves or the bike. It took another ten minutes and all Paula's concentration to navigate them down the narrow stony track, avoiding tree roots and potholes and the spiky arms of giant coconut-scented broom bushes that stretched out to bar their way.

When riding was no longer possible, they dismounted and pushed the bike, Sanders walking like a cowboy who had spent too long in the saddle.

"That was epic," he said.

"Not too uncomfortable?"

"Only a bit."

"That's why cyclists wear padded shorts. You did well though."

He blew on his fingers and pretended to buff his stumpy fingernails on his chest. "Lance Armstrong eat your heart out."

"You've heard of Lance Armstrong?"

"Doh, he only won the Tour de France six times."

"Seven," Paula corrected. "He won the world's toughest sporting event seven times in a row after beating supposedly terminal cancer. He had tumours in his lungs, brain and testicles. The doctors didn't expect him to survive, let alone ride again, but he did it – up and down the Alps and the Pyrenees, more than three thousand kilometres in three weeks, faster than any other cyclist in the world, every year for seven years. It just shows what you can achieve if you really want to."

"But he did it on drugs," Sanders pointed out.

"Yes, sadly, he did."

They emerged onto the edge of a high, grass-fringed dune. The flawless crescent of sand stretching below them was completely empty.

"This is amazing," Paula gasped.

"It's a special place, for thinking and stuff. Hardly anyone ever comes here."

"I suppose most tourists want paved roads, parking and toilets. They don't want to cycle or leave their cars miles away then cart their belongings down here. Andy took me to a beach like this further up the coast where there were seals lying about all over the place. There was no one there either."

"Most people are lazy." Sanders bent to pull a thorn out of his ankle. "They never get to see the good things. The cave I slept in is along there a bit. I'll show you later if you like."

"That was quite a walk."

"I came part of the way on the bus. Anyway, I needed to think."

Paula unclipped the pannier and chained the tandem to a solitary section of rusted metal fence that was almost hidden by the grass. Sanders took off his shoes and bounded ahead down the dune, seemingly oblivious to the razor-edged fronds.

"There's a piece of tree here we can use as a table," he called.

She picked her way to where he was sitting cross-legged on the sand and unpacked the food.

He opened his rucksack and held out a can. "It's ginger beer. I thought you'd like it better than Tizer or Irn-Bru."

She held it as far away as she could and pulled the ring. A fizzle of foam slid down the side. Licking it away, she took a long gulp. She hadn't drunk ginger beer since she was a child and it tasted as deliciously fiery and illicit as she remembered. It had always made her feel grown up when they had a picnic and her dad handed round the cans of ginger beer – it had such a strange flavour, she was sure only adults were supposed to drink it. When Pete said it was his favourite, it became hers too, even though it made her tongue hot and tingly.

She raised her can slightly. "Cheers, Pete."

"What?" Sanders was already biting into a sandwich.

"Nothing."

He brandished it in her direction. "These are nice."

Paula peeled the lid off the carrot salad and gave him a fork. "More vitamins to build you up."

He grinned. There were fragments of chicken stuck between his small animal teeth. "I've got something to show you."

He passed her a large envelope from his rucksack. It contained a letter and a certificate.

"What are these?"

"Have a look."

She read the certificate. "You've sponsored a king penguin called Bungee from Edinburgh Zoo."

He beamed at her. "The letter says it's a present from an anonymous donor. Any idea who that could be?"

Paula smiled. "None at all."

"It says he's Sir Nils Olav's twin brother."

"I didn't know penguins could have twins."

"The letter says they hatched on the same day. That's as good as twins. Someone else adopted him when he was little and chose his name, but they didn't keep up the payments, so now he's mine for good and I can visit him whenever I like."

"That's wonderful." She raised her can again. "To Bungee, the penguin."

"Bungee, the penguin," Sanders repeated solemnly, knocking his can against hers. "I was thinking I might write a book."

"Really? What about?"

"About a superhero penguin that solves crimes and stuff, you know like James Bond. I'm going to call it *Double-o-Penguin*."

Paula laughed. "That's brilliant. You should write it."

"Mibby I will." He took a swig from his can. "I've decided, you know."

"About what?" Paula asked nervously.

He gazed out to sea. "Everything."

"That's what I thought you meant. And?"

"I'm me, and that's who I'm going to stay. I don't want to be someone else just because a load of doctors think it's a good idea." He took another quick sip and turned his attention back to the view.

"So?" Paula prompted.

He spoke without looking at her. "So no drugs and no operations."

"Where will that leave you?"

He balanced his can on the tree trunk. "Where I am now, in the middle, being me."

"But you will change, whether you like it or not, and it'll be even easier for people to see that you're different. Are you prepared for that?"

"It's who I am," he said quietly. "There will always be horrible people like at the gala. At least it'll be my change, with no one interfering. I'll still be Sanders. If I can deal with it, everyone else will have to as well."

"And if you don't like it?"

"I can always have the hormones and surgery and stuff later."

"Fair enough."

When he didn't say anything more, Paula opened the cake box and took a knife out of the pannier. "Here, you cut it."

"Wow, it's got Smarties on top." Sanders cut two huge slices. "Did Nora bake it?"

"I did. It's my mum's recipe. She used to make it for Pete and me on our birthday. I got her out of bed at seven this morning to check I'd remembered it right. Then I woke Mrs McIntyre to borrow the tins."

He bit into his slice. "Yum. This is even better than the sandwiches."

"I wanted to make you something special before I left."

He laid the cake down on the leg of his shorts. "You're leaving?"

"Andy's coming to collect me tomorrow. I need to see my parents and start sorting out Pete's things. I've been away five weeks."

"Are you going for good?"

She smiled. "No, I'll be back."

"To stay?"

"Maybe. Perhaps you could keep an eye on the tandem for me while I'm away."

He thought about this. "Could I ride it?"

It was Paula's turn to hesitate. "If you want," she heard herself say. It felt all right.

"Who with?"

"Why don't you ask your mum? I'll move the front seat down for her and change the pedals."

"Okay."

They ate in silence for a few minutes. When Sanders had finished his cake, he licked the icing off his fingers and wiped them on his T-shirt. "I was thinking about that kimono dragon we saw at the zoo," he said.

"Komodo."

"I know. It was like the virgin birth, wasn't it?"

"That's what the keeper said."

"No separate mum and dad, just that one dragon on her own having all those babies."

"Uh-huh."

He helped himself to another thick slice of cake. "Well, that could be me, couldn't it?"

Paula choked as a fragment of Smartie caught in her windpipe. She cleared it with ginger beer. "What on earth are you on about now?

You're not planning to spontaneously reproduce, are you? I don't think even you could manage that. Besides, one of you's more than enough."

Sanders giggled. "Don't be stupid. I was just thinking that, you know, she seemed perfectly happy being different to all the other creatures. Just being herself in a dragony sort of way, even though she's unique. So maybe I could be happy." He cocked his head. "You know, being unique, in a dragony sort of way."

"In a penguiny, dragony sort of way." Paula cut herself a second slice of cake. "Why not. Maybe we both could."

Epilogue

Paula flipped open the laptop and checked her email. She had two new messages. Both were from Carole's address. She clicked on the first one.

Hello Paula, Carole here. Or should I say Minnie? Just wanted to check what time you're arriving. The weather's been good up here the past few days so Terry reckons we're on for the barbecue. He says to tell Andy to bring lots of wine so we can celebrate the newest additions to the Cra'frae community in style! Nora says he's really looking forward to working with Andy on expanding the taxi business – he's been talking about nothing else!

I bumped into Mrs McIntyre on Main Street earlier – she says she's got the broadband sorted out for you.

See you both tomorrow evening. Sanders is bouncing off the walls he's so excited, but I'll leave him to tell you about all his plans! Carole/Minnie x

Paula opened the second message.

Hiya PT!!! How ya doin? me and Bovis are fine – she sends her luv. School is okay. Westwick High is much bigger than Cra'frae primary and I kept gettin lost at first, but I'm gettin used to it now. My teachers are nice – mostly – and the other kids are alrite. In some of my classes I sit next to a girl called Traci. She's from Mozambique (see I know how to spell it cos she showed me). She's comin for a ride on the tandem with me at the weekend, if that's cool with yoo????? When me an Mum ride it Mum screems when we go downhill!! I went to see my psychologist last week. She says if Im happy, its okay to wait n see how things go for a bit. So thats what Im gonna do. Y'know I definitley don't want to be a girl. I mean I like them an everythin, but I don't want to be one, so we'll see. Mibby I will take the hormones an stuff but not yet. Anyway its only three weeks to half-term so I've been plannin lots of places you an me can ride to. I thought mibby, if she likes it, I could go for a ride one day with Traci, but you an me will go out the other days if you huvn't got too much work to do. Mibby we could go to that beach with the seals? And is Andy still okay to take us to the zoo to see Nils Olav an Bungee in the van??? Would it be okay if Traci comes too?????

See you l8r Alligator!!! Bovis says bye! Your friend Sanders xxxxxx

Alex Morgan was born in Edinburgh and grew up along the coast in North Berwick. She now lives in the Cumbrian town of Cockermouth, birthplace of William Wordsworth, where she works for the National Trust. She is married and has two daughters and one granddaughter. She has always loved the seaside. *Tandem* is her first novel.

Lightning Source UK Ltd.
Milton Keynes UK
UKOW04f0500080414

229579UK00008B/66/P